S0-BCJ-227

WITHDRAWN

FLIGHT OF THE HAWK: THE PLAINS

This Large Print Book carries the
Seal of Approval of N.A.V.H.

A NOVEL OF THE AMERICAN WEST, BOOK 2

FLIGHT OF THE HAWK: THE PLAINS

W. MICHAEL GEAR

THORNDIKE PRESS
A part of Gale, a Cengage Company

Farmington Hills, Mich • San Francisco • New York • Waterville, Maine
Meriden, Conn • Mason, Ohio • Chicago

Copyright © 2019 by W. Michael Gear.
Thorndike Press, a part of Gale, a Cengage Company.

ALL RIGHTS RESERVED
This novel is a work of fiction. Names, characters, places and incidents are either the product of the author's imagination, or, if real, used fictitiously.
The publisher bears no responsibility for the quality of information provided through author or third-party Web sites and does not have any control over, nor assume any responsibility for, information contained in these sites. Providing these sites should not be construed as an endorsement or approval by the publisher of these organizations or of the positions they may take on various issues.
Thorndike Press® Large Print Western.
The text of this Large Print edition is unabridged.
Other aspects of the book may vary from the original edition.
Set in 16 pt. Plantin.

LIBRARY OF CONGRESS CIP DATA ON FILE.
CATALOGUING IN PUBLICATION FOR THIS BOOK
IS AVAILABLE FROM THE LIBRARY OF CONGRESS

ISBN-13: 978-1-4328-5411-9 (hardcover alk. paper)

Published in 2019 by arrangement with W. Michael Gear

Printed in Mexico
1 2 3 4 5 6 7 23 22 21 20 19

TO
RICHARD S. WHEELER
FOR BEING OUR BELOVED
MENTOR
IN THOSE EARLY DAYS.

TO
RICHARD S. WHEELER
FOR BEING OUR BELOVED
MENTOR
IN THOSE EARLY DAYS

PROLOGUE

Of all the possessions a human being claims, ultimately, only a person's life and the demons that lurk down in the dark clefts of the soul are truly and ultimately theirs. Land, title, property, physical possessions, all will eventually pass on to others. All transitory.

For a time, all that had been left for the man called John Tylor had been the demons. And then he had found the river and employment as an engage, *a hired boatman on Manuel Lisa's 1812 expedition to the Upper Missouri.*

For the first time since John Tylor's arrest, imprisonment, and escape, he had begun to once again cherish life.

Back in Andrew Jackson's holding cell, called "the pit," Tylor had been chained in squalor, half starved, and savaged by rats. Death had been Tylor's elusive hope. An earnest prayer. Especially after word reached him that his wife, Hallie, had divorced him.

Charged with treason for his complicity in

the Burr conspiracy, Tylor had managed to escape, had barely managed to elude capture in his desperate flight to St. Louis. To the Missouri River, and finally beyond the Upper Missouri frontier.

After years of despair, self-imposed penance, and privation, he once again cherished life itself.

As to the demons . . . ?

CHAPTER 1

Under a star-shot sky, John Tylor slept in the folds of a woolen blanket. Night breezes danced out of the west, playing tenuously across the gently undulating grasslands. One moment they whispered through the bluestem, rustling the autumn-dry leaves, bobbing the heads now shorn of seeds. The next they stilled, allowing the songs of crickets, night birds, and the tremolo of distant buffalo wolves to be heard.

In his blankets, sleep-lidded eyes flickering, Tylor's dreams were haunted. The demons stirred, creeping up from their dark recesses. In flashes, Aaron Burr tormented him with an excited grin, saying, *"John, the southwest is a fallow field. Ignored by Spain, it's a paradise that needs only a firm hand to flower. An unclaimed empire that only needs to be seized."*

Burr's grin died, shifted, the vice president's face thinned into Andrew Jackson's.

The general's lips pulled thin, bitter with hate as those scorching eyes burned. *". . . Traitorous dog! A bullet's too good for you, Tylor. I'd hang you myself . . . slowly . . . but for this warrant from Washington City . . ."*

The dream faded, darkened, a scent of river caressing Tylor's nose. His heart skipped as he heard, *"Laddie, yer a debility."* Fenway McKeever's thick Scottish brogue echoed in John Tylor's nightmare. Those terrible green eyes with their merciless black pupils gave menace to the man's freckled face. Close, hard, McKeever reached out with a callused hand. The fingers were closing, trying for a hold on Tylor's throat.

With a cry, Tylor jerked back. Turned. In blind panic he ran.

All was blackness, a formless, shapeless void into which he fled. Heart hammering, he pounded on. Couldn't see his hands as they clawed at the air, felt the breath tearing in and out of his lungs.

But behind — ever closer in the stygian dark — the sound of McKeever's heavy boots hammered with each massive stride. Tylor could feel their every impact through the hard ground. Closer, ever closer.

The air stirred by his ear as McKeever reached out. In seconds that strong hand was going to clamp down and . . .

"Damn, Tylor, wake up!" At the harsh voice, the dream shattered.

A disruptive nudge to the hip brought Tylor fully awake in his blankets. He stared up at the night sky; familiar patterns of stars were black-blotched where clouds floated in silver silhouette.

He lay on his back, the bed surprisingly comfortable where the blankets mashed down thick bluestem grass. A gentle west breeze rustled through the endless dry leaves and stems, nodding them in wavelike patterns that reminded a man of the ocean.

To Tylor's right, the horses stood, head down, hobbled, and apparently heedless of his night terrors. The dung fire in its pit was burned down to red coals.

"Will Cunningham," Tylor placed the voice. "We're west of the Missouri. Three days' ride out of Manuel Lisa's camp on the river."

" 'Tarnal hell," Will Cunningham muttered. "I's back with the missus. Just shucked my boots, shirt, and pants. Anna's a laying there atop the sheets. Hot August night and all. Her hair down and spread all over the pillow. I drop to a knee, and just as she smiles up, and things start to get real interesting, ye cuts loose with a holler fit to shiver a bobcat."

11

"Sorry. Nightmare."

"Who'd a guessed?"

Cunningham's wife, Anna, was barely a year in the grave. Her loss was enough to cut the Kentucky hunter loose from any desire for the "civilized" lands of Illinois.

As if an afterthought, Cunningham asked, "McKeever?"

"Among others."

"You drowned him. Back in the river outside Manuel Lisa's camp. The dead don't matter no more."

Funny thing to say given that Cunningham had been about to make love to a deceased wife. Tylor — in a fit of good sense — figured it might be best if he avoided inserting that salient little detail into the conversation.

"We're beyond the frontier," Tylor stated simply. "I should be feeling free. Instead, every time I close my eyes, it's Fenway McKeever, Andrew Jackson, Joshua Gregg." He fingered the dog-eared letter in the breast pocket of his hunting shirt. "Or Hallie."

Tylor tossed his blanket to the side. He stood, staring around at the dark and gently rolling grassland. They were on the flat uplands, having climbed out of the incised trench of the Missouri River. It had been

12

three days since they left the new trading post Manuel Lisa and his *engages* were building on the river's east bank twelve miles north of the Arikara villages.

The new post would shelter Lisa's 1812 fur trading expedition, provide a base for the Missouri Fur Company's operations among the Upper Missouri tribes, and function as an outpost for the small trapping parties he would send out in search of furs.

More than that, the post would serve as a reminder to the western tribes that America was a solid presence, unfettered by the war with Britain that was being fought in the east. Manuel Lisa lived among the river tribes as a representative of that nation in opposition to the Spanish and, worse, the British agents who now filtered through the villages and sought to turn the Arikara, Sioux, Mandan, and Hidatsa against the new nation.

Convicted of treason against the United States, John Tylor wondered when he'd become such an ardent patriot.

The night wind caressed Tylor's thin face, flipping his long and unkempt hair. Manuel Lisa had once told Tylor that, upon first sight of him, Lisa's impression had been of a totally brown man: brown eyes, hair, and tanned skin, his medium height clad in brown clothes. Nondescript.

People wouldn't remember the nondescript. Tylor had made a point of being exactly that sort of man.

"Anything stirring out there?" Cunningham asked from his blankets.

"Just the night wind." Tylor lifted his hand, letting the breeze blow through his fingers. "Warm. Free."

He sniffed, drawing in the scent of grass: sweet and slightly tangy to his nostrils. "We're going to have to make a choice come sunrise, Will. North to the Grand River or south to follow the Moreau River. Up here, on the divide like this? We're going to be short on water."

"That's the gamble," Cunningham replied as he shifted in his blanket. "Grand or Moreau, it don't matter. We follow one of the rivers west, we'll hit one Indian camp after another. Thar's just the two of us. And, let's see. What trade did the booshway credit you with?"

Like reciting the litany, Tylor said, "Twenty carrots of tobacco, twenty ceramic pipes, fifteen traps, five pounds of powder, and four of lead, ten knives, sack of gun flints, an ax, ten hanks of beads, three bolts of red cloth, three cards of needles, four tomahawks, three blankets, a sack of flour,

14

and another of ground corn."

"And don't forget the horses."

"And two horses," Tylor amended. The Missouri Fur Company expedition clerk, John Luttig, hadn't written the credit into the official ledger. That didn't mean that Manuel Lisa *ever* forgot a debt.

The horses lifted their heads, ears pricking, as something lurked out in the grass. Sniffing, the animals dismissed it, lowering their heads and exhaling. Whatever night creature, they found it nothing alarming. Tylor had learned early to trust a horse's night sense far more than his own.

"That wife of yours," Cunningham said through a yawn, "you think you'll ever get her back?"

Tylor shifted, reaching into his worn shirt to finger the pages Hallie had written to him from a different world. "Some things are born, have their time, and die. And, Will, she's not my wife. She divorced me. Married Joshua Gregg. That she could forgive me after what I did to her? The humiliation I caused her?" He chuckled hollowly. "What a remarkable and magnificent woman."

"Wouldn't be the first time in history that a man took back what was once his."

"Not this time, Will." He looked out at the western horizon where patterns of stars vanished against the black horizon. "You see out there, just past the end of the grass?"

"I'm asleep, Tylor. My eyes are closed."

"That's my future. I'm going where no one knows me. Where no one will ever find out who I was or what I did."

"Can't outrun your skin, coon."

"No. But in the end, one can seek to atone for one's sins."

At least he hoped so.

Assuming he had finally run so far that it was no longer worth the time or effort for his enemies to run him down. They would give up now, wouldn't they?

CHAPTER 2

The mud that coated Fenway McKeever's skin and ragged clothing had dried. It flaked and broke loose as he sat up. He coughed. Coughed some more. He'd been doing that for a couple of days now since pulling himself half-drowned from the river.

How had destroying Manuel Lisa's boats and killing John Tylor gone so wrong?

He'd been more dead than alive that night. Dragged himself up on a sandbar. His fingers had clawed at the mud-rich sand, feeble as a dying kitten's. He'd barely gotten his head out of the river. Had coughed gouts from his lungs, the liquid vanishing into the damp sand. Then he'd thrown up river water.

Lying there, his chest, legs, and arms awash in the Missouri, he'd listened to the gurgling deep down in his lungs. And coughed and coughed until his throat had felt as if a splintered branch had been pulled

17

through his windpipe.

Some deep instinct, a reptilian presence, goaded him to crawl up, to battle his way across the trunk of an old cottonwood that had floated down and lodged on the beach. He'd flopped himself over the smooth wood, belly on the log, head and chest hanging, as water trickled out with each breath.

How close to dead can a man be?

Lying there, hanging like that, his cheek pressed into the sand, he'd tried to remember.

That little shite, Tylor. Backstabbing bastard that he was.

"Thought I had 'im in me hand," Fenway muttered.

Shook his head.

Tylor was supposed to have cut the line that would set Manuel Lisa's boat *Polly* loose on the current. Then they'd deal with the little boat. Adrift on the river, the boats would have grounded, holed their hulls, and sank. Any chance for Lisa's expedition would have died in the Missouri's silt-sanded depths.

"And I'd have the key to the upper river in me hand," McKeever told himself.

He blinked, thinking back to that night. To the whistling of the long pole as Tylor swung it. But for that hissing rush of air, the thing would have broken McKeever's head open like a thin-shelled egg.

He had chased Tylor all over the boat, roaring his anger. Only to have the little shite stick him in the thigh with a knife, then drag them both over the side an instant before McKeever could split the bastard's skull open with an ax.

From that moment on, McKeever would live with the memory of hitting cold water, of the blackness. And then, an instant before he finished the floundering Tylor, he'd been snagged from behind by that damn tree. The thing had fouled with McKeever's clothing, lifting him, thrusting him down into the depths. One instant he was being raised high, the next he was driven down, the air crushed out of his lungs.

McKeever rubbed his mud-encrusted eyelids. Swatted at the mosquitoes that hovered around him. Mud was a good thing. Mosquitoes couldn't bite through mud.

"Niver been so afraid in all me life," he muttered.

That had been days ago. Four? Five? He wasn't sure.

Didn't care.

What mattered was that he was alive. No

19

way he could go back to Manuel Lisa's expedition. Tylor would have told them everything.

"So, laddie" — he stared out at the wind-chopped surface of the Missouri — "yer a going to head west into the Plains, aye? Think yer gonna just up and disappear? Not with two thousand dollars a ridin' on yer head."

McKeever's smile hardened. "And not after what ye done t' me, laddie."

Thank the saints and angels above, Fenway McKeever remembered every word John Tylor had ever told him.

He pulled himself up off the bank, then beat some of the drying mud off his torn and filthy clothing.

Hiding next to the river during the day, sneaking close at night, he'd scouted Manuel Lisa's camp where they worked to build the new fort.

Tylor wasn't there. Two of the horses were gone.

That meant he was already headed west.

Fenway McKeever no longer had a keg of salt to put Tylor's head in. He wondered if just the man's skull would be enough to collect the reward.

Chapter 3

Gray Bear sat on the high point, staring out at the rolling land. The afternoon sun beat down; tall and amber grass undulated like waves under the western wind. People had taken to calling him *taikwahni,* the *Newe,* or Shoshoni, term for chief. Being a chief had never been one of Gray Bear's great driving desires. He had been happy to let his best friend, Three Feathers, serve as the leader.

Now Three Feathers was dead, killed by the Blackfeet. The little band of fifteen *Kuchendukani,* or "buffalo eater" Shoshoni, were a couple of moons' march east of their familiar territory on the western side of the Big Horn Mountains. Not really lost, just adrift in the endless sea of grass.

Over his twenty-eight years, Gray Bear had grown to an average height, stocky of build, with muscular shoulders and arms. Bowed and bandy-legged, he had the rolling stride of a horseman when he walked.

His amiable face, weather-blackened, had started to line from the effects of sun, snow, and wind. Like everyone in his small band, he'd hacked his hair short in mourning for the friends and kin killed by the *Pa'kiani,* the Blackfeet.

That afternoon he sat on a low and crumbling outcrop of white clay where it protruded from the crest of a round-topped low ridge and allowed a view of the veinlike drainages that led down toward the cottonwood-and-willow-choked river a couple of hands' ride to the north.

No one they encountered so far into the grasslands could be considered a friend. The country where they now passed was itself contested, a no-man's land between the Arikara, Mandan, Hidatsa, Sioux, Cheyenne, and occasionally the Arapaho, though they tended to stick to the west.

How have we come to this?

The question rolled around in his head. It should have been an ordinary buffalo hunt. A simple half-moon's venture into what the Shoshoni called the Powder River's Basin. Instead it had become a desperate flight from a marauding band of Blackfeet that had driven them to the supposed safety of the valleys just east of the Black Hills.

No sooner had they relaxed and dedicated

themselves to the hunt than the Blackfeet had struck, killed half of the people, stolen so many of their horses, and panicked the survivors. It had been there that Three Feathers had been killed.

Aitta, firearms, had made the difference. Especially in a lightning raid. Ride close, shoot, and dart away. A man couldn't dodge a bullet. No shield — no matter how stout — could protect him.

Gray Bear fingered his chin while the endless plains wind batted at him, flipping his short hair.

So they had come here, east, into the endless sea of grass to look for *Taipo.* White men. The foreign traders who would barter guns for fine furs and hides. But where did Gray Bear and his little band find these elusive *Taipo?* Along the Great River, yes. But that selfsame river was crowded with enemies who would kill him and the rest of the men and boys, enslave the women, and steal their wealth of finely tanned calf buffalo hides.

From his seat atop the ridge the task seemed impossible.

"Hey, how you doing?" Old Aspen Branch asked as she climbed up beside him. She was what? Almost sixty? White-haired, her face like a shriveled and wrinkled old section of hide. Most of her teeth had fallen out, leaving her jaw undershot and her lips puckered.

"Wondering how we got here."

"I told you. We need the *aitta* traded by the *Taipo* white men here in the east." She gave him her toothless grin. "I felt the *puha,* the spirit Power that filled you. And you dreamed the *Taipo* with the hawk."

"Not all dreams are real, *Grandmother.*"

He called her "grandmother" out of respect. Aspen Branch was a *waipepuhagan.* A female shaman and medicine woman. On occasion older women who had passed their last monthly bleeding would dedicate themselves to the study of spirit Power. Not that women didn't have their own Power and spirits, but when a woman was "in her *hunni*" or bleeding, she wasn't supposed to be in contact with men or a man's possessions. To do so was considered a sort of pollution. Running and hiding as they were, associating with bleeding women hadn't seemed nearly as dangerous as being murdered by the next war party to crest the nearest ridge.

"That dream was real," she told him assuredly. She gestured. "I know this place."

He shot her a sidelong glance. "You do? Here? This far east?"

"Stood right on this spot as a girl. I was maybe five? Six? I was here with my father and a party headed for the Mandan to trade."

"You are sure this is the place?"

Aspen Branch squinted her eyes, as if seeing back into the past. "We were the thunder in the world back then. The other peoples feared us. We rode where we would, having driven the *Denee* far off to the south. The *Sa'idika,* the dog-eating Arapaho, and the *Pa'ganawoni,* the Cheyenne, still grew corn and lived over east of the river. They only came here after the Blackfeet got *aitta* from those British traders up north. And even then, we might have kept all this, but for the rotting-face death. I was a young woman the first time the illness came upon us. Entire bands of people died. For every ten of us, only one or two of us were left."

"That was just the first time," he whispered, remembering. "It came back when I was a boy. Twelve years since the last time the rotting-face sickness came." He blinked at the memory. "It took more than half of the people that time, too. My mother and father, my older sisters."

"Disease and war." Aspen Branch pulled at her ear. "So few of us survived that we're no longer the thunder of the plains. No longer arrogant in our might." She shot him a sidelong glance. "We need allies, *Taikwahni*. If we can find the right *Taipo* to speak for us, perhaps there is a way."

"Power and allies come at a cost," he reminded her, watching as a couple of crows tumbled and sailed in the sere late summer sky.

"We can pay." She gestured to where the packhorses were hobbled in one of the low swales a couple of bowshots to the west. "Half of our horses are loaded with finely tanned buffalo calf hides. Beautiful things, soft as air, dyed pure white. No one tans better hides than we do."

At the moment, a rider appeared, working a buff-colored mare up and out of one of the drainages off to the east. She couldn't be mistaken: Singing Lark. Sight of the girl brought a smile to Gray Bear's lips. She rode the horse as if born on it, the wind catching her cropped black hair as she came at a canter.

"Wonder what she's found now?" Gray Bear asked absently.

"We'll know soon enough." Aspen Branch shot him an evaluative look. "You know she's had her moon?"

"When?"

"Just finished it, *Taikwahni*. Why do you

think she's been away from us so much these last days?"

"Thought she was scouting for danger."

"Yes, she's your scout, your chickadee who sees everything and keeps us safe. But she is also now a woman."

"Why didn't she say anything?"

"Why does anyone keep a secret? She doesn't want anyone to know."

"And why are you telling me this?"

"*Taikwahni,* she's afraid that if you know she's a woman, you'll order her to stop scouting for you."

"Where would she get that notion?"

"Think of the men who have preceded you. Even your good friend, whose place you've taken. All of them would tell her that she was no longer a girl, that she was a woman. That a woman's duties were different than those of a girl, and for her to dedicate herself to the tasks that would help her find a husband."

He considered that. Red Moon Man, Kestrel Wing, and the rest would expect Singing Lark to behave now in a manner appropriate to a responsible woman. But they wouldn't be nearly as adamant about it as the women in their small band.

"*Pia,* we have fifteen of us. Just fifteen. We are in a land surrounded by enemies, searching for a *Taipo* who may be a fantasy. If the Arikara, the Mandan, the Hidatsa, or Cheyenne find us, they'll kill you, me, and the men. The women they will take as slaves. I could care less if Singing Lark wants to keep acting like a girl." A pause. "And I'd be a fool to lose her skill as a scout. She's better than any man I've ever known."

Aspen Branch gave him a toothless grin. "That is why *Puha* chose you for this task. But Turns His Back, Red Moon Man, Kestrel Wing, not to mention the women, will have other thoughts on the matter."

"Then maybe we had best keep her secret, *Waipepuhagan.*"

As Singing Lark rode close, her mare blowing and sweat-covered, she pointed. "I saw them, *Taikwahni.* Two *Taipo.* Or, I think they are *Taipo.* Light brown skin, hair all over their faces. They lead packhorses with curious packs, and" — she grinned — "best of all, they each have an *aitta.*"

"Did one carry a hawk?" he asked. The man in his Spirit dreams had come in the company of a hawk.

"Not that I could see, *Taikwahni.*"

"What do you want to do?" Aspen Branch asked.

Gray Bear sucked at his lips, then glanced at Singing Lark, enjoying the delight that reflected in the girl's . . . no, the woman's eyes.

"Can you find them again, stay out of sight?"

She grinned, exposing shining white teeth. "This is me! Of course, my chief."

CHAPTER 4

Private Toby Johnson had never felt so tired in all of his nineteen years. He stood at ease, mud-spattered and smelling of his and his horse's sweat. Every bone and muscle in his body ached from the long hours in the saddle. The knot of hunger was pulled tight in his empty belly. He'd started before daybreak, driving his mount down the rutted forest trails that passed for roads in this part of Tennessee.

But he'd made it to Jackson's headquarters in Nashville where more than two thousand men had been enlisted into Jackson's forces.

At his desk, the general was inspecting the correspondence Toby had delivered. Dressed in a fine uniform, the general looked every bit as dangerous as his reputation. The shock of hair made Jackson appear like some raptorial bird; his eyes had hardened as they scanned the correspondence William Clark had penned back in St. Louis. Jackson placed the pages on the desk, leaned back.

Toby pulled himself to attention, muscles stiff. Damn, Jackson looked absolutely fierce, mouth pinched, eyes burning. Toby figured the devil himself would cringe if he had to face Jackson when he was in a rage. The man unnerved him. Had caused him to run out without saluting the last time Toby had stood before him thus.

Hope he don't remember that.

From his commander's expression, the letter wasn't good news.

Someone had told Toby that the ancient Romans and Egyptians cut the heads off messengers who brought bad news. Compared with Jackson's wrath, Toby concluded it was probably better to be a Roman.

"Toby?"

"Sir!" Toby saluted his best salute, eyes fixed on the wall behind so as to avoid the general's deadly eyes. Those black pupils would have gone through him like a pin through a bug.

"According to William Clark, the man about whom I have been enquiring has escaped. Again. We are at war, and now the black-hearted traitor is loose on the Upper Missouri to foment who knows what kind

31

of perfidy. Damn that man!"

Toby, whom most everyone considered dumber than a rock, was smart enough to keep his mouth shut. He wondered what "perfidy" was.

Jackson leaned forward, pulled his pen from the inkwell, and scratched out a quick order. He blew on the sheet of parchment and handed it over.

Toby took it, swallowing hard.

Jackson's pen was scratching its way across another sheet of paper as he spoke. "That's a field commission, Corporal. You are to take Privates Danford and Simms. Your orders are to find John Tylor if you have to pursue him to the ends of the earth. That man could single-handedly lose us the Upper Missouri and the entire northwest. Turn the tribes against us and unleash a bloodbath. Deliver them into the hands of the British. I don't care if you have to chase him all the way to the Pacific to do it, but I want John Tylor either captured and re-turned to me or shot dead."

I'm a corporal? In charge of men? On a special mission?

Toby's heart skipped, throttled only by the realization that if he failed, Jackson would have his balls. Better to just shoot himself in the head than return to report failure.

"I know this is asking a lot, Corporal, but I don't have anyone else to send. I'm filling out your orders now. You will present them to William Clark in St. Louis. Draw any stores you and your men will need from him or from the commanding officer at Fort Osage. Accept any advice either Clark or the officer gives you about travel upriver. I don't care if you have to follow Tylor through hell and back, or what steps you have to take, but find that accursed traitor, and stop him before he commits more mischief."

Jackson handed over the orders, his thin face oddly red with anger, the fingers of one hand gripping the arm of his chair so hard the nails were white. "Word is that I may be taking the command to New Orleans to reinforce that swamp-slithering serpent Wilkinson. Your duty, your only duty, is to deal with Tylor so I can focus on other responsibilities. Can you do that?"

"Yes, sir! Give you my word, sir!" Toby barked. Hunger and fatigue were gone; every fiber of his body vibrated.

Jackson sat back in his chair, shaking his head. "Tylor is up the Missouri. Last known in the employ of Manuel Lisa. Lisa's a trader and loyal to the United States. One of the partners in the Missouri Fur Company. If anyone does, he will have information on where to find Tylor."

"Yes, sir."

"What is it with that man?" Jackson knotted his jaws. "I should have shot him when I had the chance. You'd think he was water the way he slips through people's fingers."

"What did he do, sir?" Toby dared the question.

"Sold out this country, Corporal. He was in thick with Aaron Burr. Was going to use this government's resources to carve his own country out of the Spanish lands in Louisiana and Texas. The man *conspired* with the British. With Anthony Merry, no less. That pompous and poisonous prig. Asked for a British fleet to back up his invasion. And, because of Merry's intrigue, came within a whisker of getting it."

Toby blinked. The Burr conspiracy? By thunder!

"Get *out* of here and go *find* that man!"

Toby wheeled, calling over his shoulder, "Yes, sir. On it, sir!" as he hurried out the door. Only when he was in the hallway did he remember that he'd forgotten to salute again.

All the more reason to hurry. He had to

find Eli Danford and Silas Simms. Both were older than him. Tall, rawboned long hunters. And he had to get supplies. Enough corn and salt pork to get the three of them to St. Louis.

And after that?

Assuming he could convince Danford and Simms to follow his orders, assuming he could hunt this John Tylor down, what sort of man would he discover his fugitive to be? Tylor had obviously outwitted Andrew Jackson, escaped justice, orchestrated a traitorous conspiracy that included the vice president, was a known spy who was complicit with the British, and was up the Missouri unleashing havoc.

Oh, Toby. What have you gotten yourself into?

CHAPTER 5

"What is it?" Tylor asked as Will Cunningham reined his horse in. The Kentucky hunter leaned forward over his saddlebow, squinted into the west wind as it tugged his beard back. The crow's-feet tightened at the edge of Cunningham's eyes.

Tylor, not waiting for an answer, turned his attention to the endless grass that stretched to the far horizon. The haunting waves were so reminiscent of the ocean; endlessly rolling, they gave a sense of animation to the land. The plains were a place of movement: the restless sea of grass; the rising and falling wind; formations of cloud; and the endless parade of the sun, moon, and stars in the firmament.

The ground here had taken on a flatter aspect as they traveled farther from the river's broken uplands with their brush-filled drainages. But the appearance of the land deceived. It might look level at a distance, but as a person progressed, it was to find the country cut with enough creeks, dry drainages, and low swales to hide an army.

"Old Cobble smells something." Cunningham continued to scan the undulating grass. "Just caught a whiff."

"Out here it could be anything." Tylor shifted his grip on his ugly, short-cropped rifle, glanced down to ensure he hadn't snagged the pan to spill the priming. "Bear. Wolves. Lion."

"Injuns," Cunningham rejoined.

"Yep."

But the fall-yellowed grass betrayed no threat as it bent and rose under the wind's playful massage. He couldn't hear anything over the buzz of insects and flies, the rustle of the grass, the sighing of the wind. Overhead the sun beat down, the day hot. Sweat trickled down the inside of his shirt, wicked away by the dry heat. His black mare stamped at the flies, slashing her tail.

Tylor carefully inspected his surroundings, relying on his peripheral vision. His travels in the southern plains had taught him that the corner of the eye often caught the first hint of movement.

"Something's out there," Cunningham muttered, as if to himself. "Ain't big."

Tylor caught it in the corner of his eye. There, off to the right. Grass shaken as something moved it against the wind. Just a change of pattern as the endless bluestem was disturbed.

"Will?"

At the hunter's glance, Tylor indicated with his rifle. Then he reined his mare around, earing the cock back. He started his horse forward, rifle at the ready.

Tylor's mare snuffled, fully aware that something wasn't right. The animal moved warily. Tense, ears pricked.

Tylor got a good hold on the reins, unsure if the mare would shy, bolt, or buck. And, Lord knew, he had no idea how the animal would react if he shot from her. Probably pitch him on his head. He'd known nothing of the horse herd, his hours spent as a boatman on the journey upriver. He'd taken the mare at Lisa's suggestion. And if she blew up? Well, as the saying went, a fella didn't look a gift horse in the mouth. Even when he was flying past its head.

Tylor circled, trying to get a better look at whatever hid in the tall grass. The mare snorted, snuffled, and sidestepped.

"Come on, gal. Let's see."

Tylor booted the mare, clicking under his tongue, urging her forward. Clearly unhappy, she took a step. Then another.

Off to the side, Cunningham had his long Pennsylvania rifle raised, Cobble standing with pricked ears.

"Can't be too much of a monster," Tylor granted. "Might be a child or . . ."

The thing in the grass exploded upward, a blurred image of gray, brown, and yellow. Flapping. A launching streak. The thing hissed, air popping as if pounded.

The mare arched her back, leaped sideways. She did it so fast Tylor was left sitting on air. Really thin air given how fast he dropped and how hard he hit the ground. The impact knocked the wind out of him and left him stunned.

He could hear the thumping of the black mare's hooves as they hammered away across the grass. His vision blurred, cleared, and he struggled for breath.

The grass monster, whatever it had been, was vanishing in the bluestem, the heads of grass marking its passage. Tylor sucked a breath. Realized he'd lost his rifle.

What in hell?

He staggered to his feet, sucked again for breath, and charged after the thing.

Saw its path as it shoved through the grass, then stopped.

Tylor shot a glance over his shoulder, seeing where Cunningham was chasing down the mare and the two packhorses who had followed.

Tylor, still panting for breath, crept forward. Peered fearfully at the hole in the grass where the monster hid.

Some kind of big bird.

Had to be.

Easing his way, he reached out and pulled the stems and spikes back. Two fierce yellow eyes glared up at him, the pupils black and violent. The wickedly hooked beak was open, the narrow tongue flicking with each desperate panting breath.

A hawk. Young. Redtail if Tylor was any judge. The bird's yellow eyes were fixed on his, hard. Frightened.

"It's all right, Will. Got a hawk here."

Cunningham had caught the mare and was trotting his way.

The hawk tried to scramble back, one wing dragging. The bunched grass tangled around it.

Tylor's move was instinctual. He pulled off his shirt and threw it over the wounded hawk. Pressed it down. With care he managed to untangle the taloned feet from the thick grass stems and lifted the struggling bird.

"What in 'tarnal hell you doin'?" Cunningham asked. "Yer gonna get yerself sliced to ribbons when that thing comes loose of that shirt."

"It's got a hurt wing."

"Well, let the damn thing go before it lays you open to the bone."

Tylor chuckled, getting a hold of the bird's lower legs above the feet. He could feel the creature's terror through the thick folds of his old worn shirt. The hawk twisted, stuck its head through a rent in the fabric, and glared into Tylor's eyes. But for the confining cloth, it would have bit a chunk out of Tylor's arm.

"You outta yer mind?" Cunningham asked, pulling up on the horses. "Cain't keep a wild critter like that. Not on the trail anyway. Not without no cage."

"I've seen this hawk before, Will. In a dream. Like this, I was staring into its eyes. I tell you, I've dreamed this. Seen it fly again."

"Now yer tellin' me you got second sight?" Cunningham's amused smile bent his bearded lips. Cobble stamped uneasily. Tylor's mare was looking worried, nostrils flared, eyes white at the edges as she watched the bird.

"There was an Indian," Tylor told him. "In the dream, he handed me the bird.

This bird."

"Don't see no Injun, coon." Cunningham propped his rifle on the saddlebows and used his knife to cut a chew from his carrot of tobacco. Around the dry leaf, he said, "An' ye ask me? One hawk pretty much looks like another. Least a ways, I cain't tell the difference atween 'em."

"I tell you, it was this hawk."

"An' jist how's we supposed to know this Injun?"

"Round face, short hair. He's a muscular man." Tylor tightened his hold as the frightened hawk struggled to break free. "He has kind eyes, Will. But desperate. Like he needs something from us. He reaches out."

Cunningham got his quid juicing, spit a stream of amber off into the grass. With a barked laugh, he said, "Got to tell ye, Tylor. Yer hang-fire full of surprises. Now, what in hell are we gonna do with that damn hawk?"

"You've got those leather strips in your pack?"

"Yep. Them's my wangs."

"Well, step down here. Help me tie these legs. And we've got to set that broken wing."

"Do all that and not get ripped into bloody slices?"

"Well, hell, Will. I never promised you that riding with me wasn't without its risks."

42

■ ■ ■

Where she lay in the grass, Singing Lark watched the two *Taipo* as they mounted their horses.

Her heart was still pounding in her chest. Nothing, in all of her young life, compared with this. Not even the time she'd sworn she'd seen *Pa'waip,* the *Newe* Spirit known as Water Ghost Woman who lured men to their deaths. Not even the time she thought she'd heard Cannibal Owl flying through the midnight-dark winter sky.

At first, she'd figured she was either about to die, or suffer an even worse fate. Captured, raped, and enslaved. The wind had blown right down her back to the tall *Taipo*'s horse. Peering through the screen of grass, she'd seen the man's mount pinpoint her hiding place. Seen him pull the animal up and squint in her direction.

She'd been close enough to hear the *Taipo*'s soft words, uttered in a strange language. Then, just as she'd thought everything lost, the smaller rider had circled, flushed a hawk, and been bucked off his horse.

In the confusion, distracted as they were, Singing Lark had snaked her way through the grass, circling to the side, well down-wind.

"Did one carry a hawk?" Gray Bear's words echoed in her head.

Singing Lark swallowed hard, then low-ered her forehead to rest on the sweet-smelling grass. In all of her dreams, she had never dared to imagine that she would have the honor of serving a *puha*-filled *taikwahni* like Gray Bear. A leader who could dream such powerful visions.

"I have to get back," she whispered, the thrill of it tingling in her guts. "I have to tell him that, yes, these are the *Taipo* we have been sent to find."

CHAPTER 6

"What in hell ye reading, coon?" Will Cunningham asked as he sat cross-legged before the fire. They had made an early camp in a hollow, a sort of bowl in the grassy slope above the Grand River. A couple of cottonwoods shaded the depression, leaves clattering in the west breeze. The horses were hobbled down below, grazing, tails switching against the flies.

Cunningham was working on repairing one of his reins. The leather had worn where it attached to Cobble's bit. Cunningham had cut off the distressed section and was using a steel awl to poke holes, then coax sinew through them as he secured the rein to the bit.

"I'm reading Caesar. *The Gallic War.* Odd. I didn't remember his Latin being this good." Tylor closed the book. Made a face. "Either that or my own has gotten as intolerable as his."

45

"Latin, coon?"

Tylor set the book aside, glanced up at the sunset rays that shot patterns through the leaves overhead. "My father, though a fully committed American, insisted that I be educated at Oxford in England. Latin and Greek were required. I had a tutor as boy. As a scholar? Well, how about we leave it at the fact that I wasn't outstanding when it came to letters."

"That what led you to treason?" Cunningham glanced up from his stitching. "Being in England?"

"No. That was all Aaron Burr. Charming rogue that he might be." Tylor paused. "Will, tell me, if you and I are Americans, is it treason for us to instigate a rebellion among Spanish subjects in lands claimed by a foreign crown? And what is treasonous about forming a country based upon that foreign revolution? Especially if it is outside the United States? If its formation is not detrimental to the United States?"

Cunningham's beard wiggled uncertainly as he glanced at the hawk where it perched atop one of the packs. The bird's legs were bound, the wing immobilized by an improvised splint. That piercing stare missed nothing.

Tylor gestured to make his point. "It's not

46

like Aaron Burr was acting against the interests of the country by leading a revolt against the Spanish government in Texas, let alone Louisiana territory. Which, you must remember, is where we're sitting right now. Would it be treason if we declared and established the nation of Will, John, and Hawk? Wrote a constitution, and declared ourselves the government?"

"Don't know. Hadn't thought of that. Burr was tried, wasn't he?"

"And acquitted by Justice Marshall and the Supreme Court."

"So why'd it all come out so wrong?"

Tylor ran absent fingers over his book, his eyes on the hawk as the creature matched stare for stare. "Aaron Burr is an enchanting scoundrel. A true silver-tongued devil. Always his own worst enemy. But for shooting Alexander Hamilton, he'd have ended up as president. That he had no chance after the duel rankled deep down in his soul. If he couldn't be president of the United States, he'd forge his own country to lead.

"Aaron is remarkably adept at selling grand schemes, but he doesn't have a fool's clue about the details. And, ultimately, ill prepared, undermanned, and without even the basics of supply, his invasion of the Spanish lands and the creation of his new nation would have failed. Not to mention that James Wilkinson betrayed us. And there, my friend, lies the true villain of the piece."

"Why'd Burr pick you?"

"I knew Anthony Merry from my time in England. He was the British Minister to the United States. Merry hates anything having to do with America. He told me once 'Democracy is what you get when the offal of society is allowed to float to the top of the barrel.' He particularly despises Jefferson. Seems that on Merry's first state visit, Jefferson received him wearing only his bath robe. Spent the entire meeting tossing a slipper up and down with his foot, kept trying to catch it with his toe."

That brought a smile to Cunningham's lips. "This Merry. Overstuffed popinjay, eh?"

"But just the right person to approach if you want a British fleet to sail into the Gulf of Mexico to back a revolution in the Spanish lands. It would be a chance to do to the Spanish what the French did to the English at Yorktown. Think of North America like a game of checkers. Canada in the north. America in the middle. Spain in Florida on the southeast and covering the southwest. Russia in the northwest. Burr's country would carve a pro-British ally out of the Spanish southwest — a block to America's westward expansion. Not only that, the British would like nothing better than to see another country formed in North America that helps the Spanish and French empires disintegrate."

Tylor paused. "I never heard if Merry succeeded in talking the crown into sending the fleet. I was out west."

"That was when ye went to Santa Fe? Larned a bit of Pawnee?"

"Aaron was in communication with allies, people in Santa Fe, Nacogdoches, and New Orleans who were betting on his success. Wealth and power were afoot. Aaron figured to have as much as forty thousand acres of what's now Texas wilderness under cultivation within a couple of years. The trading permits alone would have made men rich."

Tylor smiled. "It wasn't just getting in on the beginning, picking my own lands, building my empire, it was the chance to see the west for myself. Learn the secrets, get a feel for the land and people." He tapped the side of his head. "Knowledge. That's where the true power lies."

"Making you what?"

"Minister of State? Vice president? One of the inner circle? One of the richest and most

49

powerful men in the western hemisphere? An American lord?" He tapped his copy of Caesar. "Like the author of this book once thought, it's not a new idea."

"Yer still looking for that? Out hyar?" Cunningham gestured around at the waving grass beyond the tree-and-brush-lined hollow where they camped.

Tylor frowned at the watching hawk. "I had my chance, Will. Gambled everything. My wife, reputation, estate, wealth, future, even my life. I lost. Spent eternity in Jackson's hole and came within a whisker of being hanged." He shook his head. "After paying that price, I'll be thankful if I can just vanish into the wilderness where no one has ever heard of me. Exile myself to the farthest reaches of men. That's my penance. The deal I've made with God."

Cunningham grunted, then tugged on his repaired rein to test its strength.

The way the hawk cocked its head, it might have been considering Tylor's words. Then, as if to make a statement, it ruffled its feathers, lifted its tail, and squirted white excrement onto the pack top.

"Looks like that rabbit you fed it done run through," Cunningham noted.

"I wasn't sure the bird would eat," Tylor told him, taking his book and stuffing it into his oiled bag.

The sounds of evening could be heard as the wind slowly ebbed, no longer rattling the leaves in the trees around their small camp. Insects shone as the slanting sun glowed in their wings. The horses stood in the grass below, heads down, tails flicking back and forth.

"The way he stripped that rabbit down to bone, I'd say that coon ain't eaten in days." Cunningham laid his repaired bridle and bit to the side. He started to reach for the sack that contained his tobacco and pipe, but then froze.

At the same time Tylor was aware of the horses as they pulled their heads up, ears pricked, nostrils flaring. Their stare fixed on the east, and they turned, shifting uneasily.

East? Downwind.

Tylor scuttled the half step to reach for his rifle. Cunningham — doing the same — collected his long Pennsylvania gun. The thing was beautiful, stocked with tiger-stripe maple, the brass work polished.

Cunningham's beard twitched as he rocked his jaw back and forth, his thumb on the forty-caliber rifle's cock.

"What do you think?" Tylor whispered, his own thumb on the cock of his crudely butchered fifty-four caliber gun. On his

51

previous trips into the west, he'd learned the advantage of a short-barreled rifle. This one, thick-wristed and awkward, appeared to have been an early attempt by an aspiring gunsmith. The original rifling at the muzzle had been worn from rust and ramrods. Tylor had had the gun shop cut the forty-two-inch barrel back to a mere thirty, and found the rifling to be quite crisp.

More to the point, when clean and tightly patched, it shot inside eight inches at one hundred paces. Good enough for a buffalo — or a man — at those distances.

"What do you think?" Cunningham asked.

Tylor followed the horses' gazes and heard his mare's soft whicker.

"Nothing moving out there that I can see. Thing is, Will, we're down here in this hollow. No telling what's just up over that grass."

"If it comes to trouble, John, we got to keep at least one rifle loaded. If'n I shoot, ye hold up lessen she's Katy bar the door. Don't touch that jack handle off 'til I'm loaded and primed."

"I'm with you, Will. No one wants to charge a man aiming a loaded rifle."

The evening sounds had gone oddly silent, the horses even more uneasy as they stomped, whickered, and shifted.

52

"Jack handle?" Tylor asked, as a nervous sweat dampened his neck.

"That damn rifle's about arse-ugly enough it looks t' be a jack handle. Reckon the feller that made it was just taking a break from his usual trade."

"And what trade would that have been?"

"Why, makin' jack handles, naturally."

Tylor grinned despite the uncomfortable feel of his heart thumping against his breastbone.

The horses reacted first, going tense. They shifted their gazes upwards, toward the head of the hollow.

Movement.

Heads appeared over the grass. East and south. They advanced slowly. Indians for sure. Warriors with bows raised, arrows nocked, they slowly descended into the hollow.

"Hold!" Tylor shouted, standing, picking the oldest and closest, a man with slightly graying hair, his face painted red with black lines on the cheeks, the left one scarred, an anticipatory grin on his face.

Tylor settled the silver-blade sight on the man's chest, again calling, "Stop!"

The old warrior lifted a hand, the others halting in their tracks.

"Who are you? What people?"

The others were looking to the older man. Good call on Tylor's part to figure him for the chief.

Cunningham stepped up beside Tylor and said, "Keep him covered, coon." Then he lowered his rifle, using hand signs to ask, "Who you?"

The war chief called a quick order; two of the young men to the side started to edge around between Tylor and the horses.

Tylor spun, covering the most threatening, crying, "Damn you, I'll kill him if he takes another step!"

The young warrior stopped, a flickering of excitement behind his eyes, as if he knew it was just a matter of time.

Cunningham was signing, adding aloud, "And yer a gonna die next, chief."

The older warrior continued to grin, signing in return.

Tylor kept his rifle pointed at the anxious youth; their eyes locked, the fool kid daring him to shoot.

"From the signs, these are Arapaho."

"Thought Manuel Lisa had a couple of traders, Champlain and Lafargue and his crew, keeping the Arapaho happy."

"Well, Tylor, they ain't hyar. They's just the two of us, four horses, and these packs full of trade. With you and me dead, who's gonna tell the tale?"

"That chief won't if he dies, and this kid goes with him. Then we're killing as many as we can before they take us down."

Cunningham signed, making the downward cut of the hand that indicated, "That's the end." Then he had the rifle back in position and settled on the chief's chest.

As Tylor let his finger caress the trigger, he experienced an odd sense of inevitability. His soul had gone airy. It would all end here. He'd shoot the kid through the top of the chest, and before the smoke cleared, he was going to charge the next young man to the right. If he could swing the jack handle, smash the young man down, he might be able to make it all the way to the third man. Might have a chance at beating him to a pulp.

"I figure I can get three, Will. You take the chief and lay into whomever you can. Maybe, we kill enough, the ones remaining might run."

" 'Bout our only chance," Cunningham agreed, no more than ten paces separating the muzzle of his rifle and the chief's chest.

At the corner of his vision, Tylor was barely aware of the chief still signing. Cunningham was shaking his head no.

"Says if we give him the packs and horses,

we can walk away," Cunningham translated.

"On foot out here? We'll end up just as dead, and we don't take any of them with us."

Cunningham let loose of his trigger just long enough to make the tapping-fist sign for "kill" and then pointed at the chief before replacing his finger on the trigger.

"Bit of a standoff, don't you think?" Tylor's mouth had gone dry. Flies were buzzing around his head. Irritating little bastards, and he didn't dare break the spell by waving them away.

With a barked order, the Arapaho chief took a step back, making the sign for "Go in peace, it is finished."

Across the short paces that separated them, Tylor could see the youth's disappointment. The kid ground his teeth, mouth working as he silently mouthed what had to be obscenities. Nevertheless, he and the others began to back away.

"Looks like we're out of the frying pan," Cunningham called warily.

"And smack into the fire," Tylor told him. "They're going to get us in the end, you know. Run us down out in the grass. Ambush us. Steal the horses in the night. Some trick."

"Reckon so," Cunningham agreed. "Think

we ought to shoot this coon while we got the chance? Open the ball and see if we can put the scare on 'em?"

Tylor hesitated. Play now or later? Here, they at least had a chance to . . .

The *hiss-thap* sound of an arrow hitting flesh startled him. With no conscious thought, he triggered the rifle. The pan flashed. His shot took the stunned youth full in the chest.

As the smoke billowed, Tylor charged forward, swinging the jack handle. The second young man was bringing his bow up, pulling back the arrow as Tylor unleashed all the strength in his body. The jack handle's barrel brushed past the young man's hastily uplifted arm. Hit the man's head with a melon-hollow thud. Tylor saw the fellow's facial skin ripple with the force of the impact.

Tylor pivoted, started for the next warrior, pulling the jack handle back.

The man was staggering away as Tylor dealt him a glancing blow with the rifle's barrel. Almost knocked him from his feet. An arrow was protruding most of its length out of his right shoulder. Ahead of him, another of the Arapaho was running full tilt up the slope.

Tylor's frantic gaze took in the camp, seeing the hawk, hissing and leaping against its ties, trying to fly with its splinted wing. The thing looked terrified.

A blue cloud of smoke was rising from where Cunningham was already pouring powder into his muzzle, his eyes taking in the three fleeing warriors.

An arrow made a blur through the air. It hissed past an Arapaho's left ear and would have been a head shot if the man wasn't jerking back and forth as he ran.

And then they were gone.

"What the hell?" Tylor demanded in terror and confusion.

"Get yer reload, John!" Cunningham cried. "We ain't out of this yet."

Tylor fumbled for his horn, bullet bag, and priming. Almost spilled the pour, dropped a ball, fished out another, and rammed it home. Raising the lock, he used his small horn to prime the pan, flicked it closed, and raised his rifle.

The chief was on his back, kicking ruts in the grass with his heels. Blood bubbled on his lips, his eyes blinking as he stared up at the yellow-orange of a dying sky. The warrior who had been next to him was hunched down on his knees, as if in prayer. His back was bowed, his hands gripping a bloody arrow that stuck out of his chest like a gigantic thorn.

Tylor spun on his heels, seeing the youth he'd shot, eyes fixed. The one he'd hit with the jack handle was staggering away, reeling. As the man slowed, bent, Tylor pulled his rifle up.

The young Arapaho threw up, his body bucking with the effort. Then he straightened and staggered out of sight.

"What the hell?" None of it made sense.

"Kai kuttih!" someone called from the grass above. *"Kai kuttih!"*

"Wonder what that means?" Cunningham asked, his rifle shouldered as he spun to face the new threat.

"Sounds like a kid," Tylor muttered, the jack handle raised.

"Kai kuttih!" And a figure slowly raised itself above the screening grass. The hands were held high, thin fingers spread wide.

Tylor shot a glance back toward the horses, seeing that they were only fixed on the single figure, not staring around as they would if the camp were being surrounded.

As if reassured, the wisp-thin youth walked down the slope into the hollow, repeating, *"Kai kuttih!"*

And then it hit him: Despite the short-cut hair, the newcomer was distinctly female.

Round hips, thin waist, slim legs and arms. And that was no war shirt, but a supple and form-fitting dress.

"Tylor," Cunningham called. "I'll be double damned if'n it ain't a girl!"

CHAPTER 7

Gray Bear lay belly-down in the grass, his heart beating like a pot drum in his chest. He gripped his bow so tightly he wondered if the wood would crush. The arrows in his left hand, he managed to treat with more care. Flies were buzzing around his head.

Above, the evening sky burned with that fading pale haze of late summer orange fading into night. Through the masking stems of grass he could just see the dead and dying Arapaho. See the *Taipo* as they stood, shoulders hunched behind their raised *aitta*. He had watched the deadly weapons spew smoke, fire, and death into the Arapaho. His own victim was on his knees, curled over the arrow Gray Bear had driven through the man's back.

"No shoot!" Singing Lark kept crying out. *Tam Apo, keep her safe!*

Gray Bear forced a swallow down his dry throat. She had volunteered, insisting that

61

as a girl, she posed no danger to armed men.

But the *Taipo* had just been in a fight for their lives. Men who had just killed — almost been killed themselves — were known to react first, think later.

"No shoot!" Singing Lark kept calling as she walked down into the camp.

The tall *Taipo* kept her covered with his skinny *aitta*. The short, mostly brown, man proved the more wary, his gaze skittering around as he tried to watch in all directions. Gray Bear had to approve. This one wasn't anyone's fool.

His heart skipped again as the hawk shrieked, unhappy with the noise, the smell of blood. The bird kept trying to leap away, forgetting its bound legs; kept trying to flap its immobilized wing.

Gray Bear took a deep breath. Trying to come to grips with the reality before his eyes.

I dreamed this!

Not this scene directly, not the dead Arapaho, or the position or sequence of events, but the man and the bird. The *Taipo* and their weapons. Dreams, his personal *puha*, had led him to this place.

"No shoot!" Singing Lark insisted loudly as she stopped in front of the tall *Taipo*.

This was the moment of truth.

Gray Bear took a deep breath and shifted his arrows, ready to rise to his knees and drive a shaft through the tall man's chest if he tried to take Singing Lark captive.

The tall man said something in an incomprehensible tongue.

The brown man kept turning, pointing the *aitta* this way and that, his gaze still roaming in search of enemies. He said something back.

The tall man lowered his *aitta*. His hands formed the sign for "Who you?"

"Singing Lark," she both signed and told him. Her hands like graceful birds, she signed, "We are *Newe*."

At the sinuous sign for the people, the tall man cried, "Snake, by God!"

"Snake?" the brown man asked, lowering his rifle. He pointed to the dead Arapaho chief and signed, "He is yours?"

Singing Lark cried, *"Kai!"* and made the sign for *Sa'idika*. Then she signed, "Enemy."

The brown man pointed to the Arapaho transfixed by Gray Bear's arrow and signed "Who kill?" — his movements jerky, his suspicious eyes on Singing Lark.

"My *taikwahni*," she told him, then turned, calling, "Stand up, Gray Bear."

Both *Taipo* followed her gaze as Gray Bear — feeling like his heart wanted to leap up

63

his throat — stood and called, *"Kai kuttih!"* He carefully left his arms at his side, the bow and arrows almost hidden in the waist-tall grass.

"How many *Newe*?" the tall man signed.

Gray Bear shifted his bow to his left hand, signing, "Five. *Haintsa!*" He made the hand sign for "friend."

The two *Taipo* talked warily to each other, glancing suspiciously from Singing Lark to him, to the surrounding grass.

"Show yourselves," Gray Bear called. "Keep your weapons down. Just stand there so the *Taipo* can see you."

Turns His Back, Red Moon Man, and Kestrel Wing stood from where they'd been concealed.

"Look at their faces!" Turns His Back said in amazement. "You think their mothers locked hips with bears?"

"I've seen *Taipo* before," Red Moon Man noted, a hint of superiority in his tone. "When the Astorians went through the Valley of the Warm Winds last year. They are all crossed with bears and very pale."

"Enough," Gray Bear told them. He signed, "I am coming to you." And as he started down the slope, he added, *"Kai kuttih!"* and *"Haintsa!"*

To his relief, the *Taipo* didn't raise their

aitta, didn't make as much as a threatening move.

"Taikwahni!" Singing Lark proclaimed with pride as he stopped beside her. As she did, she made the sign for "chief."

"John Tylor," the brown man said, stepping forward.

Gray Bear blinked, stunned. He signed, "I have seen you." Then he pointed. "I have seen the hawk."

John Tylor smiled, the expression making his beard move as if alive. "Seen you." And he pointed at his head.

Gray Bear took a deep breath. "Nothing prepares a man for a moment like this." He pointed at the Arapaho. Signed, "Dog Eaters." And said, *"Sa'idika."*

Then he turned, pointed to the west, and signed, "We go. Now. *Sa'idika* come back tomorrow. No good."

The two *Taipo* talked again.

The brown man used signs to ask, "What you want?"

Gray Bear pointed to the man's rifle. *"Aitta.* We trade. Much trade. Unlike *Sa'idika,* we no take."

And then he stepped to the side, dropping on his knees before the still agitated hawk. "Brother, it is good to see you. The day will come when once again you fly. If I have seen this, I am sure that day will come."

The young hawk met his gaze, black pupils burning in those bright yellow eyes. The bird was panting, tongue flicking with each breath.

To the others, still waiting up on the slope, Gray Bear ordered, "Go and get the horses. We have a hard night's ride ahead of us. The Dog Eaters who escaped will bring others back. We don't want to be here."

When he looked up, it was to see John Tylor bent over the young Arapaho he'd killed. The man was speaking softly, as if in apology. *The Taipo* had a pained look on his face, as if tormented in the soul.

Gray Bear hoped the kind words wouldn't cause the dead Arapaho's *mugwa* soul to follow them. Ghosts could bring terrible trouble down upon a man.

CHAPTER 8

Tylor was impressed and more than a little amazed. The girl, Singing Lark, *Denito'ai Hiittoo* in Shoshoni, had led them on their long night's ride. She'd been out front, scouting, riding ahead to vanish in the half moonlight. Sometime later, she'd appear out of the darkness, whisper instructions to Gray Bear, then fade into the night again.

It had started with Gray Bear's insistence that the Dog Eaters were going to return. Not such a hard leap to make given that half of the raiders had escaped. Let alone the fact that someone was going to come looking for the bodies. Chances were good that they'd have a real mad on when they did.

Tylor had to admit, he was just as glad to be quit of the little hollow. The fact that he'd killed that young man — barely more than a boy — kept replaying in his head.

Didn't matter that the kid was there to

cause him harm, looked forward to it, actually. Killing Tylor, striking him for coup, and stealing his horses and outfit would have made the kid a full-fledged warrior. Turned him from a boy to a blooded man of renown all in one triumph.

I just up and shot him.

He'd known what the sound of that arrow hitting home had meant. Somewhere deep in his mind, he'd probably thought it had hit Cunningham, that there was no way out.

Might not have been Cunningham who'd been hit, but Tylor had been very much correct that any chance for a peaceful resolution was gone.

Nevertheless, the whole thing was confusing. Upsetting. He'd *killed* that boy. Badly hurt, maybe killed, another. A lot of Dog Eaters had died.

Those fateful moments kept replaying. The buck of the rifle against his shoulder, the gush of smoke and the bang. The Arapaho kid had just crumpled. Dropped like lifeless meat. Alive one instant, then — like a snap of the fingers — he was dead. Broken. Destroyed.

Tylor rubbed his trigger finger, trying to understand the impossibility that such a tiny movement, the pressure on the pad of his finger, could have such horrendous consequences.

How fragile life was.

The almost magical appearance of Gray Bear added to his confusion and discomfort. The amiable-faced Indian from his dreams. The one who'd reached out in supplication, tears streaking down his face. Maybe the *taikwahni*'s face wasn't exactly the same. Could have been some difference in the roundness of cheek, the bridge of the nose, or the width between the eyes.

Sure looks close enough to be a brother.

John Tylor wasn't much for mystical visions, leaving those claims for the devoutly religious, the insane in their asylums, and the devotees of opium and too much alcohol.

But, yes, damn it. He'd dreamed it. Never had so much as a hint of foresight before. Didn't believe it now.

So, what the hell? He had the hawk. Now he was riding with the Indian.

To his and Cunningham's relief, the Shoshoni had stood to the side as he and Will had mantied up the packs and lashed them onto the packhorses, then saddled their mounts. The entire process had been accompanied by awed mutterings among the Shoshoni who rode like centaurs.

As darkness descended, the way had led

down to the Grand River, into the water and downstream, across the river, then over a ridge to a tributary stream. Sticking to the channel, they'd splashed back down to the Grand, then turned upstream. The horses had had to wade up through the shallows for what seemed half the night; the stars had wheeled most of the way across the heavens.

Then Singing Lark had led them up another creek, this one on the south bank. They'd made their way upstream until the brush closed in so densely they had to break out.

Singing Lark kept them low, following the contour of the land, keeping to drainage bottoms, hanging on the edge of the brush, having them ride single file.

The sun stood a full three hands high above the northeastern horizon when Singing Lark led them over a low ridge and down to a camp. The location was in the uplands, well hidden, a deceptive depression in what looked like a grassy flat.

"Have to tell you," Cunningham muttered as they rode into the shallow bowl, "this coon's about to slide off this old bone rack and give up my ghost if it means a nap."

Tylor blinked and yawned. He appraised the camp: small lodges laid out in a semicircle, women and a few kids staring at him with stunned brown eyes. Fires — apparently burning buffalo dung — smoldered, but cast little smoke. Packs lay about, and parfleches were stacked next to the lodge doors.

Behind the tents, a dozen horses were pastured, a tall, crop-haired boy keeping an eye on them. The animals came in all colors, looking shaggy, small, but wiry. They seemed well-cared-for, coats sleek. Now they neighed in greeting to their returned brethren.

A seep fed a patch of willows and provided water at the foot of the hollow, then the trickle soaked back into the ground from whence it had come.

As Tylor and Cunningham rode into the camp, they were the center of attention. The women, children, another couple of men, and one grinning and ugly old woman with wild-flying white hair flocked around, chattering among themselves.

The sight of the hawk, tied where it was atop the manty on Tylor's packhorse, elicited awed comments. For its part, the hawk stared around, starting to pant again, worried at the proximity of so many people.

Gray Bear dropped from his horse, face breaking into a smile. The old woman went

71

straight for him; her gaping grin exposed a couple of brown teeth in her gums and re-arranged the mass of wrinkles that was her face. She hugged him, laughing and chattering in Shoshoni.

Then she turned her dark and sparkling eyes on Tylor as he stepped off of his mare. She spoke to him in what was clearly a reverent tone. With a frail-looking hand, she reached out and tapped the barrel of his rifle with a clawlike finger.

After she'd done so, she raised the finger to her nose, sniffed, as if searching for an odor, and chuckled, apparently amused at herself. She turned to the people calling out in a singsong voice. The people laughed and clapped, looking pleased.

Singing Lark was still sitting on her horse. The girl's eyes were bright, her smile almost enchanting. As her eyes met Tylor's they seemed to warm in an oddly beguiling way.

"What do you think, coon?" Cunningham asked, his wary eyes trying to keep track of everything.

"I think it's too early to tell, but my hunch is that we're safe for the moment."

"Been cogitating on it. These Snakes, they didn't just show up. Neither did the Arapaho. My take? Them Arapaho was tracking us. Follering our trail. Maybe the Snakes

72

caught sight of us? Maybe they saw the Arapaho and was watching them to see who they was hunting. Maybe they was a watching us and then saw the Arapaho. However that worked, them Arapaho would never have braced us if they'd a knowed about the Snakes being right close."

"That gives you the uneasy shivers, don't it? You and I figured we were alone out in the middle of nowhere. Never had so much as a clue we were the center of so much attention."

"Yep. Reckon this child just larned him a lesson he ain't never gonna forget."

"Me either," Tylor assented, thinking about how blithely and carelessly he and Cunningham had ridden. Right into a mess. But for the good graces of the Snakes, it would have turned out a whole lot worse.

Gray Bear, grinning, had finished his greetings. He turned, gesturing that Tylor and Cunningham unsaddle. With his hands, he signed. "You stay. Eat. We trade."

"Trade?" Tylor asked glancing back at the packs. "Well, hell, that's what Booshway Lisa sent us out here to do."

He and Cunningham stripped the saddles and tack from the horses, then watched the young man from the horse herd lead them out to the cavvy. The usual melee ensued as the horses sorted it all out.

Tylor took care to place the hawk in the shade of a couple of packs. To his surprise, Gray Bear spoke to one of the women, and she produced a prairie dog carcass. It took the hawk a while — uncertain as it was about its new circumstances — but in the end, hunger won out and it ripped into the fresh meat.

Meanwhile, Tylor lifted the manty from their trade packs, and began laying out some of the items. As he did, one of the women approached with an armful of remarkably white, soft hides the likes of which he'd never seen.

"Buffalo calf?" Cunningham asked.

Tylor took one of the hides, fingering it, feeling the remarkable softness. The Shoshoni were standing in a half circle watching. "Better than anything coming out of the tan yards back in the United States," Tylor said. "Feel this."

Cunningham took the hide, rubbing it between his fingers. "Ain't never known the like of it."

"We'll trade," Tylor told Gray Bear with a grin and pointed to the items he and Cunningham had laid out.

Gray Bear stepped close, made the sign for "trade," and nodded happily. Then he pointed at Tylor's rifle where it was propped against the packs. *"Aitta,"* he said. "Trade." He made the sign for "many," then repeated, *"Aitta."*

"He wants our guns," Cunningham observed.

"Will, old coon," Tylor said dryly. "I think we have a problem."

CHAPTER 9

Gray Bear watched with amusement as John Tylor made a face and carefully picked a grasshopper from the bowl of stew that he cradled. The brown man lifted it, staring distastefully at the hopper where it was illuminated by the glow of the dung fire.

"Duka." Gray Bear made the sign "Eat." Then he demonstrated as he fished into his own bowl, pulled out a grasshopper to plop into his mouth, chewed it gustily, and swallowed. *"Tsaan."* And he made the sign for "good."

Tylor shot him a look — then glanced sideways at Cunningham, who was now staring uneasily down at his stew — and gingerly put the boiled grasshopper in his mouth. He chewed nervously. Swallowed hard.

Taipo, it seemed, didn't eat grasshoppers. Gray Bear wondered if they felt the same way about crickets, grubs, moths, and some of the other foods the *Newe* considered common fare.

The rest of his people were crowded around in the dark and watched every move the *Taipo* made. He had almost had to take a switch to Singing Lark. The girl — no, the young woman — had been dazzled by the *Taipo*. She'd wanted to stay and study them, but with angry Arapaho somewhere off to the east and maybe less than a day's ride away, someone had to watch their backtrail. Keep an eye out.

Three Feathers had ignored that responsibility, and he — not to mention so many of his band — had died as a result.

As the feast progressed, Gray Bear was entertained when the *Taipo* periodically stopped chewing long enough to pull out the little bones, inspect them curiously, and pitch them into the fire. People had rituals when it came to food. Maybe, by burning the bones, *Taipo* thought they were showing respect to the mice and voles who'd gone into the stew.

Must have been good though; the white men greedily finished off three helpings apiece, grinning as they placed their bowls on the ground before them.

"Trade," Gray Bear said after offering his prayers of thanks for the meal.

"Trade," Tylor agreed, leaning forward. "*Aitta.* Guns." He signed, "You have many hides. We have *aitta* at the Great River."

Then, in the grass, he drew a line, saying "Moreau River." Drew another line. "Grand River." And a third line that crossed them. "Great River, what we call Missouri." He made a dot on the Great River. "*Aitta.* There." He pointed to the packs of tanned buffalo calf hides. "*Pehe* here." He'd learned the *Newe* name for hides.

"Bring *aitta*?" Gray Bear suggested, trying to figure out the ramifications of the swap. Guns were smaller, easier to transport than the heavy bales of tanned leather.

Tylor shook his head. Rattling off a string of *Taipo* talk, Cunningham nodding his agreement.

Tylor signed, "Take *pehe* to the river." He gestured. "You, me, Will. We go make trade."

Gray Bear took an uneasy breath.

"I don't like it," Red Moon Man said from behind. "What kind of fools do they think we are? You ride off with all of our calf hides. Bang. You are dead out in the grass, and we never see the *Taipo* again."

"My friend is right," Kestrel Wing agreed. "Not to mention that we're in dangerous country here. We know the Dog Eaters are somewhere east, and at any moment a hunting party of Atsina, Mandan, Arikara, Sioux, or Cheyenne could ride over the ridge and murder us all."

John Tylor was watching him with knowing eyes. He chuckled softly. Signed: "I see your worry. How can we make better?"

"The brown *Taipo* can stay," Aspen Branch said from behind. "Gray Bear, Red Moon Man, Walks Too Fast, the three of you go with Tall *Taipo*. Tylor" — she pronounced it in two syllables as Ty Lor — "will stay with us. You have a half moon. If you are not back? We kill Ty Lor, leave his ghosts wailing in the grass, and the rest of us will try to sneak home."

"I'm satisfied with that." Red Moon Man shrugged. "The *waipepuhagan* and you have brought us this far, Gray Bear. I'll gamble my life that you can get us our *aitta.*"

"Me, too," Kestrel Wing agreed.

From where he sat in the back, Five Strikes, still moody and mourning the murder of his wife, son, and the abduction of his two daughters by the Blackfeet, called. "And if you do not return, *Taikwahni,* I will be the one who kills the *Taipo.*"

Gray Bear made a gesture with his hand. Young Eagle's Whistle hurried forward and tossed another couple of buffalo chips onto the fire.

Gray Bear wanted to be sure that he had enough light to read John Tylor's expression as he explained his counteroffer. He suspected the *Taipo* wasn't going to like it.

CHAPTER 10

"Yer sure this is a good idea?" Cunningham asked as he used his knife to cut a chaw from his carrot of tobacco. He was sitting on Cobble, his long Pennsylvania rifle across the saddlebow. He cast a sideways glance as Gray Bear — mounted on a muscle-tough and scrubby-looking horse — led a string of six horses packed with the bales of tanned calf hides.

"A good idea?" Tylor shrugged and grinned. "Hell no! But, Will, it's the best option we've got. Being a spy and a conspirator, I'm no expert when it comes to tanned hides. But you are, and you've told me that what's on those horses is worth a small fortune."

"Might make the difference for the booshway," Cunningham granted. "What with the war, the British raising hell, the poor returns on the expedition so far this year."

"Indeed, it might."

Singing Lark was listening and nodding as Gray Bear gave her instructions, waving off to the east as he did so.

"Got yer eye on that one?" Cunningham asked, a questioning tilt to his head. "She's sure been watching you."

"Not in the way you're thinking. She's too young." He grinned. "I like her. She's got grit."

Cunningham gave him a saucy wink in return. "Yeah, well, you know that woman what wears that yeller skirt? Got it outta ol' Gray Bear. Her husband's just dead. And I like her. Exactly in the way yer thinking."

"Her name's Whistling Wren."

"Watch yer hair, coon."

"Watch my hair?"

Cunningham raised a finger to his brow in salute. "Yep. Make sure you keep it on top of yer head, child. Not hanging from some savage's horse bridle."

"My hair will be fine. You keep track of your own."

Tylor watched the riders and horses as they lined out and started out of the bowl. Within moments they were gone, the only sign of their passage being the bruised grass.

Around him, the camp seemed suddenly somber, curiously quiet. The sad warrior, the one called Five Strikes, was watching him through unemotional black eyes, his short hair teased by the wind. The women, too, were giving him uneasy glances.

Singing Lark took notice, glanced knowingly at Tylor, and then called out some sort of chiding remark, flinging her hands at the people as if in remonstration. In response, the rest of the Shoshoni broke out in laughter, the tension broken.

Tylor, himself, chuckled.

Kestrel Wing was rubbing some kind of oil on his composite bow, the thing being made of mountain sheep's horn and layers of some kind of wood. Tylor had seen the power, how one of them had driven the whole length of an arrow at a steep angle through one of the Arapaho warriors. The shaft had been held in the wound only by the fletching.

The young boys, he noticed, had curiosity in their eyes as they shot him sly glances and smiles.

Tylor scuffed the grass with his worn boots. The soles had separated from the uppers and were held together by wrappings of leather. He wondered what the well-shod Shoshoni thought of that. Turning, he walked over to where the old woman was seated cross-legged on the grass.

Singing Lark was watching him with a

speculative gaze. Each time he glanced her way, she gave him an amused smile. She nodded with approval and made the sign for "good" as he turned his attention to the old woman.

"Hello, Grandmother," Tylor told her. "Mind if I sit and share the sun with you?"

She gave him that gape-toothed smile that seemed to beam light, and though she couldn't have had a clue about what he'd asked, patted the hide beside her.

"*Taipo* Ty Lor," she said.

He pointed at her. "You?"

"*Sennapin muka.*"

"Thought they called you Wipehegand or something?"

"*Waipepuhagan.*" She made a sign with her hands that Tylor couldn't fathom and added a "yes" gesture to it.

Singing Lark had sidled closer so that she could listen.

Tylor stared up at the sun, bright in the sky as it shone down in the east. "Well, Sennapin Muka, it's going to take Will and the rest more than a week at best. I have nothing to do, so while we wait, why don't you start to teach me the language?"

He pointed at the hawk, sitting in its shaded perch, head tilting this way and that as it watched everything that happened in the camp. "Hawk," he told her.

Catching on immediately, she told him, *"Kinii."*

He repeated the word, committing it to memory.

And, if nothing else, perhaps I can retire to some learned institution back in the white world and become a professor of languages.

Assuming that Cunningham made it back with the rifles and that Kestrel Wing didn't use that marvelous bow of his to drive an arrow through John Tylor's lights.

CHAPTER 11

The ride to St. Louis had been hard, the roads passable, and Eli Danford and Silas Simms — while skeptical of Toby's promotion — had been game. Especially Danford, who, though older and more experienced, realized that *Corporal* Johnson didn't care that he took a nip off his flask every so often. Not that Danford was a drunk, he just liked his corn spirits.

Toby knew exactly what his Bible-quoting blood-and-thunder father would have said about it, but figured that if Danford kept it to the occasional taste, it wasn't worth making a scene over.

Traveling under military orders, and with a discretionary purse, was a revelation. Toby had been told to keep track of all his spending. Unable to read or figure, he'd been lucky to have Danford along to keep track of it all. Then, to Toby's dismay, a sudden shower had soaked the piece of paper he kept for the purpose, and when he'd tried to extract it from his pocket, it had fallen apart.

Nevertheless, he led the way on his tired horse as he and his small command climbed the bank from the Mississippi River ferry.

Clopping through the muddy streets of St. Louis, Toby found his way to General Clark's official address and stepped down.

"We sure we can't stay here awhile?" Simms asked hopefully, his eyes straying to the surrounding buildings. "This place sure is the beat of Nashville. Me, I reckon I'd like to take a stroll down through some of them fancy houses by the river."

Toby, still a virgin, made a face. He definitely knew what his father would say to that. "Silas, how much money you got?"

"Nigh onto two dollars."

"And how much would one of them women charge?" Danford asked. "Ten cents? Up to two bits? That'd buy you a nice room with a bed an' a real roof over yer head."

"Reckon it would," Simms agreed. He carefully stepped down from his horse, stretched, and made a face. "How much they charge for a room with a roof and bed up the Missouri whar we're headed, Corporal?"

"Ain't no roofs or beds that I know of once we's past a couple of them forts."

Simms shot Danford an arched look. "So, Eli? What in hell's we saving even two bits for?"

Toby chuckled to himself. Father was a long way away. Green as he was, Toby knew a commanding officer had to keep his men on his side. "For the time being, you all keep an eye on the horses. Me, I got to palaver with the general. Soon's I get straight with him on my mission, we'll figure what we're gonna do. You done good in the getting here. Reckon that oughtta buy ye a bit of a reward."

Simms grinned at Danford.

Toby climbed the steps, feeling every muscle in his back and thighs. Too dang long on the back of a horse. Took him to the top of the steps to recover any hint of a normal stride.

His papers presented, he had to wait for close to a half hour before he was ushered into General William Clark's office. He took in the furnishings, having been there not so long ago. Nothing much was changed.

"Ah, you're back!" Clark said, rising. "And a corporal now, is it?"

"Yes, sir." Toby handed the man the correspondence Jackson had given him.

"Brandy?" Clark asked as he seated himself behind his desk and frowned down at the sheath of papers. These Toby had kept in the waterproof dispatch case. They'd fared so much better than his receipts.

Toby turned toward the cut-glass decanter. Stopped short. He'd never so much as . . .

"Pour one for me, too, if you please."

Sounded like an order. Toby winced, made himself reach for the bottle, wondered how much to pour, and filled both glasses to just a hair shy of the rim. Carrying them over, careful not to spill, he placed one on the desk at the general's elbow. That left him with nothing to do but stare anxiously at the amber liquid in his own glass.

"The devil's curse is the demon of spirits! A Satan-possessed liquid that damns men's souls to the black pit!" Father's words echoed in his ears.

I'm an officer now.

Officers drank.

And what would General Clark say? It would be downright rude to set the glass down. For the briefest of instants, he considered hiding it, maybe stuffing it behind the decanter, but Clark would find it the next time he . . .

"So," Clark said softly, "Andrew Jackson

still wants Tylor. I'd rather hoped the whole John Tylor excitement had blown over."

Toby turned his attention from the brandy problem to the general who now frowned off into some distance in his mind.

William Clark seemed much too genial and personable to be a real general. But then, this was the hero of the Corps of Discovery who had traveled all the way to the Pacific. The red hair was turning white and thinning on top. The long nose was swelling with age — the occasional broken blood vessel turning it a brighter red than the rest of his face. Those once-brilliant blue eyes had faded under the drudgery of desk work and administration.

"Uh, sir? Reckon the general give me an order. I'm t' fetch the traitor back alive or dead, sir."

"I see, Corporal." A pause. "It's a fool's errand. We're in the end of August. The last thing you need right now is to try and chase your way up the river at this time of year."

Clark paused, tapping his lips with his fingers as he thought. "How about I reassign you to St. Louis? I could find you some task more suitable, and God knows we are in need of soldiers. Especially given the machinations of the British. I curse that Robert Dickson. He's played hell up at

Michilimackinac. The defense of St. Louis is a great deal more important than running down a man who is only seeking to flee his past."

"Reckon I thank ye, sir. But I been given an order." Toby grinned in what he hoped was an inoffensive way. "An' if'n I didn't set this Tylor's carcass at the general's feet, wouldn't be no surprise if'n Jackson didn't skin me alive."

"Allow me to handle Andrew. You sure you wouldn't like a reassignment here?"

"My complemates, sir, but I cain't." He knew that was wrong. Hadn't paid attention when the officers were talking before, and now really wished he had.

"That's 'my compliments,' " Clark corrected with a smile. "I begin to see why Andrew chose you. Dedicated to a job once you've been given it?"

"Some say I'm too dumb to know when to quit. But that's Paw's teaching. Reckon it's part 'cause I was a hunter, too, sir. Best in the county. Kept the family fed while Pap made sure we was right with God."

"Very well." Clark reached for his glass, noticed it was brimming. His brow arched as he noted how full the glass in Toby's hand was. The smile, more amused than ever, widened. "To your health, Corporal."

Toby lifted the glass, gulping the drink as if it were water. Got a couple of swallows down before his throat locked up. He inhaled in surprise, only to have fire burn down his windpipe.

In the coughing fit that followed, he did his best to keep from spilling the general's brandy on the carpet.

As the tears streaked down Toby's face, General Clark threw his head back and laughed like a man possessed.

CHAPTER 12

John C. Luttig sat behind the crude table where it was jammed in the back of the rough-hewn warehouse and sorted through his journal papers. The last thing he expected that night was for Will Cunningham to walk through his door in the company of three Indian men.

Luttig's path to the Upper Missouri had been circuitous. He had begun his professional life as a successful businessman in Baltimore. His dealings there had led him to realize that St. Louis, on the frontier, was ripe with possibilities. Subsequent to relocating to the city in 1809, he found work as a clerk and auctioneer, speculator, and agent for August Chouteau.

His talent, intelligence, and ability led him into politics where he supported reforms in the ham-handed way the federal government administered the territory. In this pursuit, he was seated on a grand jury that

93

investigated the role of certain government-appointed justices. Subsequently he helped pen a presentment to the Congress in Washington City, asking that judges be required to live among those whose lives they presided over, that taxpayers in the territory have a role in determining their taxation as well as which laws were passed, and demanding better determination of land title.

Such activism, of course, brought him to Manuel Lisa's attention. Luttig's understanding of business, ledgers, accounts, and his skills as a clerk made him perfect for the perilous 1812 expedition upriver.

Luttig stared up in surprise from his papers, illuminated as they were by candlelight. Cunningham was grinning. The three Indians were staring about, wide-eyed and whispering to themselves.

The men were dressed in an unfamiliar manner, their hair cut short and unkempt in comparison to the usual Indian predilection for fancy roaches, ornate coiffure, and highly oiled and primped styles. Nor had they painted their faces for the occasion and donned their best, but looked rugged, muscular, with breechcloths of soft leather and what looked like mountain-sheep-hide cloaks hanging from their shoulders.

"Will! I thought you'd be long gone for the mountains," Luttig cried as he rose to his feet and extended his hand.

"Reckon I'm just a right fast coon. Been there and back. I brung ye a passel of trade, too." He gestured. "These be Snakes, John. Come ter trade. They got tanned buffalo calf hides the likes of which ye never seen. Six large packs. Tanned white. Soft. The sort that will raise eyebrows back home."

Luttig stared. "Snakes? From the far mountains? How did they know to come here?"

"Happenstance, coon. Tylor and I got jumped by Arapaho. Got plumb serious. Had our bacon saved by ol' Gray Bear, here, and his friends. Figger'd to repay the favor. Whar's the booshway?"

"Upriver. Dealing with that ugly business with the Big Bellies."

Cunningham's expression pinched the slightest bit. "Got a problem. The Snakes, here, they got fine hides. But they want guns, John. We willing ter make that trade? Or do ye need the booshway's okay on that?"

"Let me see the hides, and I'll —"

"We got 'nuther problem. Worked out slicker'n grease on a doorknob, us sneaking in here. Most of the Sioux and 'Ricara is

95

out picking berries, cherries, and plums. We's able to wind our way around them. Come close ter gettin' spotted a couple o' times. Sneaked into the post after dark 'cause we don't want none of these other coons to know we's here. Snakes is prime prey in this country. And they're rich. I mean it when I say them hides is prime. And John, if'n we trade for rifles, ye 'tarnal well know that half the Injuns in the country's gonna be after the Snakes and me."

"Will, what are you asking of me?"

"I want ter make this trade. Get 'er done. Come sunup, this child wants t' be well shut of the river and making tracks back to the Snake camp. After that, we got a passel of riled 'Rapaho gonna want our hair. Catch my drift hyar?"

Luttig ran a hand through his hair. "These hides better be damned outstanding. You know what a rifle is worth in trade up here?"

"Reckon I do, coon. Now, help me get these packs in. Way I figger it, I'd trade these hides fer ten guns, shot, and powder."

Luttig started, then laughed. "You're out of your mind."

Cunningham gave him a challenging grin. "C'mon, John. Help me with these packs, and then we'll see."

Luttig did. Helping the burly Snake men

96

as they carted in heavy pack after heavy pack. He'd seen the like. As fine as the best English or Massachusetts tanneries. These weren't coarse hides, but calves. Thin, light, and supple. All were finished in a remarkable, almost snowy white.

"Reckon they used that clay up White River," Cunningham told him after signing back and forth with the leader, the one called Gray Bear.

Then came the bargaining, conducted over the guttering candle as it burned low.

In the end, Luttig cried, "Whose side are you on here?"

Cunningham grinned, replying, "Coon, ye want the Snake trade all wrapped up fer Manuel? Or d' ye want 'em heading west to them British posts on the Columbia? They's talk that Lord Selkirk's building a post on Red River just north of the border, too."

Luttig rubbed his face, aware that the Shoshoni men were watching him with keen black eyes. What the hell would Manuel do? But in his heart, he knew. Lisa would be willing to cut his profits in the front end, knowing damn well that he could make it up down the road.

"Deal," Luttig muttered, extending his hand.

After finalizing the trade, Luttig stood in

the cool night, hearing the sounds of the river, frogs, crickets, and the hum of night insects. A wealth of stars frosted the velvet black above as Will Cunningham, the three Snake men, and their horses walked slowly out of Lisa's burgeoning new trading post and headed west into the uplands.

They left with ten rifles, twenty pounds of powder, lead, and the necessary molds. Each warrior carried his rifle across his horse's withers. The rest of the guns rode wrapped in an oilcloth and tied atop one of the scrubby-looking packhorses.

"Will, God help you if any of the local Indians around here figure out that you've got those rifles. They'd turn this country upside down to get their hands on them."

CHAPTER 13

Dawson McTavish, twenty-three, sat hunched with his arse on a fallen cotton-wood log, his hands busy with a needle and thread as he sought to repair a seam where his shirtsleeve was coming loose at the shoulder. He squinted in the firelight, care-fully running his needle through the heavy stroud.

"Scary being on the west bank of the Mis-souri. Think we'll find the Tetons before the Arikara find us?" Joseph Aird asked thought-fully as he shifted the pot on the fire in an attempt to get it boiling for tea. His nineteen-year-old face had a worried look as he crouched before the crackling flames. His shirt was decorated with the beaded flower patterns common to the north woods.

Their camp was located in the floodplain of a small creek that flowed east to the Mis-souri. The location was screened by thick cottonwoods, brush, and scrubby oak trees.

The fire could only be seen from close at hand. The picket line, with its horses, was tied off so as to be out of sight of anyone on the terraces to the north or south.

The fact that they were crossing through Arikara territory made their plight perilous. On the one hand, the Rees were currently at peace with the Teton Sioux. On the other — with only four in McTavish's party, plus the two packhorses loaded with gifts for the Teton Sioux chiefs, not to mention their personal rifles and supplies — who would notice if they were mysteriously murdered and their belongings turned up scattered among a handful of Arikara lodges?

Besides, the Rees could guilelessly claim that there was a war being fought, and a few missing British traders in American territory were just part of the arithmetic.

Overhead, heart-shaped cottonwood leaves rattled with the night breeze blowing down from the west. Looking up, Dawson could see the fire's yellow tinge reflected there.

An owl hooted from somewhere upstream, which immediately brought Matato and Wasichu to full attention. Both of the Santee Dakota had tensed, hands going to their medicine bundles where they hung from thongs at their necks. Most Sioux thought owls were messengers of misfortune. Silly damned superstition that it was.

"What do you think for tomorrow?" Dawson asked, hoping to distract Matato. The tall Sioux warrior stood right at six feet. He was related to Totowin, Robert Dickson's Whapeton Dakota wife. Given his kinship to her, not to mention his cousins among the Teton, Matato — along with his younger counterpart, Wasichu, or "White man" — were the perfect key to unlock access to the western Sioux.

"We need to be up at dawn. Traveling slow." Matato glanced back at the darkness, fingers still on the medicine bundle. "This time of year? People are out. It is the moon when the berries come ripe. Back this far from the river, with as few buffalo as we've seen, it is not likely that we will run into hunting parties. But we could still be found. We need to stay to the low places."

"No telling what the Tetons are gonna be like," Joseph muttered, as he wiped at his nose with a finger and tossed a small bundle of tea into the water as it began to boil.

Joseph was Dawson's best friend, boon companion, and worshipful subordinate. They'd grown up together, traveling with their fathers from fur post to fur post. In Dawson's eyes, Joseph was the little brother he'd never had. They'd been inseparable for years now.

Dawson made his last stitch, pulled the thread tight, and tied the knot. Then he bit the thread off. "There. Ought to hold until I can trade for a better one among the Teton."

Again the owl hooted, closer this time, causing everyone to jump.

"Bit spooky, huh?" Joseph asked as he used a fold of cloth to keep from burning his hand on the hot handle as he moved the teapot back from the fire to sit and steep.

"Didn't seem so scary back in camp at the Falls of St. Anthony. Sounded like a right high adventure. 'Be my agents,' Robert says. 'I need you to travel west, across the Missouri. Rally the Dakota to the Crown.' "

"Didn't think that black-hearted Lisa would be upriver. You heard the talk before we left. All that palaver that Missouri Fur Company was broke. British trade boycotted. Nobody figured the damn Americans could put together a trading party."

"Well, that greasy old Manuel Lisa did. And now, here we are. Slipping around out here in fear of our lives instead of arriving like lords of the dance at the Sioux camps."

Matato said, "You worry too much, British."

"Just hope we find the right Sioux camp," Dawson added. "Wouldn't do to be seen sneaking in and find out later that your kin were all away hunting buffalo someplace else."

Matato chuckled at that. "Robert Dickson is family. Makes you family, too. Dickson asked me to keep you out of trouble. This I will do. Once we find Crooked Hand's village, all will be well. But we must find him first. If Lisa has been here, he will have sent presents to Chief Black Buffalo. He is a respected leader. Many will listen to him. If we can reach Crooked Hand, he can make our path smooth, perhaps even talk Black Buffalo and his band into joining us."

Matato could not have been a better choice to accompany the mission. He'd been with Robert Dickson for years. Had traveled to Montreal and Quebec. Understood how important it was for the South West Fur Company to keep the Americans at bay. Especially with the North West Company and Hudson's Bay Company tearing each other apart up in the north. Drive the Americans out of the Upper Missouri, and that entire fur trade would be the South West Company's to profit from.

The only obstacle was Manuel Lisa.

Dawson was considering that as he watched the steam rise from the pot of tea. Once their stash of leaves was gone, with the war on, he wondered when he'd get another good cup. Have to make do with local substitutes, he suspected.

It wasn't an owl this time, but a voice. "Hallo the camp!"

Dawson lost himself in the scramble to pull up his rifle — a once-fine Philip Bond of London gun of sixty caliber. Over the years it had taken a beating, but still shot straight.

"Who comes?" Dawson called.

"Fenway McKeever! I'm a friend, laddie."

"What kind of friend?"

"The kind that's damn happy t' have found ye. I bin' oot looking for some of Robert Dickson's agents. Bless me fer being me poor mother's son, but I think I found ye."

"Come in, but you'd better be alone."

"Aye, laddie. I'm alone, and sore for the sight of yer likes." From behind the brush, a solitary figure emerged, stepping forward with his hands up.

The man who eased into the firelight was big, thickly muscled through the shoulders, his face and hands freckled, sun-reddened, and his green eyes hard and knowing. He was dressed in muddy and torn rags that barely qualified as clothes. Worn boots, separated at the sole, shod his feet. Thick red hair had been gathered into a ponytail that hung down his back.

"What happened to you?" Joseph Aird asked.

"Manuel Lisa happened to me, laddie." The big man lowered his hands. "Him and a mon named John Tylor. But that's a story for another time. I heard ye mention Robert, that'd be Dickson, eh? Yer working for South West Fur Company. Sent by Dickson to ally the tribes to the British cause. Deny the Americans their hold on the Upper Missouri?"

"And if we are?" Dawson asked, his rifle still at the ready.

Where he sat slightly to the side, Matato had slipped his knife from his belt, holding it low beside his leg as he gathered his feet beneath him, ready to spring. Wasichu, having read his fellow Sioux's subtle signs, had shifted to the left. The young man's hand had found his war club.

"I serve John Jacob Astor, who owns South West Fur Company in association with William McGillivray. Ye ever heard o' him?"

105

"Of course. I was born in the trade. I'm third cousin to Robert McTavish, of the North West Company. Through my mother, my other cousin is Robert Dickson," Dawson claimed.

"Ach, an 'tis good I found ye. I got here by way of the North West Company meself, and the XY Company before that. Me job was to spy on Manuel Lisa, and if possible, wreck his expedition. I was betrayed. Which, sorry to say, leads me to this state of squalor."

Joseph shot Dawson a questioning glance.

Dawson said, "I never heard any of this."

"So Robert Dickson's yer cousin, eh, laddie? D'ye think he told you ever'thing he's aboot? Perhaps give ye an inside to his plans for his Indian troops what he be marching east to fight the Americans? I reckon not. Ye, see, it's the things ye don't know that can get ye killed."

"And you'd know these things?" Joseph asked uneasily.

"Aye." The big Scotsman grinned, showing yellowed teeth. "And, laddie, ye'd best order yer Indian, here, t' let that knife drop. If'n he'd make a wrong move, I'd have to take it away from him and shove it sideways up his arse. Same with the young laddie yonder and his war club."

Dawson made the desist gesture with his hand. Something about Fenway McKeever indicated that, unarmed and ragged as he might appear, the threat wasn't empty.

"If you're an agent sent by Astor, why'd you want to wreck Lisa's expedition? Astor's an American, too."

"Aye, one with a financial interest in fur companies like yers, laddie. Ye think he could care who wins this war? When it's all over, he wants the American Fur Company in control. Right now, the Missouri Fur Company stands firm in his way. Has blocked him every time. What better excuse than a war to be rid of it? It's aboot owning the trade. Governments can go play with the devil."

Dawson hesitated. Something about the man sent a shiver up his back. Still, he was a Scot. His words about the North West Company and the XY Company before it rang with truth. The fight between them had been as vicious as that between the Hudson's Bay Company and the Nor'westers that was currently being fought out in Canada's plains, forests, and prairies.

"Ye kin shoot me . . . or let me have a cup of that marvelous smelling tea, laddie. Make yer choice." The green eyes had narrowed.

Dawson, still nervous, wondering if he was

107

making a mistake, tossed the man a cup. "Do come and join us."

As the big Scot sat, Matato was slowly shaking his head. The feeling Dawson had was like a giant cobra had just coiled itself in their midst.

CHAPTER 14

"Kuchu'na," Singing Lark said.

"Kootsoo nah." Tylor tried to pronounce the syllables.

"Kuch," Singing Lark corrected, emphasizing the *ch. "Kuchu'na."*

Tylor repeated the word as he looked out at the grazing *kuchu'na*. The word meant buffalo. The herd consisted of cows, calves, and a couple of young bulls. Fifty-six of them in total. They dotted the gentle grassy slope to the west, upwind. Not more than a quarter of a mile away.

He fingered his rifle, wondering if it was worth trying to sneak close, shoot one. The camp could use the meat.

From where he and Singing Lark sat on the grassy rise, he could worm his way down, ease along the shallow bottom, and come up just under the slope where the bison grazed. Crawling up the drainage, he could rise, take a knee, and have enough clearance above the grass. Close enough for a solid fifty-yard heart shot.

They were a couple of miles east of the Shoshoni camp, having ridden out on a scout. Singing Lark had invited him, asking him to leave the hawk in Aspen Branch's care. Five Strikes and Turns His Back had objected to his leaving camp with the girl, but Aspen Branch's snapped rebuke had silenced them. Then the old woman had waved Tylor and Singing Lark out of camp. Odd that the old woman would blithely entrust an attractive young girl into the care of an unknown and completely foreign man. No wonder the others had disapproved.

On the other hand, maybe the old woman, with her Spirit possession, was able to see into Tylor's soul, read his character. Knew that his particular chivalry wouldn't allow any impropriety with the bright and charming Singing Lark.

That, or it was a test, and Kestrel Wing and Five Strikes had circled around, were waiting to see if he'd try anything inappropriate.

No, that was silly and way too elaborate and convoluted for the people he'd been living with for the last week.

Seemed like every time Tylor turned around, Singing Lark was making use of the moment to question him, tease him, watch him. As if fascinated. That her preoccupation with him annoyed all the others except Aspen Branch was obvious. Tylor did his best to treat the girl with respect. Went out of his way to answer her questions, laughed at her jests at his expense.

Girl? Odd, but she didn't act like a girl. Rather she had a hard side to her personality — as if she were mature beyond her years. Nothing was childlike about her ability as a scout and tracker. She might be young in years, but not in actions.

Well, maybe but for the teasing. She seemed to take great delight in his foibles and ignorance about all things Shoshoni.

Better yet, he had come to enjoy her company. Damn, how long had it been since a woman looked at him with anything other than disgust in her eyes? She was just easy to be around.

So, maybe he ought to sneak over and shoot her a buffalo. He was on the verge of suggesting this when she clamped a hand to his arm and squeezed. In the Shoshoni way, she nodded instead of pointing.

He followed her gaze, looking north down the gradual rolling slope toward the bur oak in the drainage bottom that led down toward the Grand River.

Tylor thought he had sharp eyes. Nevertheless, it took him a couple of seconds to pinpoint the distant dots, and then to realize what they were: riders.

"Think that's Will and Gray Bear?"

"Sa'idika," she told him. Despite his commitment to learn Shoshoni, the rattled words that followed came too fast for him to grasp.

"Which way they headed?" Tylor wondered, squinting, trying to discern their direction.

"Antsi Newe."

"Did you say they're looking for us?"

She turned her dark brown eyes on his. *"Ha'a.* Yes. Look for us."

He wondered who was learning the other's language faster, him or her. And he had the advantage of being immersed in it. Hearing it all day long. Having to try and use it, even if his fumbling attempts brought amusement to the Shoshoni.

Tylor pulled a dry stem of grass, chewing absently on it as he watched the distant riders.

"Which way they go?" he signed.

"Tapaiyuanankute." West. *"Antsi.* They look for, yes. Along river. Places we might leave . . . um . . ."

"Tracks. Sign," Tylor finished. "Makes

sense. If we didn't have the seep up at the camp, we'd have to send somebody for water. So, if you're Arapaho, you send parties cutting for sign along both sides of the river."

She gave him a knowing sidelong glance, and her clever smile bent her full lips. She made the signs for "We see first."

"Still, it's worrisome," he told her. "Wish Cunningham and Gray Bear would make it back. They could ride smack into those hunting Arapaho. Worse, the Arapaho could cut their trail, follow them right into camp. Wish to hell we were all headed west as fast as we could go."

Her eyes were fixed on the distant riders, the wind teasing her silky black hair. The soft hide dress she wore conformed to her shoulders and slender back. He tried to ignore the way it molded around the rest of her.

Which made him return his attention to the distant Arapaho. He knew what they would do to Singing Lark. She would be taken, raped repeatedly, and then sold into the worst kind of slavery. He'd seen enough slave women throughout his time in the west.

"That isn't going to happen. Not to this girl," he promised around the grass stem he chewed.

How can you prevent it? If they find us, attack the camp, what can you do if we're overrun?

She was watching him, a question behind her dark eyes. *"Hinni?"* What?

"Worried about you, girl. That's all."

"Don't know words." She'd picked up that phrase early.

He made the signs for, "I want me to make you safe." He pointed to himself. "Me. I want to keep you." He pointed at her. ". . . Um, protect. Yes?"

She studied him, a curious confusion behind her eyes. Her lips pursed. She signed back, "You want me. *Manapuih.*" A pause. *"Ni kwee?"*

Tylor could see her surprise. She seemed to be considering him with a new intensity.

"Me. Keeping you . . . um . . ." What was the sign? "Protect? Take care of?"

She bit her lip, wary eyes on his.

Tylor pointed at the Arapaho. "I don't want them catching you. Understand?"

She glanced back at the Arapaho, talking rapidly to herself. He caught the word *taipo* as it popped up in her soliloquy. Then she laughed to herself and shrugged.

Singing Lark studied him in a way she never had before, a churning behind her eyes. Accompanied by a rapid-fire string of Shoshoni, she reached out and distastefully fingered Tylor's beard. Gave it a half-hearted tug. Then she lifted the cuff of his shirt, tapping his skin where it remained white and protected from the sun.

"I want you . . ." he signed and stopped short. "Not hurt."

She seemed to be arguing with herself. *"Nakweekktu?"*

"Girl, I just didn't want harm to come to you." He used his most earnest voice, hopefully communicating his serious intent.

She took a deep breath, seemed to reorder her thoughts, and said, *"Nihannih napaisai."* She made the sign for "Later." And in English, said, "Understand?"

"Understand what?"

"Nakweekktu." She made the signs for "Not now."

In the distance the Arapaho had crossed the drainage, headed west along the broken slope above the Grand River.

"Come," she told him in English. "Go back. Tell others."

But he could tell that he'd upset her as they rose to their feet and walked silently back to where the horses had been hobbled down in the low lee of the ridge.

In the distance, the *Kuchu'na* watched,

heads up, alert.

Tylor tightened his cinch and stepped into the stirrup. He had inalterably changed his relationship with Singing Lark. But what the hell had he done?

CHAPTER 15

The morning sun still lay beneath the eastern horizon when Dawson McTavish awakened to the sound of the tin pot being placed on hearth stones in the fire.

He blinked, aware of how cold the morning air felt compared to the warmth in his blankets. He'd always found mornings hard. Some part of his makeup was naturally lazy. But, he did have his family legacy to live up to. The great trader, Robert McTavish, three times removed as he was from Dawson, cast a large shadow, one that Dawson had to be worthy of. People expected that of family. Not to mention his maternal relationship to Dickson and the trust that his mentor had placed in Dawson's ability as an agent.

It's up to me to be the leader.

He sat up, looking around in the gloom to see that Fenway McKeever had breakfast cooking. Across the fire, Joseph's blanketed form indicated that he was still asleep. From

117

his blankets, however, Matato was watching the big Scot through dark and gleaming eyes. Wasichu's bed was empty, the young Sioux no doubt having excused himself beyond the brush for his morning toilet and to check the horses.

Dawson sat up, yawned, and stretched as McKeever set the stew pot on the renewed flames where they leaped around freshly placed wood.

"You're up early."

"Much t' do, laddie. I figure we can made nigh onto thirty miles by nightfall."

"Thirty miles? We can't travel that fast. Not through Arikara country. They'll see us for sure."

"We're not going through Arikara country. We're headed west, laddie."

"My duty is to find the Teton Sioux, to induce them to give their loyalty to the crown and make war on the Americans. If the Sioux side with us, so does the whole upper river."

"Yer not the only agent Robert Dickson has workin' oot here, are ye?"

"Well, of course not. James Burke was sent south. And Jacques Molier and his party were dispatched —"

"I told you who I be, laddie." McKeever was staring at him from across the fire.

"Who I work for. And I daresay, John Jacob Astor and William McGillivray outrank yer Robert Dickson like a king trumps a jack. Now, I give ye an order. We're going west. And we're going to make good time at it."

Dawson threw off the covers, climbing to his feet in a half panic. "You can't just drop into my camp from nowhere, giving orders. I don't have the faintest idea who you are. You claim to be Astor's agent, but for all I know, you're just some boatman. Maybe a madman on the run."

The Scot's eyes had turned a frigid green, the pupils like tiny dots. "Laddie, yer aboot t' become a debility."

"A debility? What kind of talk is that?"

"The kind that gits a mon killed."

Dawson's gut had that queer liquid feeling of fear. "You threaten me?"

"Aye, and it's more o' a promise actually. Ye'll obey, or not. But soon's breakfast is over, we're heading west. At least yer horses and plunder are going wi' me. Ye can stay here and look fer yer Sioux if'n ye want. But I got Comp'ny business in the west."

"Matato," Dawson said, "escort this man out of my camp."

The big Indian rose from his blankets like a wraith, silent, fast. One second he was in his bed, apparently somnolent, the next he

119

was on his feet. Dawson was already grinning his victory when the big Scot, like lightning, shifted, hammered a blow with a freckled fist, and punched Matato in the throat.

Dawson saw the wide expression of disbelief in Matato's diamond-shaped face. His jaw worked, tongue protruding. The big Sioux's shoulders hunched, jerked.

McKeever backheeled him, slammed the big Sioux to the ground with a resounding thump. Hard enough to stun him. Even as Matato's body bounced, McKeever launched himself, driving the point of his knee into the Sioux's chest, the Scot's full weight behind it. The sound of popping ribs could be heard. Matato's body bucked and jerked. His legs twitched, arms fluttering and fingers spasming.

McKeever, just as quickly, rocked back and up, regaining his feet in a single fluid motion. He leaped high; his booted foot stamped down on Matato's throat. A crackling and snap could be heard. Matato's eyes and tongue protruded in a ghastly caricature; his limbs twitched, a rasping came from his throat. Then the bugged eyes stilled in his head. The body went limp.

McKeever wasn't even breathing hard as he said, "Now, laddie, be aboot yer business. I mean t' be on the trail by sunup. That means we need to eat, have camp packed, and be gone."

Unable to take a breath, Dawson reached for his throat; his gaze remained riveted on Matato. The big Sioux's wide eyes were fixed on the lavender morning sky; his expression empty and slack.

Joseph Aird stirred in his blankets, yawned, and sat up. Hair mussed, he rubbed his eyes. "Is it morning?" he asked, voice muzzy.

"Aye, and git yer arse oota them blankets and to work, laddie."

"You giving orders? Or did I miss something?" Joseph blinked, then shot McKeever a confused look.

"Jist a wee rearrangement in the chain o' command," McKeever told him. "Change o' plans. Now, roust yer young arse and give me a hand w' the horses and packs."

Joseph blinked, looking confused. "What?"

"You heard him," Dawson said, trying to keep the fear from his voice. "We're . . . we're heading west." He should do something. Get up. Fight.

Instead, frightened in a way he'd never been, Dawson just wanted to throw up. His blood seemed to melt in his veins.

"What? Why?" At that moment, Joseph's

wandering gaze fixed on Matato's corpse. He gaped, as if trying to understand why the big Sioux was sprawled so.

Because if we don't, I have no doubt but that McKeever will kill us all.

CHAPTER 16

Possessed by an uneasy feeling, Gray Bear fundamentally understood that his world would never be the same. That it had been forever altered. Without any chance to go back.

He had started this mad journey with the simple goal of accruing enough wealth that he could trade buffalo calf hides for a good sheep-horn bow to replace the one he'd broken.

Since that spring day when he'd left the Valley of the Warm Winds, he'd been forced far to the east, watched his best friend and so many of his people die, been made a chief, and been saddled with the uncomfortable responsibility for his little band's safety. He'd killed *Sa'idika* and was now being hunted by them. Had found himself face to face with *Taipo.* He'd traded with them at the Great River, actually been in their log village: what they called a "post." He'd seen

123

their boats. Huge floating wooden lodges. Inconceivable compared to a bullboat. Stood inside their remarkable wood-and-stone structures. Unbelievable compared to a wickiup. Seen their remarkable clothing, goods, furnishings, and wealth. Miraculous things that — had he not experienced them with his own eyes — he'd never have believed.

That late afternoon he didn't ride with a new sheep-horn bow, but with a shiny new *aitta* held crossways on his horse's withers. No, not *aitta,* but *rifle. A gun.* Those were the *Taipo* words for the gleaming weapon.

Gray Bear ran his fingers along the smooth wood and metal. It felt like nothing he'd ever touched before. Will Cunningham had picked this one special for Gray Bear. Said it was better than the "trade guns" the others had. That this one "held true."

If he hadn't trusted Cunningham, Gray Bear would have insisted on one of the trade guns. They had gleaming brass work, a snakelike creature inlaid in the wood beside the metal tube. His rifle, in contrast, looked drab, had dull iron fixings, and a smaller cock.

"Trust me, coon," Cunningham had told him. "It be a better gun. More accurate. What's pretty ain't always strong."

Yes. The world had changed. Inexorably. Gray Bear fingered his rifle, distressed by the knowledge that what he once had known, the world he had lived in, was gone. That those easy and simpler days of just being *Newe* and living in the mountains were finished. Much as his father must have felt when the rotting-face sickness first came and killed almost all of the people.

No going back. No recalling the dead. No reclaiming the endless plains that the Shoshoni had once dominated.

"No way to be a simple hunter," he whispered to himself as Moon Walker led the line of horses winding up out of the narrow drainage and onto a shoulder of the rolling slope that led to the uplands south of the Grand River.

The western sky brooded in an ominous way, thick with high-piled bruised-looking clouds. Beneath them, the storm's black skirt flickered from hidden lightning. Huge as the thunderheads were, the setting sun was hard-pressed to outline the limits of the monster bearing down on them.

I am taikwahni. *I have traded our prized calf hides for a fortune in rifles. If I can get them back to the* Newe, *I will be a great man. The other leaders will come to me. People will never look at me the same way again.*

"I never asked for this," he whispered.

He pulled Moon Walker up, letting the west wind play across his face and tug at his cropped-short hair. Carefully he took his time, searching the endless grass, the gently rising and falling country, trying to read each slope, each undulation, searching desperately for any hint of an enemy.

"Camp's just over thar," Cunningham said, pointing in a most un-Shoshoni way. The action always jarred Gray Bear, and was considered rude; but *Taipo* did a lot of rude things without even a hint that it might be upsetting to their hosts. *Newe* probably did the same among *Taipo*. He'd seen the stern looks, the uncomfortable expressions, as he and his warriors had wandered around the post, oohing and aahing, as they fingered the magical and mysterious belongings, and lifted the lids from barrels and peered inside.

"Yes." Gray Bear told him. "We close." In Shoshoni he added, "Time to be extra wary."

"We have all these rifles," Red Moon Man said arrogantly. "What fool band of *Sa'idika* would dare attack us now."

"Rifles we barely know how to use," Gray Bear reminded. He'd been itching to shoot his gun. Instead, Cunningham had carefully

126

explained that, like a bow, one didn't just pick up a rifle and shoot "center."

After Cunningham demonstrated how the gun worked, Gray Bear, Red Moon Man, and Walks Too Fast each had been allowed to prime his rifle, cock it, aim, and pull the trigger. And each had jumped half out of his skin as the flash of fire, smoke, and smell had exploded in front of his face. But for a quick catch on Cunningham's part, Red Moon Man would have dropped the rifle onto the ground.

"We can't fight with a weapon we do not understand," Gray Bear insisted. "Cunningham said he'd teach us. First, we have to be away from the Arapaho, the Arikara, the Mandan, Hidatsa, and Sioux. Then we will learn this new thing."

"The wait is eating at me like a thing alive," Red Moon Man declared and shifted his grip where he held the lead to the pack-horses.

"Me, too. I want to feel this *Taipo*'s *puha*. I want to control it. See the rifle kill." Walks Too Fast's expression was filled with frustration.

"What's up?" Cunningham called, pulling up next to them.

Gray Bear signed, "Too many wants. Want this. Want that."

Cunningham and the rest laughed. "All in good time."

"We're going to get wet." Walks Too Fast jutted his chin at the storm.

"Be nice to get to camp," Gray Bear told him. Then he took one last glance back. Let his eyes scan the backtrail. Almost missed the slight black dots.

He pulled Moon Walker around. Squinted. Yes, the dots were moving. "Look. There." He pointed like a *Taipo.* Figured it didn't matter as long as they saw the same thing he did.

"Riders," Cunningham muttered. "Somebody found our backtrail."

"How many?" Walks Too Fast asked. "I count five, ten, maybe eleven. No, look. There's another three. That's fourteen."

"And a couple of outriders. Call it sixteen," Red Moon Man said. "And they're all traveling light. Men. War or hunting party. Not a moving village."

Gray Bear wheeled Moon Walker around. "So much for stealth. We go straight for camp."

"How will we see them coming in the middle of that storm?" Walks Too Fast asked.

"How will they see us fleeing through it?" Gray Bear asked in return. *"Mayanuhi!"*

128

Move it!

He put heels to Moon Walker, wondering if it would hurt his new rifle to get wet.

Move it.

He put heels to Moon Walker, wondering if it would hurt as new rifle to get well.

CHAPTER 17

The last three days had been confused, exhausting, and had left Tylor's body aching, chafed, and sore like he hadn't been in years. Strike that. He'd *never* been this sore. Not even on his long ride to Santa Fe across the southern plains.

But then he'd never ridden like this, either.

To everyone's surprise, Gray Bear, Cunningham, and the two warriors had appeared in the middle of the storm's first downpour. They brought with them news that an enemy war party was hot on their heels. Gray Bear, as *taikwahni,* had left no doubt: They were packing up and running.

Right through the crashing downpour of the storm. In the dead of night. Surrounded by eye-searing flashes of lightning, deafened by thunder, blasted by wind that hit them like a hammer, and hail that might have been grapeshot fired by a field piece. Of them all, the hawk, tied atop the packs, seemed to have suffered the most until young Eagle's Whistle figured out a wrapping to protect the bird.

That they'd managed to pack as the heavens opened, that they'd cinched the packs, lodges, and tipi poles onto the balking horses, and headed straight into the maelstrom without a wreck, seemed — now that he could look back — like a miracle.

He didn't wonder that they could keep their course through the misery, chaos, and slashing black rain: Singing Lark rode up at the head of the cavalcade, leading the way. What was it about that girl? She just seemed to have a sense for direction that left him in awe. However she'd done it, she'd led the little band safely through the tempest.

In the days since their departure, they'd traveled in the uplands, south and away from the Grand River. The route had stuck to the contours of the land, and Singing Lark carefully threaded them through herds of bison, her keen eye able to read the ebbing and flowing of the herds. She kept them well away from the masses of animals where they blackened the land. Individual old bulls, the occasional cow and calf, might flee from their path, but the Shoshoni made it clear that they didn't want to be trapped in the center of a large herd.

But why get close to the herds in the first place? What if the animals stampeded?

Looking back, Tylor finally understood the tactic. He had seen the herds grazing across their backtrail. Covering and obliterating any signs of their passage.

"Be hell fer the 'Rapaho to track us through that," Cunningham had noted. "Never seen so many buffalo. After they pass, won't even be a horse apple left to mark our trail, let alone a track."

Their rate of travel was determined by the horses. The Shoshoni, Tylor realized, were superb horsemen. Seemed they could read their animals with a sixth sense. Nor was it the stubby, hairy, Indian horses with their awkward confirmation and heavy loads that slowed the party, but Tylor's black mare and *Taipo* packhorses that dragged at their pace. Though Cunningham's mount, Cobble, seemed to hold his own.

The bison weren't the only wonder. Mixed in were miles of prairie dogs who stood and yipped on their mounds, the occasional deer, foxes, and coyotes, the odd pack of buffalo wolves, small herds of elk, and bands of pronghorn antelope. These were composed mostly of does and fawns, the erstwhile buck running along behind, wary lest one of the does escape his harem.

Tylor had grown used to the barking *kau!* called in curiosity as a lone antelope buck watched them pass. Of all the plains creatures, Tylor decided that the pronghorn were the most beautiful with their tan, white, and black-patterned coloring. They had a stately grace, and when they ran, the speed and movement were pure poetry.

Abruptly, yesterday, Singing Lark had turned them due south. The way traversing uncharted hills and ridges, some topped with occasional sandstone outcrops. Then down across shallow valleys with occasional patches of buffalo berry along the higher slopes. Streams here were bordered by bur oak, their bottoms thick with willows and the sentry-like cottonwoods. But beyond it all was the grass. Endless. Waving on the wind.

Tylor remarked to Cunningham: "This country's all the same. One ridge looks like the next. One creek like every other one we've passed. The only difference is size. One flows a little more water than the other."

Late that afternoon, reaching the top of a ridge from which five drainage heads radiated like fingers, Singing Lark — at the head of the column — pulled up. Her horse stood like a sentry in the wind, its tail blowing.

133

The young woman remained fixed, leaned forward over her horse's withers. She seemed to be contemplating something. Her look studious.

One by one, they rode up beside her, reining in the blowing horses.

Tylor followed the girl's gaze to the southwest. The dark lumps on the far horizon brought him a feeling of relief.

"Them black clouds?" Cunningham asked.

"Mountains," Tylor told him. "You've never been this far west, have you?"

"Nope."

"Trust me. Those are mountains. Reminds me of the first time I laid eyes on the Sangre de Christos. Knew that Santa Fe was real."

Gray Bear slouched on his indomitable Moon Walker, the horse looking as fresh as ever. The chief pointed with his chin. "We call *Aingakwe Hengard Oyabi.*" Red Fir Tree Mountains. "Others call *Duhubiti Katete.*"

"Black Hills," Tylor translated, thinking of the crude maps he'd seen on Lisa's desk.

Looking to the west he could see successive lines of ridges, some with stands of pines that lay like dark shadows. The wind gusted, pulling at his hair and beard. Compared with the ocean of grass they'd crossed in the east, he liked this more rugged land, uplifted, with rocky outcrops of sandstone.

"Country sure looks a sight more broken, John," Cunningham told him.

"*Newe* here?" Tylor asked, gesturing to the land before them.

"Mostly Crow, Arapaho, and some Black-feet," Gray Bear told him.

"How far to *Newe*?"

Singing Lark finally broke her stare, shooting him a speculative look. "Long way, *na-dainapettsi.*"

The Shoshoni broke out into laughter, as if the stress of the long days on the trail had suddenly broken.

"*Nadaye* . . . What in 'tarnal hell?" Cunningham asked.

"Got me." Tylor rubbed the back of his sunburned neck. The direction of the wind had pushed his long hair over his left shoulder, exposing skin that hadn't seen the sun for months. "She's been calling me that. Not sure what I did wrong, but it's changed everything."

Whatever it was — going back to that day when he'd told her he wanted to make sure she was safe — it really chafed. Bothered him deep down. He wanted to apologize. Wasn't sure what for. But, hell, he really missed the girl's company. When, exactly,

135

had that happened? And why did it seem so all-fired important?

Singing Lark kicked her horse into a trot, leading the way down the long grassy slope.

The grass was subtly different here, shorter, harder, and not as thickly packed as it had been further east. The soil, too, had changed — sandy and buff in color, the ridge tops being weathered from sandstone. In places down in the bottoms, however, the soil was gray, more clay, often layered with thin sheets of sandstone and shale.

The air, too, was drier. The sun seemed to have a brighter shine, the light harshly crystalline and sharp.

In the far northwest, two large plumes of smoke could be seen burning beyond the horizon.

"Big fires," Tylor speculated, using any distraction to take his mind off the way his bones ached; his tendons burned and his thighs felt as if they'd been pulled out of socket.

Gray Bear signed, "Burn buffalo range."

"Who?" Cunningham asked.

Gray Bear shrugged. *"A'ni? Dua'ni?"* Crow or Hidatsa.

Tylor asked, "What did Singing Lark call me? *Nadainap* something?"

Gray Bear spared him an amused look.

He balanced his rifle and used both hands, signing, "man" and "woman" and then locking the fingers together. "*Nadainape.* Yes?"

Cunningham, watching from the side, asked, "Coon? There something you want to tell me about when you and that little gal was alone?"

"What? No!"

Gray Bear was giving him a questioning look. He gestured first toward Singing Lark, then at Tylor, and laced his fingers together again.

"I have always acted with respect."

Gray Bear signed, "What you ask her? *Nakweekktu?*"

Tylor remembered that word. "Yes. She said something about that."

Gray Bear made that same maddening sign, locking his fingers together. He seemed to find something funny in the whole thing.

"You asked her to marry you?" Cunningham gave Tylor an incredulous look.

"No!" Tylor cried. He gestured his frustration. "Listen, I like the girl. I sure don't want to marry her."

"No tell her," Gray Bear said, his look going studiously blank. His hands made the sign for "Bad" and then "Insult."

Tylor felt his heart drop. "No. I just told

her I wanted to keep her safe. That I didn't want her to get taken by the Arapaho. Didn't want to see her get hurt."

"Maybe that ain't how she heard it, coon," Cunningham said laconically.

"She's just a girl."

"Wa'ippe," Gray Bear told him, that emotionless, disapproving look on his face. The word meant "woman."

"Damn it!" Tylor growled, his gaze going to where Singing Lark rode at the head of the procession. "What do I do?" He followed it with signs.

Gray Bear shrugged, that amused look back in his eyes. "Give horse. Maybe beads." Signed: "You could do worse."

"Reckon I'd go fer the beads," Cunningham suggested. "Cheaper."

"Yeah, got to fix this," Tylor said with a sigh. "How could she think I was proposing?"

"She's a pretty thing."

"She could be my daughter."

"Then I'd say you started at a right young age. Would have made you what? Nine? Ten at the most?" Cunningham chewed at the bottom of his mustache. "Coon, Gray Bear called her a woman. That's what *wa'ippe* means. How old was that Hallie when you married her?"

138

"Seventeen."

"What's a couple o' years." Cunningham squinted. " 'Course, yer makin' the assumption she'd say yes. Now, my take? That gal's somethin' special. Figgering that, she's smart enough to take yer proposal and tell ye a flat-out no. Hell, she could have any man she wanted. Why settle for the likes of you?"

"She's too young."

"Out hyar?" Cunningham laughed. "Think it through, coon. She's been scouting fer this party. She's survived an attack that kilt half of her people. Not mention she got us plumb across the plains. You've seen how the rest treat her? Ask her opinion? Listen when she speaks? That ain't a child."

"And I ain't interested in a wife," Tylor mimicked Cunningham's drawl.

"Me? I been hoping that Whistling Wren might smile back at me. Lot of woman, that one. Strong. Figure she'd be a comfort of a cold night."

"I wish you success."

"Yep, well, like Gray Bear says, ye've insulted young Lark, there. Whatever you give her to make it up, it better be something really valuable. Maybe that bolt of cloth, or hell, a whole hank of them red beads."

Tylor winced as he shifted on his horse.

He felt like his body was one giant bruise. How long did it take a man to toughen to the saddle? If only they could stop for a couple of days. Rest. Let his bones and joints heal. Was this really him? A couple of years back he'd lived on horseback for days while making the crossing from the Pawnee to Santa Fe.

And yes, the time would allow him to apologize to Singing Lark without having the whole damn band watching him do so.

He would give her a fine gift. That would solve the whole mess.

CHAPTER 18

Upon General Clark's suggestion, Toby, his small command, and their horses had managed to commandeer a ride by keelboat as far as Fort Osage. The cargo had consisted of military supplies for the fort, and being an army charter, the patroon had made room for Toby.

They were offloaded on the banks of the Missouri just below the post where it dominated the river's southern side.

The fort, built in 1808 to serve the Osage, was a pentagon-shaped, wooden-walled enclosure with blockhouses on four corners. It contained the officers' quarters, enlisted men's cabins, and blacksmith shop.

Like a large triangle, the Osage factory, or government agency, was an attached, palisaded area with its own blockhouse on the north. It was here that Toby left Danford and Simms while he reported to a private at the gate. The man saluted, took Toby's orders, and led him to Blockhouse One. Inside, the private knocked on a plank door, and opened it to announce, "Corporal Toby Johnson, Captain. Jist arrived with orders."

"Come in," a rather cross-sounding voice called.

Toby was ushered into a cramped office with a small desk, tiny glass window, and a couple of chairs. Not that Fort Osage — crude as it was — really impressed. As the government factory, or trading and political embassy to the Osage nation, it served as a center of trade and ration distribution, as well as America's outpost on the frontier.

"Captain Eli Clemson," the captain said, taking Toby's salute before rising and offering his hand. "Welcome to Fort Osage." Then he reseated himself, scanned Toby's orders, and read the letter of introduction from General Clark. Clemson looked up.

He tapped the orders, saying, "You come well recommended, Corporal. I am asked to provide you with every assistance. I've never met Jackson, but know him from his record. That William Clark speaks for you, however, carries a great deal of influence. So, who is this John Tylor? A British spy? And why is he headed upriver with Lisa's expedition as a mere *engage*?"

"Sir?"

"It's a simple question, Corporal. William Clark asks me to outfit you and your men to go chase this man up the Missouri. Provide you with supplies that might prove vital to this post's survival and the defense of the western approaches to St. Louis in the event of an attack by either a British expedition or their Indian allies. Assuming, of course, they can unite the western tribes against us."

Clemson continued to tap the papers with an insistent finger. "So, explain to me how this man is a threat? As a mere *engage,* how can he act against the United States?"

Toby experienced a tingling tightness in his chest. "Sir, I reckon I'm just the hunter. Ain't my place to be asking no questions like that. The general wanted me to go find him, and bring him back. That's all I know, sir."

"And if I refuse to supply you for this mad adventure?"

The sense of panic was building. Having nothing better to fall back on, Toby snapped out another salute, saying, "Reckon I'll foller my orders, sir. Me and Danford and Simms. We'll just saddle up and ride on up the river."

"Sheer stubborn guts and stick-to-itness, eh, Corporal?" Captain Clemson asked with a thin smile. "Very well. I'll issue the orders. But, Corporal, think this through. Know what you're getting into. It might not have occurred to Jackson, but he's sending you and your boys up the Missouri in late fall. Smack through the Kansas, the Otoe, the Ioway, the Omaha and Ponca, the Teton Dakota, and the Arikara. Some of the most dangerous Indian nations on earth. Not to mention that Robert Dickson — vile creature that he is — will be using his Santee Sioux contacts to turn the river tribes against us. The son of a bitch has already captured Michilimackinac, and he's in the process of taking Detroit as we speak."

Toby frowned, licked his lips. "Sir, I got my orders."

Clemson nodded. "Corporal, I sincerely respect your dedication, but have you considered that what goes up the river, eventually comes down. As will this John Tylor when Manuel Lisa brings his expedition back next spring. You are welcome to bivouac here, augment my command for the time being, and capture your man when he shows up here with Lisa's party next spring."

"Thank you, sir." Toby couldn't help but salute again, figuring that doing so was the best way to keep the captain from getting mad. "But me and the boys, we got our orders."

Clemson raised his brows in defeat, handed the papers back, and said, "Your funeral, Corporal. See the quartermaster. Listen to his advice. Then stop at the interpreter's cabin. He'll have the latest news on what's happening upriver."

"Yes, sir!"

"Dismissed."

Toby grinned as his boots clumped on the hollow-sounding wooden floor. "Why, hell, this is turning out to be easy as chewing apple pie. Bet we have Tylor within the month."

CHAPTER 19

They called it the *Dsaa Ogwee,* or Pretty River. It ran through the lowlands just north of the Red Fir Mountains. The rest of the world knew the creek as the Belle Fourche, and the mountains as the Black Hills, a name the latter had received because their thickly timbered slopes appeared black when seen from a distance across the plains.

Gray Bear felt a distinct relief. He'd camped on this very spot before. Knew this bend in the stream's course where it ran through uplifted beds of soft red rock, white gypsum, and darker brown and resistant sandstones.

From the heights where Red Moon Man now kept watch on their backtrail, a man had a grand view of the highest peak down south in the Black Hills. And looking north, he could see far into the broken uplands and plains with their occasional patches of pines, buffalo berry, and rolling grass.

A hand of time's ride to the south was the ancient buffalo trap. A curious hole on the crest of a low hill. Steep sided, it had been used for generations. A place where, if the buffalo runners were careful enough, and the hunt well planned, entire herds of bison could be slowly worked into position, then stampeded up the drive lines. If the stone cairns, called "dead men," were placed right, if the people were courageous enough where they stood behind them, waving blankets, the bison would be running full out as they crested the hill, expecting to escape over the other side. They would have no warning as the ground dropped away; in a mass they would tumble into the pit.

Gray Bear's grandfather had been a boy the last time the trap was used. Now the drive lines were falling apart, the timber fencing between the cairns mostly rotted. He wondered if any of the *Kuchendukani*, being horse people, still had the knowledge, patience, and skill that the old buffalo runners had. Those young men had dedicated their lives to studying the bison. They had known how to work an entire herd, putting pressure here, easing them there. They used their perfectly trained dogs to maneuver the mass of animals. Never enough to stampede or frighten the lead cows, but just enough to nudge the herd in one direction or another.

And all the time, a *puhagan* — his souls set free by spirit plants, fasting, and prayer — would sing from a high place, communing with the souls of the bison.

These days bison hunting was done from horses. At speed. With animals left scattered far and wide. Butchering took place all over the plains, conducted by people in ones and twos. To Gray Bear's way of thinking, it was careless and inefficient compared to the old buffalo trap. There, the entire village set up on the site, butchering their way down until the meat soured. An entire winter's kill in one spot: efficient.

So many changes.

Gray Bear contemplated this. For the first time in days, he allowed himself to relax. They had been on the trail now for a full quarter moon. Seven long days.

Bellies were gaunt, tempers short, and the horses worn. Time for a well-earned rest. Besides, Tylor and Cunningham had shot a couple of antelope with their rifles. Two banging shots. The antelope had run no more than a hundred paces before falling.

Gray Bear sat with his back to a young bur oak, periodically staring at the hawk, now perched atop a branch on a conveniently fallen tree. The bird was tied but seemed content to sit in his lordly spot and survey the camp.

Gray Bear ran reverent fingers down the smooth wood of his rifle and remembered the feeling as he had shot it. Fire had flashed before his eyes, and the gun had spoken. The thing had bucked against his shoulder like it was alive. Better, through the fire and smoke he'd seen the dirt jump. Knew he'd hit the patch of white that was the target. He'd dug the flattened ball from the soil.

"Always recover yer lead if'n ye can, coon," Cunningham had told him. "Ye can melt it down, shoot it again."

Much like an arrow could be reused.

They all understood Cunningham's lessons now. His insistence that they wait. Why he had made them practice "flashing the pan." They had learned to ignore the fountain of fire. To hold steady until the bang.

Gray Bear sniffed as the scent of baking antelope came to his nostrils. They had seventeen hungry people and two antelope. Many of the others were out collecting berries along the river, some digging for roots, others seeking any game that might fall to their rabbit sticks or flung stones.

Across from him, John Tylor was cleaning

his rifle, using the ramrod and bits of wet cloth to scrub the black sulfur-smelling soot from the inside of the tube.

Guns, like a good bow, needed to be taken care of in order to make them last.

Tylor was something of a problem. The *Taipo* didn't know it, but he'd had the entire band in an uproar. Had they not been running for their lives, it would have exploded like steam from a geyser. Ignorantly, the *Taipo* had ridden along for the entire journey, missing the barbed remarks, the catcalls, and the derisive jokes at his expense.

Whether he had intended to or not, Tylor had asked Singing Lark to marry him. That wouldn't have been a problem except that most of the people had still considered her a girl. Men didn't marry girls. But Singing Lark had been a woman at the time. She just hadn't bothered to announce that fact. Yet. Which meant that John Tylor hadn't committed a breach of etiquette by asking a girl to marry him. She'd been a woman. A fact no one had known.

The upshot was that as his band had traveled along, Gray Bear and Aspen Branch had quietly informed everyone about Singing Lark's status. Which, of course, made everybody mad and left them feeling duped that Singing Lark had misled them.

So Gray Bear had explained why the young woman had wanted to keep her status secret. Had taken it upon himself to accept the blame, saying he had agreed because he wanted her to stay a scout. But that he hadn't known a stupid *Taipo* would ask the girl, um, woman, to marry him.

Before the coming of the *Taipo,* it would have been a major issue and the topic of a great deal of drama.

Now, with the *Taipo* traveling among them, not to mention Cunningham's obvious interest in the just as obviously uninterested Whistling Wren, no one said a thing about forcing Singing Lark to change her behavior and accept the responsibilities of womanhood.

Somehow, Gray Bear had kept a lid on it. Barely.

He shook his head. "When I am old and all my teeth have fallen out, I am going to laugh about this."

He was thinking this when Singing Lark appeared, slipping between the shadows of the bur oak. She came at a trot, a curved rabbit stick in one hand, a collection of three sharp-tailed grouse gripped by the feet and hanging from her other hand.

The hawk watched her with keen yellow eyes. The bird always got fed when game was brought in. To ensure no one forgot this practice Hawk issued a grating shriek of anticipation.

John Tylor looked up from where he was cleaning his rifle on the other side of the camp, his expression oddly pained, as if he hurt and didn't know what to do about it.

Singing Lark tarried only long enough to place her feet, one by one, on the grouses' wings, grab the birds by the shanks, and jerk. The action ripped the birds in two, exposing the guts. Plucking out the hearts, livers, and gizzards, she threw what was left to the screaming hawk. As the bird gulped down the entrails, Singing Lark flopped down beside Gray Bear.

"Got three. Two got away." She indicated the grouse. "I think we should pack them in mud, toss them in the coals to bake overnight. Be a good addition for the morning meal."

"You look preoccupied, white man's wife." She gave him a look of disgusted rebuke.

Gray Bear arched an eyebrow. "Do you think that maybe you should go talk to him? Tell him that you understand that he didn't mean to ask you to marry him? Make peace?"

"He hasn't done anything since." She was staring at her hands, stained as they were with grouse blood.

"Meaning?"

"A man should do something. Everyone knows that."

"Maybe *Taipo* don't. What are you trying to tell me?"

She took a deep breath. "Yes, I am a woman now. Everyone knows. If John Tylor hadn't asked me to marry him —"

"That was a misunderstanding."

"— by now Red Moon Man or Walks Too Fast would have come asking me themselves."

"They are both good men."

"Kestrel Wing is still grieving over his wife's murder by the *Pa'kiani*. Walks Too Fast can't think beyond the next meal. Being married to Red Moon Man would be as exciting as being married to a juniper tree."

"Why are you telling me all this?"

She gave him a thoughtful glance from those large eyes. "My parents are dead. You are chief."

"Why don't you ask Aspen Branch?"

"She says I should marry John Tylor. Thinks he'd be a kind and caring man. Says his souls are all good, and that I would be cherished. Like he said that day, that he'd take care of me like no *Newe* man ever would."

153

"And?"

"He's a *Taipo*!" she cried. "He has hair on his face! His skin reminds me of a . . . a *fish's*. Do I want such sick-looking skin rubbing against mine? And he's, well, really stupid. He does the dumbest things. If he just showed the simplest of courtesy."

"I was in his people's post, as they call it. We were there just long enough that I could tell they thought we were ill-mannered and rude, and really stupid. Cunningham spoke for us. Without him, we would have walked away with nothing." He fixed on her eyes. "The point I am trying to make is that people have different ways of behaving. John Tylor might act inconsiderate at times, but he is not trying to."

"Then why doesn't he either tell me he no longer wants me as a wife, or offer me a token of his interest? A man who wants a woman to marry him should give her a gift. Everyone knows the value of the gift a man offers is symbolic of how much he values the woman he wants to marry."

"First, Tylor worries about your age. He has concerns that you might be too much a girl. That you are not a woman in all ways. You should respect that. Like us, he believes a man should not engage in *yokog* with a girl. Second, if you were so against it, why don't you tell him no in front of others? Hmm? Or is he right, and you are still a girl playing a game?"

She made a face. "If he just wasn't a *Taipo.*"

"You saw him when the *Sa'idika* would have robbed and murdered him. The man is brave, and he's a warrior. He killed one, counted coup on two others. Hard to say he's not a good hunter when we're eating his antelope. Can't say he's lazy or can't provide. Not to mention that he's rich. So, do you enjoy his company?"

She nodded, brow pinched. "Before he asked me to marry him, I enjoyed him. He's honest. It's . . ."

"Go on."

"It's like everything is new to him. Like each thing he learns is a revelation. Like he has just discovered some hidden and special surprise."

"And you like that?"

She pulled her knee up, propping her chin as she stared across the camp to where Tylor was studiously ignoring her. The man seemed uncommonly preoccupied with his rifle. The hawk, now full of grouse guts, kept glancing between the two of them as if some drama were playing out.

"I don't want to be a woman," she told

him. "Life is a lot easier as a girl."

Gray Bear laughed. "Ah, so you would flout all of our accepted and expected behaviors. Rudely ignore the proper role of being a responsible woman and act like a *Taipo* who didn't know any better?"

"I'm trapped."

"Only if you want to be. People are just people. They always expect you to be someone you may not want to be. Think I wanted to be *taikwahni*?"

"You are a very good one. Everyone says so."

"Then maybe . . ." He didn't finish the thought as John Tylor placed his rifle, the one he called "Jack Handle" — whatever that was — to the side. He stood, looking self-conscious. The man took a deep breath, came walking straight for where Gray Bear and Singing Lark sat.

Beside him, the young woman froze.

Tylor walked up, laughed as if amused at himself, and said, *"Denito'a Hittoo,"* taking a stab at Singing Lark's Shoshoni name, "Taikwahni."

"John Tylor," Gray Bear said back.

"Singing Lark," Tylor used signs to fill in the words, "I am sorry that I have caused you discomfort. I would make it right. If you and the chief would come with me, I'd like to offer you a gift. Something to show you that I didn't mean to hurt you and offer you my heart in its right place."

Gray Bear blinked, wondering if he'd gotten the translation right.

"You are offering me your heart?" Singing Lark asked, astonished, forgetting to sign.

"Ha'a," Tylor told her. Yes.

She got warily to her feet, shot an unsure glance at Gray Bear, and followed Tylor across the camp to the *Taipo* packs. All the goods, tobacco, the cloth, the needles and beads were arranged on the spread manty. The rifles had been set out to one side and gleamed in the sunlight.

She'd seen the remarkable goods before, fingered the fine red cloth, ran her fingers over the hanks of remarkable beads, felt how sharp the iron awls were.

"Choose anything," Tylor said, signing to make sure she understood. "I give you horse if I had one. I just want you happy to make." He frowned. "With me."

Gray Bear wondered, "Tylor, you know what you're doing?"

Tylor launched into some complicated explanation, failing to sign. The *Taipo* words were too much to follow. But the man sounded so sincere.

Singing Lark, her face gone pale, looked

157

up at John Tylor, her expression almost beseeching. "Anything?"

"Anything," Tylor asserted with a positive sign. In broken Shoshoni, he said, "Whatever . . . you need . . . to take . . . for me to have."

"If you take this . . ." Gray Bear warned.

Singing Lark stood in silence, her brow furrowed in deep thought. "What we were just saying? About people. About not having a choice. The *Newe* will make me a woman. They'll know when my *next hunni* comes. I won't be able to hide it."

"It's not like you have a penis and testicles down there to give you a choice."

She chuckled at that. "I suppose not. I heard you say the other day that our world is changed."

"Tell me it isn't."

She took a deep breath, squared her shoulders, and stepped over, picking one of the rifles off the magical waterproof *Taipo* cloth. She lifted it, turned, and with a happy smile said, "Yes. I choose the *aitta* for my wedding gift."

To John Tylor, she said, "I accept your proposal. I take you as my husband, and from this day on will live in your lodge. I call you *gwee* and you call me *kwee.* Let it be known to all, John Tylor, that we are *nanakweennewe.* "

"What just happened?" Tylor asked. "What's that last? *Nanakwee* something? Tell me that doesn't mean" — he winced — "what I think it means."

Gray Bear sighed, wondering what consternation this was going to cause. Singing Lark had married a *Taipo.* He'd given her one of the people's rifles. Worse, Gray Bear suspected the clueless Tylor had no idea what he'd just done.

Taking the man's hand — and prying one of Singing Lark's from the rifle — he carefully fitted their reluctant fingers together, interlocking them.

The look on Tylor's face might have been the same if he'd swallowed a prickly pear. Singing Lark just looked terrified.

CHAPTER 20

How did this happen to me? And worse, *What do I do about it?*

Tylor stared down at his fingers where they interlocked with Singing Lark's. Hers were cold, stained with blood, but supple, and tightened in his. Her grip was firm, committed. He wouldn't have been more stunned if he'd been hit in the head with a club.

Through that first miscommunication, she thought he'd asked to marry her. In the Indian trade, when a mistake was made, a gift was given in restitution. Now, somehow, through some additional inadvertent error, she and Gray Bear had taken the giving of the gift as bride price.

What are you going to do, John? Say, "Hell no!"

That might be a deadly insult.

Might get him and Cunningham killed.

Worse, what would it do to Singing Lark?

She'd taken the rifle, obviously agreed to the marriage, unintended as it was. If he spurned her now, it would be an irreparable act. She'd hate him.

And it might get him and Cunningham killed.

Wait. Don't make things worse.

Tylor stared down at the slim brown fingers interlaced in his, at the girl standing beside him, her eyes now filled with unease. She looked as worried about it as he was. And then a resignation filled her gaze, and she laughed, tightening her fingers in his.

"Glad you find this funny," he told her, a slow smile coming to his lips. "I guess I couldn't make it any worse."

His thoughts kept coming back to that part about not getting him and Cunningham killed.

Gray Bear said something to Singing Lark, indicating the rifle.

She replied in a sassy tone of voice.

Gray Bear threw his hands up, muttering to himself as he stalked back to his tree, resettled himself in the sunlight, and retrieved his rifle. The chief had a thoughtful look on his face as he went back to inspecting its fine lines.

"What was that?" Tylor asked.

"You make trade for rifle." She met his

gaze from under an arched brow. "Anything? I choose."

He felt his gut sink. Technically the gun belonged to the Shoshoni. It was trade for their hides. Somehow, she'd thought he had included the gun when he told her "anything." So, now he was indebted to the Shoshoni for the worth of the gun? But, she, herself, was one of the Shoshoni. Her work had gone into the accruing, tanning, and finishing of the hides. How did that work?

"One thing at a time," he told himself.

He glanced at the hawk where it sat on its branch. Was it just the light, or did the normally fierce-looking bird look oddly amused? Then its feathers stood out, it lifted its tail, and shot a stream of excrement onto its perch.

Tylor couldn't think of a better commentary on his current situation.

"Come over here," he told Singing Lark as he turned loose of her hand. "Let's talk."

She gave him a sober look, the gun clasped tightly as she followed and settled onto his blanket next to him. She appeared torn, half of her seemed entranced by the trade rifle with its polished brass work, the waxed grain of the wood, and the gleam of the metal. The other half of her was fixed on him.

"Gwee."

"Husband." Tylor rubbed his tired face. "And I call you *kwee.* Wife." He paused, using his fingers to turn her chin so she had to look at him. Her skin was smooth and soft. "Do you really want this? *Nakweettu?* To me?" He gestured to his chest. *"E'mmi suan?"* You want? Thankfully he knew those words.

Her face was a serious mask, reflecting the thoughts as she wrestled with herself. She started to say something, hesitated, then launched into a string of Shoshoni much too fast and difficult for him. She stopped short, the quiver of self-amused smile teasing her lips.

She looked away, staring as if into the distance. A sadness reflected in her soft and dark eyes. Her fingers played along the rifle, as if feeling the strangeness of it.

For once, since this whole mess started, Tylor was smart enough to hold his tongue.

Both Gray Bear and the hawk were watching him from their various locations in the camp. The hawk could think what he wanted, but what was going on in Gray Bear's head? That here came this strange *Taipo* to barge in and beguile a child to take to his bed? It sure as hell would have been awkward if some Indian waltzed into a white community and "married" a little blond girl.

Tylor's gut was starting to feel that squirmy unease.

Singing Lark nodded to herself, as if in decision. She turned, staring thoughtfully at him. Laying the rifle across her lap, she said and signed: "I don't want to be *Newe* woman. I want to scout. To hunt." She tapped the rifle and said, "Shoot rifle. You let? You not make me *Newe* woman?"

So that was it. Tylor had noticed that the Shoshoni women acted nothing like Singing Lark did, seeming to dismiss her outright. They did the camp work, attending to the chores. He was Singing Lark's way out. But at what price?

"What about . . ." He made the sign for "copulate."

"Yokog," she said, gave the sort of nervous shrug that hinted that it was an unpleasant inevitability.

"Yes, well, I'm not so keen on it myself," he told her, laughing at himself. "I shouldn't be. Girls are married as young as twelve back in the settlements. But after being married to Hallie, after living with a woman?" He shook his head.

"Married?"

"Nakweekkante newe? Married people? Yes. *Yokog?* No," he told her.

164

Her lips twitched, that old sparkle of amusement back in her eyes. Her smile was like a beam of light. "Yes. I hunt? Scout? Shoot?"

"Yes."

"Deal." She stuck her hand out, mimicking the way that Cunningham made the gesture.

Tylor took it, shook, saying *"Nanakwee-hennewe."* Married couple.

"Gwee," she told him back. And, eyes alight, she tapped the rifle. "Go shoot. Now."

"Yes, Mrs. Tylor," he told her. "Damn, I'm already henpecked."

She gave him a questioning look, then literally bounced to her feet, asking, *"Hinni?"*

"Nothing, my dear."

But, by trying to get him and the girl out of one mess, what in hell kind of trouble had he created for them now?

CHAPTER 21

Tylor sat in the dying light of day, desperately trying to read his copy of Caesar. Around him, the camp was abuzz, people staring openly at him, whispering behind their hands as if that wasn't as blatant as out-and-out yelling, "He married Singing Lark!"

Tylor snapped the book closed and rubbed his hot and embarrassed face. He felt like exploding, but what did he do? Gray Bear, not to mention Singing Lark, had made it more than plain that, according to Shoshoni law, they were man and wife.

He wasn't sure where Singing Lark had disappeared to, having packed her robes and belongings, and moved them over next to Tylor's.

Only Aspen Branch, the old shaman, had approached, a beaming smile on her old lips. "This is good, yes. You treat her right."

"Ma'am," Tylor had told her, "I promise

you I will not take advantage of that little girl."

She'd had no idea what he'd said, but seemed to read his most erstwhile sincerity. The gaping grin still dominating her face, she'd reached out, patted his shoulder with an age-gnarled hand, and said, "She has *puha* you know."

Tylor had nodded, all the while his guts being in an uproar.

So, what was he going to do when night fell? The girl had made a point of putting her bedding next to his. For the moment Tylor stared at it with dread, as if the rolled buffalo robe she slept in were some sort of hideous and malignant monster. Her parfleche might have been filled with water moccasins, or leprosy, given the threat it suddenly posed.

"Married, huh, coon?" Cunningham called as he strode into the camp, his saddle under one arm, rifle and bridle under the other. The tall Kentucky hunter had a lascivious grin on his bearded face, evil merriment in his eyes.

"Will, this just keeps getting worse. I was trying to make amends. Thought I'd give her a gift. Show her I wasn't an inconsiderate brute. I even took Gray Bear with me, you know, to make sure there were no misunderstandings."

Cunningham dropped his tack, laid his long Pennsylvania rifle carefully against the log that Tylor leaned back against. Then he lowered his lanky body to recline next to Tylor. "Fancy bit of work that, catching a young'un like her."

"Stop it." Tylor leaned his head back, taking a deep breath. "I feel like an idiot."

"That's a might bit of an accomplishment for an educated gentleman planter. Went to Oxford, you say? Fancy place for larnin' and all. And with yer copy of Caesar in yer hands, to boot." The hunter paused. "Peer's they didn't teach ye nuthin of sense, coon."

"What am I going to do, Will?"

"Tylor, think about whar ye are. Look around."

"I see bur oak, cottonwoods starting to change colors, pretty scenery, and a lot of Shoshoni looking at me like I'm some sort of bug. A predator who showed up to feed on one of their defenseless little girls."

"What I'm trying to get across t' yer thick-headed way o' thinking is that we ain't back east no more. This ain't high and mighty North Carolina whar ye's a landed gentry. This is their world. Their ways. And even back east, girls marry young. If'n they hit

168

twenty, twenty-one, they's considered old maids."

Tylor pulled his beard, nodding. "Had a neighbor, James Sutherland. His plantation was ten miles down the road . . . fifteen hundred acres in cotton and tobacco. Forty slaves. Nice mansion. Was kin to some sort of lord back in England. He was in his late forties when his wife died. Had grown children. When he remarried, it was to a twelve-year-old girl. You should have heard the tavern talk, the jokes at that poor girl's expense. And worse, the quips and barbs, the ribald winks, that passed behind Sutherland's back."

"I can imagine." Cunningham pulled out his pipe, cutting tobacco from a carrot to load it.

"As if that little girl Sutherland married had a clue of what she wanted in life, or if she even wanted to be married at all. When did she ever have a chance to find herself, Will? To even know who she wanted to be? And at that age, to be bundled into an old man's bed? I often wonder what her wedding night was like, and cringe at what she endured." Tylor paused. "I *will not* subject Singing Lark to such crude exploitation."

"So, ye gonna divorce the girl? Better do it quick, coon, 'cause the sun's slanting down t' the west."

"I do that, and I'll humiliate Singing Lark. As heartless an act as that would be, I wouldn't blame Gray Bear, Five Strikes, or any of the rest of them if they walked over and caved my skull in."

"Care for the gal, eh?"

"I really do. She's precious, Will. I'll do anything to keep her safe. Most of all, I don't want to see her hurt."

"Tylor, fer a cussed traitor, a fugitive, a treasonous bastard, and a damn landed gentleman, yer actually a decent human being. So, I'll tell ye. That little gal worships you. Her eyes light up when yer around. So, seems to me, she's got a say. If she wasn't sure, why'd she marry ye in the first place?"

"Says she wants to scout, hunt, shoot. That if she married a Shoshoni, she'd have to act like a woman. That, and no one is going to pry that rifle out of her hands. I think she married me to make sure that no one took that rifle back after I gave it to her."

"Makes this coon wonder who's using who? But set that aside, what's she say about when yer both under the robes?"

"She's made it clear she's not ready for consummation."

Cunningham rose, went to the fire, and used a twig to light his pipe. Returning, he

170

settled himself by Tylor, and said, "So, what's the problem? It's yer wedding night, right? Seems t' me that no one would raise so much as an eyebrow if'n ye was to pack up yer robes and hers. Head out beyond camp. No one would know if ye did or didn't 'cept the two of you."

"That's a thought." Tylor nodded. "Will, I need you to keep an ear open. If any of the Shoshoni think I'm doing anything to hurt that girl, you tell me so I can fix it. I don't want any of them to think I'm taking advantage."

"It's a deal."

"Good. I have to be the caretaker, the mature and responsible one."

CHAPTER 22

For the time being, life was good. The leaves were turning on the bur oak and cotton-woods, falling like yellow flakes as the mild west wind eased them from their branches. Tan grasses, cured hard and dry, rustled in the breeze. The skies had been remarkable — a crystalline and eternal blue overhead. From the high places, the plumes of distant range fires could be seen, and they were up in the north. Most likely the Crow burning buffalo range.

That no one was burning the Powder River Basin reassured Gray Bear. Normally the grasslands were burned every ten to fifteen years to clear them of old grass and the influx of sagebrush, greasewood, and woody plants. Burning ensured that next spring lush fresh grass and succulent flowers would spring from the ash-rich soil. New growth that would bring in great herds of bison. Let the ranges go too long, and the herds would migrate out of an area, into another territory where the people were better stewards of the land.

But there was another reason to set range fires. One did it when in enemy country to destroy critical winter pasture. Ensure that the bison had to go elsewhere to find winter grass. Hopefully to the Shoshoni winter range. It was a trade-off. That range would be lush come spring. But it might starve the enemy in the short term.

Fire could be used to drive the bison, when the herds were downwind and wind was high. At that time, riders towing burning shocks of grass behind their horses would try and incinerate a whole range, hoping to drive the bison out of the enemy's country and back into their own.

And fire was a weapon. Sometimes, if the wind was strong enough and the fire moved fast enough, it was possible to catch an enemy camp by surprise: scatter their horse herds, burn their curing meat and their lodges before they could escape. Ruin the winter hunt and send the enemy broken and fleeing for some other refuge, perhaps among distant relatives, who might also be short of winter food stocks. And, obviously, the hope was to burn the people themselves.

That Gray Bear could see no plumes in

the Powder River Basin left him with a feeling of contentment. It hinted that the basin was empty of people. At least for the moment. He'd lived too long to think that this would last.

It didn't mean that he took any of it for granted, either. The moody Five Strikes, Turns His Back, and Walks Too Fast shared scouting duty, taking turns watching from the high and forested peak just to the south. From that vantage every approach to the camp was visible.

Life was good enough that his small band of people could involve themselves in their own drama. Nothing too divisive, but just good enough for prime and entertaining gossip.

First, of course, there was John Tylor and Singing Lark. The notion that she'd consented to marry a *Taipo* was downright shocking. When she could have had any *Newe* man she'd wanted? That was gist for hours of whispered discussion . . . so long as Singing Lark was out of earshot.

And, of course, the newlyweds had been spied upon. They slept in separate blankets. What could be wrong with the *Taipo* that he wasn't warming his *wean* in her *ta'i*? Did John Tylor have a problem?

The women, in particular, wondered if his

174

wean was broken or soft; maybe it wasn't capable of *matuhu-pekkah.* Or was it just that the white man didn't know how to engage in something as simple as *yokog*? And maybe they didn't. It was ventured that no one had even seen a female *Taipo,* let alone heard of one, which begged the question of how they reproduced.

The men thought it might be Singing Lark, that she wasn't smart enough to slip her hands into his pants. If she'd stroke her fingers under his two *noyo,* they'd tighten and his *wean* would rise. Red Moon Man declared that not even a dead man could keep from *matuhu-pekkah* when a woman stroked his eggs like that.

Next on the list for conversation was Will Cunningham. Red Moon Man — to the tall *Taipo*'s sorrow — had moved his bed into Whistling Wren's lodge. No secrets there. From the sounds issuing from their lodge, there was enough *yokog* to make up for the lack of it in Tylor and Singing Lark's blankets.

Other events of note included Gray Bear's, Kestrel Wing's, and Walks Too Fast's first hunt with rifles. Cunningham had carefully orchestrated it. He had laid out an ambush, hidden each hunter in a steep-walled drainage so that they had a clear shot. Told them where to aim, calmed them as the bison walked past their hiding place. Then let them shoot.

Afterward, the whole camp dedicated itself to the butchering, skinning, and curing of the meat. The hides were staked out. Twin Sun Woman, Whistling Wren, and the youngsters had pitched in with the fleshing. Singing Lark was gone someplace with John Tylor — a fact that was a topic of considerable biting debate given that she ought to be acting like a responsible married woman and bending her back to the work.

For two days after the kill they'd feasted, smoked and dried meat, repaired their gear, and watched the horses recover from the long ride. Life on the Pretty River was indeed good.

Gray Bear was sitting in camp, enjoying the sunshine. The day was warm, and he had stripped down to a breechcloth. It was relaxing to just sit back and feed the hawk. The bird had recovered enough that they were able to remove the splint, knowing that if left for too long, the joint might fix. Then the bird would never fly again.

"How about that, my friend?" Gray Bear offered the hawk another strip of meat. He had to be careful. Any lack of attention and the bird would take a piece of finger along with the treat.

Overhead an eagle was circling on the thermals.

"You'll be back up there soon, little one. When you do, you need to tell your brothers. 'I was rescued by a *Taipo,* and the People made me well again.' "

Across from him, Twin Sun Woman carried in a load of firewood, dropping it next to the big central hearth. She walked over and settled herself respectfully to one side, looking up at the eagle.

"Kestrel Wing is curious. He wants to know what you're going to do about the rifle that Tylor gave Singing Lark. The *aitta* belonged to the people. It wasn't the *Taipo*'s to give away."

"This is a problem," Gray Bear agreed. "I mentioned it to Tylor. He said he'd make it right, offered his half of the trade he has. But then he pointed out that Singing Lark did her share to make and tan those hides we traded for the *aitta*. That's a valid point. She scouted the bison, helped skin the calves, worked as hard as all the rest of us to tan them. Then she was the one who first found the *Taipo.*"

"You know why she's been missing?"

He shot her a look. The hawk screamed, figuring Gray Bear wasn't paying enough attention to giving the bird scraps of meat.

"She's out there during her *hunni*. Doesn't want anyone to know," declared Twin Sun Woman.

"That's her business. It would only be ours if she were here acting in a way that tainted us with her woman's blood. Yes, we've got a proper menstrual lodge." He pointed at the brush-covered wickiup downstream. "If she were here, I'm sure she'd use it."

"You give that girl too much leeway. You know she's just using him to get her own way. She's got the stupid *Taipo* wrapped around her finger. She got him to give her an *aitta*. He's teaching her how to shoot it. Letting her get away with acting like an irresponsible girl. And what does he get out of it? Nothing! She's not even sharing his robes like a responsible wife should. And where are they? Gone. Constantly. Out there." She waved at the distant hills.

"Maybe she and Tylor have been gone so much because they're tired of having people spying on them? Maybe they want to be alone to get comfortable with each other?"

"Doesn't the *Taipo* know that he's a laughing stock? People *pity* him because he lets her exploit him like he was a fool." Twin Sun Woman gave Gray Bear a skeptical look. "But then, he isn't the only man who lets Singing Lark get away with any kind of irresponsibility. How could you let her trick the poor dumb *Taipo* into marrying her like that?"

"Well, it wasn't exactly a trick. Though I'm not sure that Tylor knew what he was getting into."

"She *using* him. It's a disgrace."

Gray Bear sighed. "They *like* each other. They're happy spending time together. As to what goes on in their bed, I know it's a scandal that they're not sharing the robes. But it's their business."

"Doesn't she know that by refusing him, she humiliates him before the people?"

"My understanding is that Tylor thinks *yokog* with a woman her age is somehow disrespectful."

"Why? She's a *married* woman. She's had her moon. That's what has everyone tied up in knots. A *responsible* woman would insist her husband . . ." Twin Sun Woman threw her hands up. "Why do I even try? Listen. You are Tylor's friend. He trusts you. When they come back, would you have a talk with him? Explain that even though he's new to our ways, he might want to act like a responsible man?"

Gray Bear caught himself before he made

a face. "Yes, yes, if it will make everyone happy."

"They've been gone a long time. Don't you worry about them?"

He smiled. "Aspen Branch says Singing Lark has *puha* in her soul."

"*Puha* and menstruating women are a bad combination. You know it as well as I do."

"Aspen Branch says that only *puhagan,* who are men, say these things. And she makes a point. How many fertile women go out and seek *puha* from Water Ghost Woman, or ask guidance from the *nynymbi*?"

"Asking guidance from the little people isn't like . . ." She shook her head. "Oh, I don't know. The girl is trouble, that's all."

He chuckled. "We wouldn't be here today if it wasn't for Singing Lark, for Aspen Branch's dream. We would all be dead somewhere out in the grass east of the Black Hills. Singing Lark acted as my chickadee. She was the one who cast her eyes up, saw the way to go. She was the one who led us safely here so that you could complain about her."

"Perhaps. It's just that . . ."

The pounding of horse's hooves could be heard.

Gray Bear tossed the hawk the rest of the

meat. The bird snapped it out of the air.

Walks Too Fast, his rifle over his horse's sweaty withers, slid his gelding to a stop at the edge of camp. "*Taikwahni!* Riders coming. *Pa'kiani.* They are just to the north, maybe twenty of them. They don't act like they know we're here, but they're going to. They're going to stumble right into our butcher site. Maybe in the next hand of time or so. After that, they'll be here in another couple of hands' time."

"Find everyone. Let them know. I want us packed and moving. Now."

"What about Red Moon Man and Kestrel Wing?" Twin Sun Woman asked.

"They will see us ride out," Gray Bear told her. "We've planned for this. They know the route I want to take and where to meet us. They will bring Cunningham with them."

"That leaves only Tylor and Singing Lark," she noted.

"I haven't a guess where they've gone." Gray Bear looked around, seeing Whistling Wren where she was starting to pack the piles of jerked meat.

"Leave most of it," he ordered. "The same with the buffalo hides. Take only enough for a week or so. We'll hunt along the way."

"Just leave it?" Whistling Wren cried. "Are you mad?"

"That hasn't been determined to anyone's satisfaction yet. Maybe I am, but I'm hoping the *Pa'kiani* are hungry. Would you chase after us and just leave a camp full of meat? All those perfectly good hides?"

She frowned, clearly reluctant to abandon the product of so much hard labor.

"It's all right, old friend. Leaving all that work may very well buy us our lives. Come, let's get packed."

They'd have to be careful, do their best to hide the trail. He doubted that he'd do as good a job as Singing Lark would, but . . . well, she'd have to figure it out herself.

He hoped she really did have her own special *puha,* and that it would keep her and John Tylor alive.

Chapter 23

Weta Kahni. The Bear Lodge. Tylor glanced over his shoulder to see the giant pillar of gray stone where it thrust up into the translucent blue of the afternoon sky. He'd never seen anything like it: a massive towering column of rock rising up into the heights like the trunk of some impossibly huge tree. Parallel lines of squared and angular fractures, like gouged flutes in a Doric column, gave the sides a textured and grooved look.

He could almost believe the story Singing Lark told him, that a giant grizzly bear in the Beginning Times had scratched those furrows down the pillar's sides while trying to get a woman who'd climbed to the top to escape being eaten.

He couldn't help but marvel at the wonders he'd seen to date. Magical things like the Bear Lodge.

Beside him, Singing Lark shifted. He returned his attention to the bison grazing no more than forty yards from where he and the girl lay belly-down against the side of a gully, their heads and guns screened by the scrubby sage. Dry yellow grass waved, teased by the wind. It carried the warm scent of soil and sage, almost felt like a tonic in comparison to the sun beating down on their backs.

Tylor laid his cheek against the jack handle's stock, and squirmed slightly to the right, his leg and hip touching Singing Lark's. Where the rifle was laid across the sage, the sight's silver blade was resting on the hollow just behind the buffalo cow's front leg.

"Ready?" Singing Lark asked through a whisper. Her head was snugged to her trade gun, her breathing easy. Nevertheless, he could feel the tension in her body.

"I'm left."

"I'm right," she told him. "Three, two, one."

Tylor triggered Jack Handle. Fire leapt before his right eye. Both guns banged, rocking their shoulders back.

"Reload," Tylor told her, keeping his watch as the sulfuric smoke blew back over them.

The two cows — the closest of the fifty or so that grazed their way down the slope just north of the Pretty River — had both hunched at the impact of the balls. Tylor's cow took a step. Then another. The rest of the herd had raised their heads, now alert, but with no idea of the threat.

Singing Lark's cow trotted forward, then slowed, staggered, and sank onto her belly. A pained rattling, almost a lowing, issued from her throat.

Tylor's cow stood, legs braced, head dropping lower. Then she tried to take a step, sank, and thrashed. The lungs worked, the tail flicked. Her head slowly settled onto the grass.

"Loaded," Singing Lark told him as she slipped back up the slope and re-laid her rifle over the sagebrush.

Tylor shinnied down out of sight, pulled his horn around, and poured his charge. He patched a ball with a bit of old cloth from the wreckage of his shirt, used the rod to ram it home, re-primed his pan, and flicked the frisson closed.

Wiggling up next to Singing Lark, he laid his rifle across the sagebrush. Both cows were down, unmoving. The rest of the herd, unconcerned, had gone back to grazing, moving ever so slowly south toward the river.

"That's two," Tylor told her.

"Work starts." She reached down for his belt, flipping out his knife and handing it to him. "I hunt. I shoot. I get horses. You skin."

"Imp."

"What is 'imp'?"

"*Taipo* word for small person who is trouble."

"Imp," she told him happily. "I like."

He chuckled, climbed to his feet, and walked out toward the closest cow. He approached carefully, and crouching down to the side, reached out. The brown iris was wide, and it seemed like he looked into a bottomless eternity where the buffalo's soul had fled.

He got no reaction as he laid his finger on the cow's eyeball. If she'd had any life in her, she would have blinked, flinched.

"I'm sorry, beautiful girl. Hope your soul dances among the stars. Your death gives us life."

Straddling the animal's thick neck, he made his first cut in the thin skin behind the jaw, working his blade up and around the neck. From there he sliced back along the top of the neck to the hump, then down the backbone to the top of the tail.

White men gutted from the belly up. When it came to bison, Singing Lark had taught him that Indians started at the spine,

186

split down the back, and worked their way down. Given that the animals generally died upright instead of on their sides, it made a lot more sense. The hide was then skinned down the shoulders, ribs, and hips and laid out like a mat on either side. The hump roasts, back straps, hips, and shoulders were cut off and laid on the clean hide.

The ribs were chopped out whole. The backbone removed in one piece. The guts they took — organ by organ — and the last thing to go was the brisket. The hide was then split down the belly into right and left halves. Given the weight of a green bison hide, a half was a lot easier to lift, pack, flesh, and tan. When finished, if a full robe was needed, the women would whipstitch it back together along the back.

He had the hump roasts and backstrap cut free by the time Singing Lark arrived on her buff-colored mare. She was leading his horse and the two packhorses. Hobbling the animals, she came to help. Working together — with the help of his ax — he figured it took them four hours to render the cows down to bloody piles of meat.

He recovered both bullets from where they'd lodged on the far side under the hide. To his delight, Singing Lark's shot had been straight through her buffalo cow's heart.

Just out of throwing range, a couple of wolves had shown up, and now paced back and forth, noses working.

These were big animals, rangy. They watched him with wary yellow eyes. Singing Lark called them "Grandfather."

"Why?" Tylor asked, taking a moment to pick the clotted blood from under his nails. His hands ached from the effort of pulling down thick hide as he sliced away the connective tissue.

"From Beginning Time," she told him. "Wolf and Coyote. They make world, yes?"

"That's a story I want to hear."

She made a face as she straightened, her back apparently as kinked as his. She brushed her hair aside with blood-blackened fingers. He thought she'd never looked so beautiful.

"Tell come, um, *egi do'mmo.*" She mimicked shivering, her arms clasped to her.

"Cold. Winter," Tylor guessed. "Winter story."

She grinned, taking only long enough to slice another piece off the liver and plop it in her mouth. A deep-seated joy lay behind her enchanting eyes.

My God, I'm really coming to love her. The notion hit him like a thrown rock.

In the weeks since their "marriage" he and

Singing Lark had done everything together. Part of it was their mutual need to get away from the prying Shoshoni. It should not have come as a surprise, but they had become the absolute center of everyone's attention. A sort of freak show.

For the Shoshoni, the notion that Tylor had given Singing Lark a rifle was almost scandalous. That she had married a *Taipo* added to the titillation, and the whole band — including Cunningham — was obsessed with a curiosity about what was happening in Tylor and Singing Lark's bed every night.

Then had come Singing Lark's insistence: "We go hunt." That she'd packed the bedding, taken the two packhorses and their saddles, indicated that it was to be for an extended time.

They had no sooner ridden out of camp than Singing Lark had taken to the bushes, warning him away. *"Hunni!"* she had cried.

What?

No, the word for "what" was *hinni.* Hunni was an entirely different word. Something new.

Took him a bit to realize it was her woman's moon. Took her a bit longer to accept that he wasn't nearly as terrified of it as a Shoshoni man would have been: something about bad *puha* if a man came in contact

189

with menstrual blood. Once that mutual amazement had sunk in, they both relaxed and enjoyed a four-day hunt that brought the horses back to camp loaded with deer and antelope. Tylor didn't even mind that he'd had to do all the butchering and packing after Lark explained to him that it was "forbidden" for a woman in her *hunni* to touch the meat.

Didn't take much for Singing Lark to talk him into leaving again for the buffalo hunt.

Tylor tilted his head back, letting the westering sun warm his face. Was this really him?

The sensation was as if a terrible weight had been lifted from his shoulders. That his body had turned partially to air; a giddy sensation of floating permeated his breast.

"Hi'i?" Her equivalent of "What are you thinking?"

"I never thought I'd ever feel this way. Absolutely delighted to be alive. After all the terrible things I've done, survived. For the longest time, I wanted to die. Would have killed myself more than once, but the chains made it impossible. After so much suffering, is this much happiness possible?"

She was squinting at him, the look filled with skepticism as the wind tossed her collar-length hair. She might not have understood the words, but she caught the sentiment. Lark stepped across the piled meat, reached out, and ran gentle and bloody fingers down his cheek. "I have good husband, John Tylor."

He took her hand in his, that feeling of love beaming through him. "I have a good *kwee*."

An image of Hallie rose in his mind, and he was cognizant of the letter that lay folded in the pocket over his left breast. She'd divorced him. An action so heinous in American society it took his being charged with treason to goad her to it.

What would she say? Tall, blond, elegant Hallie? She had always been a regal lady, dressed in the finest of fashions, the perfect hostess, her manners impeccable.

And as different from Singing Lark as ice was from fire.

Tylor cocked his head, aware that Singing Lark was still watching him, almost reading his mind. Not that she could. But she was so observant that she could pick up his mood from the slightest inflection of expression.

In so many ways she was a contradiction. One minute she was a teasing girl, giggling, almost awkward in her innocence. When he angered her, she reacted with a child's pique. In the next moment, some circumstance would send that veil of maturity behind her eyes, as if an old soul — one battered and weary — looked out at a world that held no more secrets or magic. She could be soft, coquettish, only to walk up behind a dying antelope, kneel down, and slash its throat, washing her hands in the hot and spurting blood.

Hard to believe that she and Hallie were even the same species.

And yet I love them both.

Now there was a conundrum for priests, scholars, and philosophers: Was he civilized or savage? Fire or ice? Up or down? In or out?

"Savage," he declared. "I tried civilized. It hurts too much."

"Talk too much. Eat," Singing Lark told him, playfully pressing a bloody slice of liver past his lips.

"Talk too much," he agreed as he chewed, bending down to the task of rendering more of the meat.

Singing Lark showed him how to use half hides to pack the meat. How to lay the various cuts onto the hide, and then bind it up into a container. In that moment, he understood why she had insisted that certain muscles be cut from the bone either whole or just so. It made packing the slippery meat so much easier.

When they had packed as much as the horses could carry, the sun was slanting in the western sky. By the time they were winding down the long ridge toward camp, it lay like a bright orange orb just over the irregular horizon.

Singing Lark led the way. Gray Bear's camp was situated in an old oxbow of the Pretty River. Terraces sheltered the location from the prevailing winds; the bottoms were rich in willows, cottonwoods, and downed wood for fires. There the band was engaged in drying meat, tanning winter hides. The horses had plenty of forage, and lookouts could keep track of the entire valley and surrounding land from a pine-thick peak a short distance south of camp.

Tylor would have ridden right into camp — and into disaster.

Singing Lark pulled her mare up, then raised a hand. She stared. Then said, *"Kai-kaittsaa."* Wrong.

"Wrong? I don't see anything wrong."

She indicated the horses grazing up above the terrace. "Not our horses, *gwee.*"

He squinted over the distance, picking out the animals where the dying sunlight illuminated them. No. Not right. That splotched white wasn't one of theirs. Neither was the gray with what looked to be a black mane.

He could just see two distant figures. Guards for the horse herd?

"*Pa'kiani,*" Singing Lark told him.

"Across this distance? How can you be sure?"

She turned on her mount. "*Pa'kiani.* See horse? Stolen last summer. I know these *Pa'kiani.* Killed our people."

"So, what do we do? You think they attacked the camp? Took some of our people prisoner?"

She shook her head, eyes squinted as she studied the distant camp. "*Taikwahni* got away."

"How do you know?"

"Our horses gone. Just *Pa'kiani.*"

"Why wouldn't they follow?"

"Camp full of drying meat and tanned hides." She made the sign for "What more you want?" and gave him one of those sidelong glances that hinted that he was an idiot.

She took her time, carefully scanning the country to the east. "*Aahku!* Look. See them?"

"See what?"

"Horses and riders."

194

"Ours?"

"*Sa'idika.* Dog Eaters."

"How do you know from this distance?"

"Same horses as back east. Still hunting us."

Tylor could just make out the dots of color. How could Singing Lark make out individual horses, let alone identify them? Damn, but that woman's eyes were sharp. "I see. So, what do we do?"

"Run."

Chapter 24

The way Fenway McKeever figured it, both of his companions were of stout Scots ancestry. And being such, they should have had a much tougher constitution. Not like those French dogs he was familiar with on the river. They were a lazy lot with their Gallic inclinations to wine and pork. Scots, by contrast, were born and bred on whiskey and beef.

Dawson McTavish and Joseph Aird, however — and young as they might be — had McKeever's ire up. He expected more bottom, less whining and complaining, even if he had shanghaied them from their mission for Dickson.

Now, the Indian boy, the one who called himself Wasichu — young as he also might be — was a different sort. He'd taken one look at the dying Matato, given McKeever a sober inspection, and done whatever he'd been asked to do. Hard to say what the savage's true thoughts might be. He never let them show.

Why, then, were the two South West Fur Company agents so sullen? Given what Mc-Keever had done to their big Sioux, the lads should have gritted their teeth, consigned themselves to the long haul, and determined to gut it out. Dawson McTavish had some notion that he needed to take care of the younger Joseph. That he was somehow responsible for the boy. It made McKeever wonder what Robert Dickson had seen in Dawson that he'd have entrusted the lad to a task as important as swaying the Teton Sioux. Fact was, McKeever knew he scared the shite out o' the lad. A fact he'd use until McTavish became a debility.

McKeever considered these things as his little party rode into the teeth of a cold west wind. To his relief, Matato's beaded coat had fit. Bit tight through the shoulders, but the length was good, and the flannel-lined elk hide was plenty warm. So, too, was a pair of buckskin pants from the dead Indian's pack. They'd proven to be a reasonable fit. The man's moccasins, however, were way too large. The good news was that they could be stuffed with grass to make up the difference.

To that add a good quality Nor'west trade

rifle, lead, mold, and powder, not to mention the Sioux's knife and tomahawk, and Fenway McKeever was fully outfitted for the trail.

He rode in the rear, the trade gun across the horse's withers. That damn Sioux hadn't used a saddle, so McKeever had to make do bareback. He'd never been much of a horseman, but if it meant running down Tylor, chopping off his head, and earning that two thousand dollars, he'd become a goddamned centaur if he had to.

But what did he do with the two South West men? For the time being, McTavish was cowed. Not beaten. The moment would come when he would try something. Aird wasn't that kind. His answer would be to slip away in the night, take his chances on a run for the river and the east.

McKeever wrestled with the problem as their horses plodded ever west, following the ridges above the Moreau River. That was the best route. And if McKeever figured it correctly, Tylor would have headed for the Black Hills and the Arapaho. Lisa had men with the Arapaho: Champlain and Lafargue's party had been hunting with them for a year now. It made the most sense that Tylor would seek them out for protection and companionship.

McKeever found himself awed by the immensity of the grassland. His early years in the north had been filled with birch forests, firs, willows, and aspen groves in a land of water, shallow and rocky soils, and clouds of hellacious black flies and mosquitoes. Travel was mostly by canoe, from post to post, as the vicious fur wars were fought between the Hudson's Bay Company and its rivals. There he had developed his cunning, but in the end, had killed the wrong man. Escaping the consequences had led him to New York and Joshua Gregg. The east he understood: forests, rivers, those were his environments. A man could step off a trail and be hidden.

Out here?

He stood out in a universe of grassland and sky. Indeed, it had its ups and downs, hollows and distant rises, but everything looked the same. One rise was the exact repeat of the last, one drainage, brush-choked and shallow, but a perfect predictor of the next, right down to the bobbing heads of endless grass.

Over it all, the sky was without bounds. Not even on the ocean, with its waves of water, had the sky seemed so large, so encompassing as it did over these undulations of grass.

Makes a mon feel wee and weak.

The only thing that gave him hope was the river. An hour's ride off to the south, the Moreau was his guide in a land without direction.

"Follow it west to the Black Hills." That had been Wasichu's suggestion. Without it, and but for sunrise, sunset, and shadow, Mc-Keever would have had no clue as to which direction was which.

He squinted between his horse's ears, past the packhorses with their load of trade. Centering his thoughts in the middle of Dawson McTavish's back where the laddie rode up front, he had a feeling he should shoot the man square in the back. Be rid of whatever trouble he was sure to hatch. And McKeever would inherit that fine Philip Bond rifle as well as the man's horse and saddle.

Aye, and ye can't be killing every man who might be a problem, Fenway. There'd be none left.

Besides, this was the wilderness. Together they had three rifles and a young Santee with a bow. Hardly the makings of a mighty war party that would strike fear into the hearts of savage warriors. He needed McTavish's rifle, his wilderness skills, and his understanding of Indians. Robert Dickson wouldn't have appointed the lad to entice the Tetons to side with the British if he didn't have some sort of talent. Not even because the boy was kin. Dickson was too pragmatic when it came to results.

The land might look flat, endless, and monotonous. Just about the time a man convinced himself that he was a mote under God's eye, and alone in infinity, the error of his ways was made clear.

Dawson McTavish was leading the way up a long grassy incline, and just as he topped out and started down the other side, he came face-to-face with five mounted men on horseback headed east.

Neither side had any warning. Both parties topped the summit at the same moment, stopping short in surprise, each as unprepared as the other.

"Whoa!" McTavish cried, pulling his horse up, staring into a similarly alarmed Indian's face. The man had been half asleep in the saddle, and now jerked upright. Behind him, the other four riders pulled up short. The horses were prancing, whickering.

"Tell 'em we be friends," McKeever called. "You, Wasichu, ease forward. Tell 'em we're not here to hurt 'em none."

"Arapaho," Wasichu called back, letting

his horse walk forward. Everyone was milling, fighting to quiet their equally surprised mounts. Seemed that horses meeting strange horses were just as wary of each other as men.

McKeever wondered what trick of the wind had kept his mount from smelling the others.

The lead man — maybe in his thirties — had raised one hand, chattering away in some language McKeever had never heard. It might have been similar to one of the Algonquian tongues from back east.

McKeever urged his excited horse forward, pulling up beside McTavish, and smiling. "Greetings, to ye all! I'm Fenway McKeever, in service t' His Majesty King George. Bless 'is royal arse. We mean ye no harm."

Wasichu was speaking slowly in Sioux, signing as he did.

The five Arapaho had stilled their horses, gotten themselves over their surprise, and were muttering softly among themselves. To date, none had pulled out their cased bows, but two had grabbed up their war clubs.

Wasichu called out something, bringing the Arapaho to attention. The leader, the older man, his face lined and already weathered like old walnut, asked something, making signs with his hand that McKeever had no clue about.

Wasichu said, "He wants to know what we want, and why we're here."

"Tell him we're kidnapped," McTavish muttered, shooting a sidelong look at McKeever.

"Ye'll tell him no such thing," McKeever growled, then lightened his tone, saying, "Tell him we're in pursuit of a white man. One of Lisa's. That he's a killer and a thief who's fleeing west. Brown hair, brown eyes, and beard. Carries an ugly rifle. A short one with a cutoff barrel."

Wasichu translated, adding occasional words in Arapaho.

A young man on the right said something, the others listening and then nodding.

The lead Arapaho held up two fingers, then replied softly.

"They chased two white men, one short and brown. The other was tall. They had four horses, two packs. They killed four Arapaho and allied themselves with a party of Snakes. The smaller man had the ugly rifle."

"Where'd they go?"

Wasichu translated. The Arapaho replied.

"He says they tracked the Snakes west for many days. The trail was difficult, but they worked it out. To their surprise, they found Blackfeet in the Shoshoni camp. They fought, had four men killed and another three wounded. They killed three of the Blackfeet and drove them off. They took what was left of the meat the Snakes had left drying and headed east. Most of his party took the wounded men to an Arapaho village east of the Black Hills on the White River. He and these four were headed back to their band on the Missouri where they want to trade."

"What about the white men?"

Wasichu translated the answer: "They are with the Snakes. He says they worked out the tracks. The Snakes got away. Went west. After the fight with the Blackfeet he says the Arapaho had wounded to care for."

"Sounds like your John Tylor's managed to escape," McTavish noted dryly. "Since he's gone, maybe we can get back to what we're supposed to be doing?"

McKeever ignored him. "Ask the Arapaho if they will take us back to this place. Tell him we've got trade. That we'll give him one of the trade packs back there if he and his warriors will lead us to the white men."

"What?" McTavish cried. "That's not yours to . . ."

McKeever shifted his rifle, the muzzle

pointed at the young man's midriff. "Say another word, laddie, and yer guts is gonna be blown all over poor Joseph there. An' ye better get it inta yer thick head that I work for Astor hisself. Yer on a company job, laddie. You'll either sign on, or I'll leave ye to rot in the grass here."

McTavish swallowed hard.

The Arapaho had watched, missing nothing.

Wasichu gave them McKeever's offer.

Heads nodded as they spoke, each man glancing speculatively at the packhorses.

"What're they saying?" McKeever asked, barely above a whisper.

"Two want to go, two want to leave, one cannot decide," Wasichu answered.

The leader considered, rocked his jaw, not staring at the packhorses like the others, but at McKeever. He seemed to be taking his measure. McKeever gave him a wicked grin in return.

The Arapaho laughed, a genuine appreciation behind his eyes. As he spoke, Wasichu translated. "He says his name is Stone Otter. He and two others will take your trade, and then he will lead you to the white man."

"Tell him he will get the trade after he leads me to the white man. That the trade will ride along wi' us 'til the deal be done.

Then he can take it and go where he will."

As Wasichu translated, the Arapaho continued whispering among themselves.

Stone Otter reached out with a hand, made a smoothing motion, and, looking McKeever in the eyes, said, "It is good."

"That's a deal," McTavish needlessly said.

"Aye," McKeever said happily. "Now, how about . . ."

Two of the Arapaho, most likely the dissenters, called something disagreeable, and kicked their horses off to the side. They didn't look back as they cantered off toward the river.

"Guess they didn't like the terms," Joseph Aird noted where he leaned over his saddlebow.

"Lot of that going around these days." McTavish gave McKeever a hard look. "All right. I won't try and stop you. That's my word. Now point that rifle another direction."

"Why, laddie, ye've a lick o' sense in that cussed head o' yern after all. See it through, and ye'll come out of it all ahead. Me promise on that."

Stone Otter barked some command, wheeled his tan horse around, and started back the way he'd come.

"You sure that old Stone Otter there is

worth half the trade? That's enough to *buy* the entire Teton Sioux nation." McTavish was giving him that troubled look.

"Aye, especially if the mon can really track down John Tylor fer me. They'd o' not made that claim if'n they couldn't. There's money to be made for all of us, laddie. As well as stopping Tylor in the process."

And Stone Otter apparently had his own ax to grind with Tylor.

CHAPTER 25

The fire burned low; a small eye of redly glowing coals rendered down from a stack of buffalo chips. Singing Lark preferred dung fires since they didn't smoke, didn't flicker with dancing flames that could be seen across a distance.

Their camp lay in a copse of ponderosa, the pines whispering as night breezes blew through the long needles. On their picket, the horses shifted, standing hip shot, heads down. The temperature had dropped, a chill riding the wind.

Using a pointed stick, Singing Lark had excavated a body-long trench in the duff. Then she'd insisted that they build a shelter, a low-angled lean-to crafted out of pine branches, shocks of twisted grass, and sagebrush. Tylor had been surprised at how tightly she'd showed him the branches could be woven together.

In the distance a pack of coyotes yipped,

cried, and squealed, while off to the west buffalo wolves howled in their eerie tremolo. Clouds obscured the frosting of stars that would have glowed from the soot-black heavens, this being the dark of the moon.

Beside Tylor, Singing Lark had just finished tending to her rifle. Now she laid it aside and pulled her knees up. She'd hung one of the hair-on buffalo hides over her shoulders, heedless of the brain matter, fat, and urine on the wet side. Propping her chin in a pensive manner, she stared into the coals.

Given the dropping temperature, Tylor suspected that it wasn't going to be long before that curly-haired warmth overrode any concerns about a little odor.

"Should have cut tracks," she told him in mixed English and Shoshoni. They were getting pretty good at patching together each other's languages. "Gray Bear would have headed south. We follow Pretty River. Maybe he take Powder River."

"Why the river?"

She gestured to the east. "*We'shopengar.* The Gourd Buttes. From the top a scout can see the entire basin. Anyone traveling on a ridge. But down low, no one can see."

"Like the route you've taken us on," he realized.

He glanced over at the meat where it lay protected by the second cow's hide, most of it sun dried, the rest of it smoked. That had been Singing Lark's doing. He'd have abandoned the fresh buffalo meat as a burden. She'd shown him how to thin-slice and smoke it over sagebrush fires at night. How to air-dry strips atop the packs during the day. The same thing with the quick-tan on the bison hides. It wasn't pretty, but the skins were still mostly pliable.

He chuckled at himself.

"What?" she asked.

"I must seem simple to you."

"Don't know simple."

"Not smart. Not capable. Like a child."

She didn't acknowledge it. Maybe to spare him the humiliation.

"I wouldn't have known. I would have ridden right into those Blackfeet. Wouldn't have had the first clue about how to hide a trail. You've kept us alive, *kwee.*"

"You are a warrior. Killed that *Sa'idika.* Struck coup on two more. You let me be me. You're a good hunter. You and me, different but same."

"Going to be cold tonight."

"Takkapi." Snow.

She'd taught him that word by mimicking flakes with her fingers, saying, "white," and pretending to shiver.

"Hope that lodge is enough to keep us from freezing."

"We sleep like this." She crossed her index finger with her middle finger. "Close. Warm."

"You sure. Being that close?"

"You afraid of *yokog*?"

"Not if it's going to be that cold."

They both laughed at that.

Tylor followed directions as he crawled into the shelter and lowered his body into the trench. Nor did he feel uneasy as she carefully settled the quick-tan hides, hair down on top of him. Like a snake, she wiggled in, slipped her body next to his, and fiddled with the final arrangement of the hides.

For a long time, Tylor lay there. Eyes closed he inhaled her scent: smoky, with a taint of horse, and a subtle fragrance that was all hers. Their shared warmth filled the robes. He carefully extended his arm to draw her close.

To his immense relief she didn't tense, but snuggled herself against him, sighing with content.

It wasn't his will, anything but. His body acted of its own. He tried to wiggle away as he felt himself stiffen.

She giggled, didn't pull away. Said, "It's a *wean.* They do that. Go to sleep."

With that, she took a deep breath, exhaled in contentment, and began to breathe deeply.

Yes, sure. They do that. I am not James Sutherland. I will not be James Sutherland.

It took Tylor hours to drift off, and only then when a gentle rain finally lulled him to dreams of nubile young women and the possibilities of what they might share with a man.

CHAPTER 26

That first storm had left a couple of inches of snow. The one that followed, two days later, dropped almost six. Each time Singing Lark managed a different kind of shelter that, with the buffalo cow hides, allowed them to sleep warm and dry.

With the arrival of cold weather, Singing Lark had immediately changed her direction of travel, turning them west. Or as near to it as they could come. She would follow a drainage to its head, hurry them across the open summit, and into the head of another drainage on the other side. When that one began to veer in the wrong direction, she hustled them over the divide and into yet another drainage.

It was sinuous work, but that night they camped under a tilted sandstone outcrop that was barely wide enough for both of their bodies.

The following day they reached the Powder River, as Singing Lark called it. When they crossed the leaf-strewn floodplain they found tracks winding through the sagebrush just back from the cottonwoods. A lot of horses moving at a quick clip. Fresh in the still-muddy silt.

After studying them for a bit, Singing Lark told him, "Four tens of horses. Not long ago. Maybe a hand of time."

"Ridden?"

"Yes. See how straight the track lines? Horses, left to themselves, go back and forth." She made a sinuous motion with her hand. "Take their time. Some go here, some go there."

"Headed north. *Pa'kiani?*"

She shrugged, worried eyes staring at the cottonwood-choked bottoms down which the horses had vanished. "Can't tell, *gwee.* Crow horse? Arapaho horse? Blackfeet horse? All have the same shape feet, yes? Only men make different style of moccasins."

Didn't matter that they might have already passed. For all Tylor and Singing Lark knew, the riders could be waiting just on the other side of the trees, or someone might be following. Maybe to catch up with the rest.

Singing Lark pushed them forward mingling their tracks with the others, then after a couple hundred yards to confuse their trail, veered off onto the carpet of fallen cottonwood leaves. Winding through the gray trunks, she crossed to the river, splashing into the Powder. Tylor stared at the water as they crossed. The stuff looked opaque. Like light brown milk. He couldn't see so much as an inch into the surface.

"What's the plan?" he asked.

She jerked her head back. "Moving horses make tracks, *gwee*. We keep making tracks and someone will follow. We go to a place where we don't make tracks."

She took them into a small creek, then turned the horses upstream, splashing in the little brook and occasionally forcing their way through the overhanging brush until she encountered a low gravel bar. She dismounted, leading the horses, one by one, around the back side of the gravel bar, then up onto the bank. Tylor watched in amazement. From the stream, given the way Singing Lark threaded the horses around the gravel, not a single track could be seen.

From there, she led the way up out of the little valley, keeping to outcrops of sandstone, or following cobble surfaces, always places that the hooves wouldn't disturb. Tylor challenged himself to pick the route, looking ahead, trying to anticipate where she'd take them. By afternoon, he was getting a feel for it. Starting to learn.

A couple of hours before sunset, she ground-reined her horse in the lee of a long ridge, its sides sagebrush-studded and dotted with juniper trees. The looming flanks of what she called "Powder River's Mountains" rose in the west, the slopes timbered; high on the mountain, slabs of bedrock tilted at steep angles above rocky talus.

If he had to guess, they were still a half day's ride away — past the foothills — and then into the mountains themselves.

"Come," she told him. "Tie off horses. We look."

After securing their mounts and pack animals, they scrambled up the slope. Tylor's hard-leather soles slipped and slid on the grass despite the wrappings that held his boots together. He felt the chill in the bitter wind as it drove through the rents in his shirt. At the crest, Singing Lark used a scrubby juniper for cover, beckoning him up beside her. Settling, she turned her gaze to the east.

"What are we looking for?"

"Anyone," she told him. "See who follows."

Tylor arranged his butt on the rocks, shaded his eyes, and carefully began his survey of the broken land that led down to the distant Powder River's timbered bottoms. One by one, he let his eyes trace out each of the drainages. The black spots he recognized as buffalo. In other places, patches of pine or juniper could be discounted.

"There," she said, gesturing with her chin.

He tried to follow her gaze. "I don't see."

She gave him that "you're impossible" look, then grabbed his finger and used it to point.

Tylor sighted down it, recognizing the creek she'd made them wade on the way up from the Powder. Back where they had crossed the Powder itself, he made out horsemen. The tiny dark dots of men on horses stood out because they moved. Hard to confuse, even over the distance. They were combing their way back and forth, looked like they were searching.

Tylor's gut sank. "Who?" he asked. "Recognize the horses?"

"Too far."

"But most likely enemies," Tylor muttered.

She kept her eyes on the distant riders, what, maybe four, five miles away? "*Gwee*, snow comes. Tomorrow."

"How do you know?"

"I know." A pause. "We watch for now. See what others do. If they find trail."

"And if they do?"

"We ride hard all night. South. For Sweet Water River. Hope tomorrow snow hides trail. Cold ride."

"And if they don't find our trail?"

"We ride hard all night. West. Hope tomorrow snow hides trail. But then stay in warm place. Wood, water, good grass for horses."

"Either way we're riding hard all night."

"Reckon so, coon," she mimicked Cunningham's voice.

Tylor laughed, happy to break the tension. "Hope he and Gray Bear and the rest are safe."

"I think yes. *Taikwahni* is smart. He got away. *Pa'kiani* didn't chase him. Those *Sa'idika* would have ran right into *Pa'kiani*. Maybe they killed each other. My bet, *Taikwahni* got everyone back to *Pia'ogwe*."

"Where's that?"

"Across the mountains. West. You and me go long way. Go here. Go there. Have to hide trail. Keep from getting caught. *Taikwahni* has scouts to see danger first. Can go fast. We have to go slow."

Tylor resettled his bottom on the flat stones that covered the ridge top. The wind up his back sent a chill through him. Damn, he wished he had his coat. Hoped that Cunningham had bothered to pack it. One of the buffalo hides would have sufficed, but they were wrapped around their supply of cured meat. He was on the verge of shivering, but Singing Lark seemed immune.

And more snow was coming?

"For out in the middle of the wilderness," Tylor muttered, "there sure are a lot of people out here."

"It is fall. Time to hunt. Maybe catch the *Newe* by surprise. Kill a few men, steal their meat, and capture some women and children. Do it often enough and the *Newe* will stop coming to the Powder River to hunt. Make it too dangerous and the Crow, or Blackfeet, or Arapaho can call it theirs."

"Politics, by any other name . . ."

"Hinni?"

"People are all the same, *kwee*. Europe, America, or the upper Missouri."

She stiffened. "Look."

Tylor concentrated. One by one the distant dots were moving. Heading away from their search. Looked like they were going north.

"Think they gave up?"

"Maybe."

By Tylor's reckoning, they sat for another

half an hour. In the end, she took a deep breath. "I think we're all right."

"So, we ride all night? What about the cold?"

"Storm comes. Warm ride tonight. I know a place we can hole up. Stay warm. But, *gwee,* we need hides. Have to make *kutta.*" She mimicked putting on a coat.

"All right."

"So you say now, *Taipo.*" She shot him a sardonic grin. "Wait 'til the work starts."

"Think I'm not up to it?"

"Once the drying and stretching has to be done, most men find something important to do. Like going hunting for a couple of weeks."

"I won't."

"We'll see."

She kept him there for another hour, just to be sure. During that time, nothing moved on their backtrail but a smattering of bison, a few bands of antelope, and a herd of about thirty cow elk followed by a majestic bull.

"Come, *gwee.* Now we ride all night."

He considered, looking up at the clear sky. Snow tomorrow? And warm enough to ride all night.

At least they had enough moon to keep them from riding off a cliff. Or so he hoped.

CHAPTER 27

Cunningham came riding up from the rear, his big black horse mud-spattered and blowing. The man was dressed in a composite of *Taipo* coat and pants with a buffalo-hide cape over his shoulders and a fox-hide hat on his head. His hands were covered with mittens, sewn fur-in. Whistling Wren had made them for him, perhaps a token of apology for spurning his advances.

Their trail had taken them around the southern flank of the Powder River Mountains, then west across the occasional creeks and broken uplands to the head of the Bad Water River, so called for the bitter taste leached from the clays over which it ran.

The way led down a rocky slope from the foothills and onto a flat above what the *Newe* called the Big River, or *Pia'ogwe.* The basin stretched south to the distant Sweet Water River Rim, the land marred by the occasional butte, low ridges, and the cottonwood-lined meander of the *Pia'ogwe* as it flowed north. Upstream, a day's ride to the south, the river hooked back to the northwest and the Valley of the Warm Winds.

"Some country," Cunningham said. He'd been dedicated to learning as much of the language as he could, although his pronunciation was oftentimes so abominable as to be incomprehensible.

Gray Bear gestured with his chin, indicating the distant mountain range to the west. The high peaks gleamed whitely in the sunlight, the flanks of the mountain range clad in timbered slopes. "Snow is already deep up on Mountain Ram's Seat. What we call that highest peak. But the Valley of the Warm Winds will let us hunt some before the deep cold. And, Will, we have rifles to trade for all the food we need."

Gray Bear glanced back to where the hawk rode on the mantied trade pack. The bird was so used to traveling by horse, sitting atop the pack, that he wondered if it ever would want to fly again. What was the point? Here, among the people, the hawk was fed, cared for, carried from place to place. All it had to do was sit there, look regal and beautiful, and the people did everything for it.

Cunningham followed his gaze to the bird.

Grunted. "Think Tylor's all right? He set store by that bird."

"I asked Aspen Branch last night at the Bad Water camp. She said that neither Tylor nor Singing Lark had come when she called them to her dreams."

"What does that mean?"

"When a person dies, the dream soul, *navushieip,* is set free. Someone with great *puha,* like the *waipepuhagan,* can call the wandering dream soul. Her own *navushieip* can talk to the dead person's soul."

"So, she thinks they're still alive?"

"*Seepa kia.* Maybe."

"Why *seepa kia*?"

"Just because Aspen Branch called to Tylor or Singing Lark's *navushieip* doesn't mean either will come. Think about it. When you are asleep, does your dream soul do what you tell it to? Mine doesn't."

"Not sure I foller where you're going, coon."

Gray Bear had to concentrate as he eased Moon Walker down where the terrace dropped off in a steep descent to the floodplain; rounded river rocks and dirt cascaded from under the horse's hooves. He glanced back, making sure the pack animals didn't lose their loads on the scramble down, and that old Aspen Branch kept her seat as the band followed. The hawk, with its superb balance, didn't even sway.

Satisfied that they had all made it, Gray Bear said, "When I go to sleep, I can tell myself: 'Tonight, I will dream of a warm lodge, two beautiful wives to snuggle with, and elk steaks dripping fat as they roast over the fire.' But what does my *navushieip* do? It takes me to a dream place where I am freezing in a blizzard, naked, hiding in a snowdrift, with terrible hungry grizzly bears hunting me while *Pa'kiani* warriors are searching for me from every high place. Then, just as I freeze to the point I can't move, the bears will find me. The *Pa'kiani* will be charging down, knives ready to cut my scalp off my skull. At the moment when I'm ready to scream, my *navushieip* will fly back into my body. I snap awake shivering and scared."

Cunningham laughed, glanced off across the flats toward the river and the line of cottonwoods along its bank. "Hell, and to think I got enough trouble just having one soul."

"You have told me this before. I have thought about it a lot. Discussed it with the *waipepuhagan*. When you are alone, who do you talk to?"

"Huh?"

224

Gray Bear pointed at his head. "In here. If there is only one, you can't talk to yourself. Like the sound of one hand clapping."

"I talk to myself all the time. We call it thinking."

"Then who listens?"

"Why, I do, coon. I ask myself: 'What do I think about doing so and so?' And another part of me answers: 'Well, that'd be 'tarnal stupid. How about doing this instead?' And I figger it out."

Gray Bear lifted a skeptical eyebrow. "Does that not indicate that there are at least two souls inside you? One asks. The other answers. And if you dream of other places, of distant people, and other times, that dream soul must exist as well."

Cunningham frowned, chewed at his lips, which made his beard bunch and pucker. Finally, he said, "Coon, when the first preachers come here, they're gonna raise hell. They're sure they got it from on high that ye've only got one soul."

"What is this word, 'preacher'?"

"Hard to explain. Like a sort of *puhagan*, I reckon. But without the visions and *puha*."

"That makes no sense."

"Given that preachers don't take to drinkin', whorin', gamblin', and a little knuckle-and-skull every now and then, I guess you

225

an' I see eye to eye on preachers, Chief."

As Gray Bear had listened, too many *Taipo* words in Cunningham's answer were unfamiliar. Tylor spoke one dialect of English, Cunningham another. At times they sounded like different languages.

Not that the dialects of *Newe* weren't as varied. In the far west, out in the Great Basin, "Sheep eater" was pronounced *Tuku-dika*. Here, in the east, it was *Dukurika*. *Muqua* in the far west was pronounced as *Mugwa* in the east. Unlike the *Taipo* — who the Salmon Eaters called *Taiboo* — the *Newe* had a fluent sign language to fill in the differences.

"What?" Gray Bear asked as they rode across the sagebrush-thick flat. "You still look worried."

Cunningham shrugged. "You don't know it yet, but this is the last free place, Chief. Here, in the high plains and mountains. No forts, posts, or preachers. But they're coming."

"What does this mean?"

"Sort of how it is." Cunningham stared out at the distant Wind River Range, voice soft. "My great-grandpap was one of the first long hunters. Crossed the Appalachians from North Carolina to hunt in Tennessee and Kentucky. My grandpap moved the family into Tennessee after the Revolution. Then my pap settled west of the Cumberland. Raised his family. And here I be. Plumb inta the middle of the wilderness. 'Bout as far as a coon can go."

"I don't know these words."

"You will, Chief. I'm sorry, but the day will come when you will."

At that moment, Turns His Back, who had been scouting ahead, broke from the cottonwoods. He came charging back, riding flat out on his buckskin gelding, his rifle held low and to the side. His hair was flying, and he whooped.

"Trouble?" Cunningham asked, shifting his rifle.

"That is not the way he rides when he has discovered trouble. Not a single look back. And see, he is smiling."

"I have just talked to Flat Finger!" Turns His Back cried as he slowed his horse. "*Tukanih Punku*'s band is camped on the *Pia'ogwe*, a day's ride south! We have found the people!"

Night Horse's band! Of course his old friend would be camped here on the *Pia'ogwe*. Gray Bear's heart skipped, and as it did, he experienced a warm and filling glow inside. *We have done it. Made our way to the great river in the east, traded a wealth of calf hides for a greater wealth of guns.* Guns that would at least give his small band a chance against the *Pa'kiani.* The few remaining guns would be an incentive for others to do as he had done.

He glanced back.

The hawk was watching him with evaluative eyes.

What do you know that I do not, Grandfather?

And where was Singing Lark? Part of this was her success. She had been the chickadee, the far-seeing eyes, the scout who picked the path. The one person more responsible than any other for his success as *taikwahni.* Since he had taken the leadership, he hadn't lost a single person.

Please, be safe. He sent the prayer her direction.

CHAPTER 28

Most men find something important to do. Like going hunting. The memory of Singing Lark's words that day up on the ridge echoed in John Tylor's mind. His hands hurt: fingernails feeling like they'd been bent double and backwards; his knuckles worn raw and bleeding. In his forearms, the muscles burned, as did his shoulders and back. The slanting sun shone down, casting long shadows on the slope to the west; he puffed a breath in the cold air, watching it rise in the weak light.

Immediately to the east, the uplifted red wall of sandstone had taken on a gaudy, almost crimson hue. The stark light accented every detail of the blocky layers of rock that gave way to steep cascades of red dirt and tumbled stone. Tawny with fall grasses, the slopes below the wall were dotted with sage as they fanned out into the valley bottom.

To the west, a tan-sandstone hogback rose flat and steep. Like a giant's table canted at a forty-five-degree angle, the uplifted sheet of bedrock inclined toward the sky. Juniper and scrubby-looking pines at the foot of the slope were scattered in an irregular blanket, giving way to thicker stands of ponderosa and fir in the distant heights.

The camp, or "hole" as Singing Lark called it, was everything she'd said it would be. Here part of the red slope extended out into the valley; in its side a stone overhang — like an arched brow — had eroded out of bedrock. Beneath the arch, a shallow cavern extended back into the sandstone. A deep cleft in the slanted bedrock behind the camp provided security for the horses: a box canyon from which the animals couldn't wander. Perfect to pen them in at night.

A stone's throw to the west, a small, willow-and-cottonwood-choked creek ran down the valley, joining the middle fork of the Powder some two miles to the south. There the river ran east through the red wall and wound its way out into the basin. Cottonwoods, narrow-leaf cottonwoods, willows, and chokecherry lined the river's banks along with stands of rosebushes. Currents, wild plumb, and raspberries flourished in cracks and crevices.

They'd been able to bathe. What a relief that had been. Tylor might have had reservations the first time. But the way Singing Lark divested herself of her dress and splashed into the water deadened any of his inhibitions. After he'd shucked himself free of his rags, she'd studied his body thoughtfully, totally unconcerned, as if nudity had no more consequence than the sun rising in the east.

He remembered how they had no more than arrived at the camp before the storm had come blowing down from the mountains. As Singing Lark had predicted, snow had fallen for two days. In their south-facing rock shelter, a crackling fire in its narrow entry, Tylor and Singing Lark had kept mostly warm. Right up until those occasions when they had to venture forth and break branches for firewood from the juniper and pine on the slope across the way.

That had been a week ago. Since then, they'd been constantly at work. Driven by the knowledge that winter was coming, and they weren't prepared.

Tylor winced, and worked his poor fingers. Wished he could make the excuse that he had to go hunting. Wouldn't be in this fix if he'd had his coat and blanket. But he didn't. And, besides, the hunting was over.

He and Singing Lark had attended to that the third day they'd been here. Had killed six mountain sheep on the slope above. Had packed them down, and under Singing Lark's tutelage, had begun tanning the hides.

Hard damned work that. First came the skinning. And as soon as the meat was put to smoking, they began to flesh the hides. Not a quick job like they'd done with the buffalo cows. No, this was a complete fleshing. Then came the job of removing the brains from the mountain sheep skulls. A job made easy with the ax. Singing Lark had cooed in appreciation as she fingered the keen steel edge with a careful finger.

Once the brains were obtained, Singing Lark had dug a hole, lined it with one of the green hides, and put the brains and some water in. They had taken turns, reaching in and mushing it all between their fingers until it reached a thick soup-like consistency.

Singing Lark had used sticks to drop hot stones from the fire into the mess to bring it to a boil.

Then, one by one, the fleshed hides had been staked hair-side down, and the concoction was smeared on, scraped off, re-smeared, re-scraped, over and over.

"Can't do too much brains," Singing Lark had told him.

Drying the hides presented its own problems. She'd shown him how to use curved chokecherry sticks to squeegee the moisture out of the stretched skin.

"Slow dry is best," she'd insisted.

Hadn't been that tough, just a little tedious. Right up to the moment she'd retrieved the lash ropes from the packhorses. She'd tied them between two of the cottonwoods and the graining and stretching had started. She'd taken one side, Tylor the other, and for hour after hour, they'd pulled the hides back and forth over the tight rope. Pulled for ten, maybe fifteen minutes, turned the hide, and began the process over again. From dawn to midday for one hide, midday to nightfall for the next. Five hides in all.

He thought his hands would become crippled claws.

To clench his fists sent an agony through his fingers, forearms, and shoulders. But they'd finished the last of the hides. And, to his amazement, they had come out remarkably soft. Every square inch was pliable. Because she'd insisted.

And, well, yes, he hurt, but he'd enjoyed it. Because they'd done it together. When he reached that point where he'd wanted to stop, he needed but look over. She'd shoot him that secret smile of hers, her white teeth flashing. Something devilish, almost challenging would flicker behind her dark eyes. A hint that they were sharing some great secret. Something special and forbidden to most of the world. Tylor had never known the like.

As Singing Lark packed the last hide back to the safety of their shelter, Tylor worked his fingers and glanced up at the sun in time to catch the last rays of it as it dipped behind the high slope. The cold was coming now. Time to call it a night. His stomach was growling, empty, and squirming for something to fill it.

"I take hides. You catch horses," she told him with a smile hinting at curiosity and promise.

By the time Tylor had laid the poles that served as a gate on the narrow mouth of the box canyon, Singing Lark had the fire stoked up. Once the brains had been used up, the hide-lined hole had been turned into an ad-hoc cooking pot. Filled with water, it had been the container for an ever-evolving stew. She employed her charred sticks to fish hot stones from the fire, then dropped the hot rocks into the liquid. Hissing and steaming, they brought the contents to a low boil.

Tylor called it a stew, a mixture of the last chokecherries and the few squaw currants, rosehips, and plums they could find. Juniper berries and pine nuts had been collected from the slope above. Some roots that Singing Lark had identified from the remains of their dried stems, along with bits of sheep liver, heart, and meat, made up the rest.

Not much in the way of diversity, but filling, nutritious, and surprisingly tasty.

"Tomorrow we smoke the hides," she told him as he stepped under the shelter and settled himself to one side of the fire. She used a quarter-curl horn from one of the young rams they'd killed and scooped some of the stew from the hide-lined pit. This she handed to him, then used the second horn to scoop her own supper.

She slipped over, seating herself beside him, sharing the view as shadow filled the valley. "Once they are well smoked, it's time to cut and sew."

"Just like that," Tylor noted. He glanced around at the fittings for their camp. But for the rifles, powder, and lead, his horse tack, their skinning knife, his clothes, and the ax, nothing was American. Their bedding, cooking utensils, the drying rack, everything else was made from the land. Even the "water bottle," which was crafted from a section of mountain sheep intestine.

She drank lustily from her horn, eyes on the canyon before them. The last of the light had faded from the brilliant red wall, the gloom deepening. Tylor could feel the chill as if it were dropping like a blanket.

The first hooting of a great horned owl could be heard up the canyon.

"Have to take the horses and pack in more wood tomorrow if we're smoking hides," he noted.

"We do. Need the right wood. Got to smoke good." She turned her speculative eyes on him. Studied him thoughtfully as he finished sucking down the hornful of stew.

"What?" he asked, turning to look at her.

"I want you."

"You have me."

She took his hand, removed the empty horn, and stared at his raw knuckles, then raised them to her lips. "You know, no *Newe* man would dare help a woman with hides."

"Then they're idiots."

"No *Newe* man would lay next to a woman, night after night with his *wean* hard and aching."

"I'll never —"

236

"After all this, do you still think of me as a girl?"

"I think you're all woman."

She placed her fingers to his lips, pulled him to his feet, and led him back to the bed in the rear. The old buffalo hides, gone stiff now, had been placed on the ground hair-side up for a mattress. The new sheep hides had been laid atop them, just like a real blanket.

She met his questioning stare, and with a flourish, slipped her dress up and over her head, laid it to the side. She kicked off her moccasins, then told him, "Take it off."

"Singing Lark, I . . ."

She stepped forward, her quick fingers working to loosen the ties on his fly before jerking his pants down over his hips. Then she attacked his shirt.

"For too long now, my *ta'i* has been aching for you. Such a longing can cause soul sickness. You are my husband," she told him in English. "It is time that I am your wife."

And with that, she pulled him down and held up the hides as he slithered in beside her.

Neither of them slept much that night. The next morning they were late getting the fires started to smoke the hides.

CHAPTER 29

The weather was foul when Corporal Toby Johnson's small command reached the mouth of the Platte where it flowed into the turbulent Missouri River. Call it plain miserable.

Toby squinted out at the falling rain, his breath fogging before him. He hadn't grown used to cold feet. Seemed like with his coat, oilcloth slicker, and hat, he could stay mostly dry. Dry was warm. But his feet down in the stirrups were always cold. Maybe because his boots were always wet.

He led the way down from the riverside trail, hearing Eli Danford's big gray horse slopping through the mud behind him. Each hoof lifted with a sucking sound. Didn't need to look back. Private Simms would be there, steady as the North Star; and behind him the two packhorses that Captain Clemson had provided would be following on their leads, heads down, ears flat in the drizzle.

The pack animals should have been doing better. Their loads had been diminished as Toby and his small command had eaten their way west. About half the flour and most of the cornmeal were gone. The salt pork hadn't lasted even as far as the mouth of the Kaw.

Toby stared out at the Platte. Didn't look like much of a river with the thin ripples of shallow-running currents braided across its wide mouth. Still, several trails split off from the main one, each running down to the bank.

"What do you think, Toby?" Danford asked from behind. "Cross or make camp?"

"Cross." He tilted his hat enough to stare up at the dismal clouds. "No telling how it's raining upstream. Water could be up in the morning. Besides, you've heard tell. It's supposed to be big doings, crossing the Platte. A special high jinks."

"Yep," Danford said woodenly. "I'd be up for a high jinks, all right. 'Cept my jug's been empty for nigh on two weeks now."

"The privations of army life, Private," Toby told him with a grin.

"Could be quicksand," Silas called from the rear. "You gonna cross, you don't take

239

no time, Toby. It's supposed to have good bottom, but looking at that water, I wouldn't trust it."

"Hiya!" Toby cried, slapping his cold boots to Buck's sides.

The big horse bolted forward, slipping and sliding down the trail, then out into the river. Toby kept him going, muddy water splashing with each pounding of the horse's feet. Then Buck was climbing the far bank, digging hooves into the black mud. Toby reined the horse up through a narrow opening in the trees and bushes to find a trail ahead of him through the brush.

He stopped, resettling his oilskin cloak so that it protected the lock on his musket from the rain.

Eli and Silas were following, their mounts splashing and thundering through the water, both of them whooping like wild Indians. The packhorses seemed a little more subdued.

But the whole outfit made it. Across the Platte. Beyond the last portal of anything anyone considered civilized.

Taking stock, horses blowing, water streaming from their flanks, they were all grinning.

Around them, the last of fall's leaves were still twirling down, the branches on the cottonwoods, oak, and ash, mostly bare.

"How much farther, ye reckon?" Simms asked, hunching slightly over the saddle as his sorrel mare shook.

"Beats me," Toby told him. "Why, for all I know, we could run into Manuel Lisa any day now."

"No," a voice called from the other side of the thick stand of brush that lay between them and the banks of the Missouri. "You have a hell of a way to go. Who'n tarnation are you? And what in hell was that damn racket about? Thought we's under attack."

Toby shifted in his saddle, heart hammering at the surprise. "Who're you?"

"Louie Lajoie. With me is Joseph Joyal. There is a break in the brush up ahead. Come to our camp."

Toby glanced at the others — who both shrugged, water dripping from their sodden hats.

Toby lined Buck out, found the hole where the thick brush parted, and rode out onto the banks of the Missouri. Sure enough, a stone's throw back downstream a low fire smoked. A large trade canoe — what they called a pirogue — was pulled up and piled with tarped packs. A sort of shelter had been strung up with ropes to keep two bedrolls dry.

The two men watching him held weathered rifles crossways under their coats to protect the priming. Both were grinning.

Toby led the way forward, calling, "I'm Corporal Toby Johnson, on special detachment for Andrew Jackson. With me are Privates Eli Danford and Silas Simms. First Tennessee Volunteers."

He glanced at the packs in the canoe. "I take it you're traders?"

"*Oui,* I am Lajoie," the big one said, a wool cap at a slant on his head. "We work for Manuel Lisa, the man you were talking about on the other side of the brush. We are headed to St. Louis. From upriver, yes?"

Toby pulled his horse up. Wasn't much room here for the animals. "How far to Mr. Lisa's camp?"

"Many days' ride." The smaller man, who had to be Joyal, cocked his head. "What is your business with the *bourgeois*?"

Toby tapped his breast where the orders were hidden in their waterproof pouch. "Got a warrant for a man."

Both of the *engages* laughed at that. "As long as it is for neither of us, we are relieved."

"It's for a man called John Tylor. You know where he is?"

"*Oui,*" Joyal told him. "He is now a free

242

trapper. The *bourgeois* outfits him and Will Cunningham. They are headed to hunt and trap the lands of the Snake, yes? Far to the west." He pointed west over the trees. "At the headwater of the Platte. In the mountains. But God help them. The Arapahos have killed Champlain and his hunters. Word is that the Indians are killing any small party of hunters and trappers. Tylor may already be dead. The Rees tell that a party of Arapaho are hunting him."

"I don't understand. I'm ordered to go and find him."

"Then it is good you run into us, no?" Lajoie told him. "Maybe you find him before the Indians can kill him."

Joyal nodded his agreement, and meeting Toby's eyes, added, "Fastest way to Tylor? You follow the Platte west. Go wide through the Pawnee lands. Stay back from the river. When you get as far west as the short grass, you can return to the river. You cannot miss the forks of the Platte. The two rivers run side by side for many miles. Take the north fork. It will lead you to Snake country. Word is that the North Platte runs at the foot of a huge black mountain. From there you head west. To the Big Horn River. There you will find Tylor and Cunningham."

Toby's heart skipped a beat and felt curiously heavy. "Why did Mr. Lisa let him go west?"

"Something mysterious, yes?" Lajoie said, a smirking kind of smile on his lips. "Per'aps the *bourgeois* learns of your warrant. Per'aps that is the reason Will Cunningham rides so far. Per'aps he has beaten you to Tylor."

Toby growled, " 'Tarnal hell," under his breath. Figured that Pap would have whaled him within an inch of his life if he'd ever heard such profanity pass his lips. Not only was soldiering a constant temptation to sin, but the chase after Tylor was putting its own strain on Toby's upright and righteous ways.

"What did Tylor do?" Joyal asked. "Murder most foul?"

"I say he stole something from a rich man," Lajoie countered. "Maybe from some governor or such."

"Treason," Toby muttered.

The two *engages* stopped short. They seemed to digest that, then broke out into laughter. "Tylor? Treason? From who?"

"He conspired against the United States. But you know the man, did he ever talk about Britain? Maybe that he was a spy? Did he ever speak against the United States? Try and subvert the Indians?"

"Tylor?" Lajoie asked incredulously. "The *bourgeois* watched him. Had Latoulipe watch him, and the *bourgeois* is no one's fool. Manuel Lisa trusts John Tylor, or he would not have outfitted him and turned him loose from his contract. I tell you what, my young friend. Save yourself a long hard ride that is likely to get you killed, scalped, and chopped up for the prairie wolves. Go back and tell whoever sent you that Tylor is dead."

"What do you think, Toby?" Danford asked.

Toby scowled, pursed his lips. Damn. To the *engages* he said, "Many thanks. I'm obliged. Good thing we ran into you. Hope you have a safe trip back to St. Louis."

Toby carefully reined Buck around, watched as Silas got the packhorses sorted out, and headed back to the trail. Just before he kneed Buck forward through the gap in the brush, he looked back. The two *engages* were still standing there. Both men waved.

Toby touched a finger to the wet brim of his hat.

Leading the way back, he stopped short on the north bank of the Platte, turned Buck so he could see Danford and Simms. "I believed them right up to the point about treason."

"Meaning?" Danford asked.

"If Tylor's up the Platte, that's where

we're going."

"But you heard. Tylor might be long dead a'fore we get there."

"Eli, I gave Jackson my promise. Now, I ain't much. Folks say I'm dumb as a rock 'cause I never give up. But I can't hold the two of you to this. Not headed out into the wilderness. Either of you wants to turn back? I'll relieve you. Let you get back to Jackson and the army."

Simms and Danford locked eyes, both men shrugging at once.

"Hell, Toby," Danford said, "we're having the time of our lives. My family's long hunters like yers. Same with Silas, here. Back with the army, we'd be taking orders, marching, eating that swill they fix up. Prob'ly get shot at by lobsterbacks. I'll head upriver w' ye."

Simms chimed in, "I'm game for the Platte, Toby. They's a heap worse duty than this. Let's go see the mountains and find Tylor."

"Might be some more miserable days than this," he pointed out. "Winter's coming."

"Bet there ain't nothing ol' man winter can throw at us what we can't take," Simms answered. "Might mean making duds as we go."

"Reckon we're in, Corporal." Danford was

grinning.

Toby turned Buck's head west, hoping that the trail he took through the brush would lead him out of the trees, give him a view of the country so he could figure out the best route.

It was one thing following upriver to find Manuel Lisa's expedition. But heading out into the emptiness?

Toby sucked at his teeth, water dripping from the brim of his hat. "So be it. I give Jackson my word. And it's up to a man's honor to do his duty."

With that he spurred Buck forward.

CHAPTER 30

If Dawson McTavish didn't think too hard, allowed himself to forget Fenway Mc-Keever, it was possible to marvel about his current situation. He was west of the Black Hills. Having heard tell of them for years, they'd been almost mythical. Now he'd seen them with his own eyes, passed to the north of their wooded slopes.

The trail he and the others now followed paralleled a narrow cottonwood-and-willow-studded stream. Its course led them southwest into a wide basin, its eastern side bounded by the Black Hills, the west by a stunning, even higher range of mountains that rose in snow-capped splendor against the distant horizon.

The land was drier, the grasses shorter, ridge tops rocky. This was a different land from the plains of grass they'd crossed since leaving the Missouri. The feel of the country differed so much from the forests of his youth that it might have been another world. Back in the Minisota River lands, the earth had been wet, forested, and pulsing with life. A land of green where spirit-power seemed to emanate from the earth beneath his feet. Even the occasional boulders — found inexplicably in the flats between the gravel ridges and potholes — grew thick moss. Here any exposed stone was lucky to sport a couple of lichens.

High ground in the basin produced a short and curly combination of grasses, the soil pale, hard, and thin. Even the sagebrush looked stunted, ugly, and stressed. The ridges with their exposed bones of sandstone couldn't even grow the scrubby sage. The lower slopes and bottoms along the drainages sported a thick growth of short grasses in a variety new to Dawson's eyes.

But scrawny and wilted as the grass looked in comparison to what he was used to in the country of his youth, it nevertheless must have been nutritious, for it supported great herds of bison. It seemed like they'd see a herd or two a day — a mass of dark animals that seemed to flow along the rumpled and drainage-cut uplands.

When Dawson asked Wasichu about the distant mountains, the young Santee shrugged. Only when Dawson insisted, did

Wasichu ask this, through signs, to Stone Otter.

"Those mountains the Crow call Big Horns. The Shoshoni call them Powder River's Mountains," Stone Otter explained through signs and limited Lakhota. "Powder River is still west. We follow Pretty River to its source. It takes us to Pine Ridge, then we cross to Powder River. It takes us to the Shoshoni lands. There we find the *Ni'otho* you hunt. There I get my trade."

"How d' ye know that?" McKeever had spared the man a sidelong look.

Stone Otter had given him a humorless stare in return. "Your *Ni'otho* rides with Snakes. They are a simple and weak people. Always go back to find other Snakes." He made the sign for "safety in numbers."

"What do you make of all this?" Aird had asked when he and Dawson rode just out of McKeever's hearing.

"Joseph, I figure we're the same as hostages. McKeever's happy to let us live as long as we're of use to him. He's playing his own game, one where we're an asset to his ultimate goals. He could have killed us back at the river. Taken our trade, the horses, all of it."

"What makes us worth anything to him?"

"We're two more rifles."

"You think he really works for John Jacob Astor?"

"That's what he says."

"Maybe he's a madman," Aird suggested. "I keep coming back to that."

"There's a war on," Dawson told his friend. "Back east, they had to know it was coming. Astor would be a fool if he didn't have agents on the river looking after his interests. That said, we know that he hopes to use South West Company against Manuel Lisa and the Chouteaus. And there's the Spanish to consider, too. No telling what that governor, Salcedo, might do."

"What the hell do the Spanish matter? They's way down south."

"Joseph, you heard tell. The Spanish been mad ever since Napoleon sold the Americans all of Louisiana territory. This country we're riding over, all of it, used to be Spanish. They only ceded it to the French 'cause they thought they had the French between them and the Americans. Now there's a story that an American trading company is on its way to Santa Fe. No way that Spain can protect Texas, New Mexico, or, God forbid, California from way off in Madrid. And if rumors are true, the Mexicans are already half in revolt."

"Well, if McKeever's out here to keep an

eye on Astor's interests, why's he got us clear off west of the river? Dickson's gone to fight the Americans in the Great Lakes, we're supposed to make allies of the River Sioux and get them to attack Lisa. If Governor Salcedo was to take this moment to send a military expedition against the Americans, he'd be coming from the southwest, not out here in the mountains."

"Reckon he would," Dawson agreed, letting his eyes take in the low hills to the west. These were topped by a curious burned red stone that flaked away as if it were a kind of shattered ceramic. Funny country, this.

"So, instead, we're headed for Snake country." Joseph made a face. "To chase down a single spy. Guess that makes me wonder what threat the Snakes is to the river trade? They might have been the terror of the plains once, but since the smallpox, they're broken. Weren't enough of them to keep even a part of the plains east of the Black Hills. All that country was left empty. So empty that the Arapaho, Cheyenne, and now the Sioux is moving in without so much as a fight. They took it. All the way to the Black Hills."

"Uh-huh. So?"

"So let's say this John Tylor is holy hell when it comes to converting the Snakes.

That somehow he's got enough trade to win them all to Lisa and the American cause."

Joseph pointed at the distant Big Horns. "Their home country is clear over there. Other side of them big mountains. We're what? Two months travel from the Missouri? With winter coming on? And let's say they got a couple thousand warriors. We're supposed to believe that John Tylor can convince those couple thousand Snake warriors to ride across the plains in the dead of winter to attack the river? That they'll whip the combined Santee and Teton Sioux, the Arikara, the Mandan and Hidatsa, and the Atsina thrown in?"

Dawson chewed on his mustache where it hung down from his upper lip. "Doesn't make sense, does it?"

"Not for any agent in John Jacob Astor's employ. I tell you, this is something else."

Dawson considered their situation. "I had a couple of chances to shoot him back before we got tied up with these Arapaho. You know, moments when my rifle was pointed his way. When he wasn't paying attention. I just couldn't do it. Killing a white man? Who might be working for the company? Just shooting him out of the saddle? That was stone-cold murder."

The thing he couldn't tell Joseph was that

Fenway McKeever scared him. Scared him in a way no man ever had. Ever since that morning when McKeever had killed Matato. Done it so quickly, quietly, and fast that the man didn't even have to breathe hard.

And McKeever watched him with a knowing look in his evil green eyes. That slight smile on his lips. It was as if the man could read Dawson's mind. Knew him clear down to the soul.

In that deadly green stare had been the promise: Try it, laddie, and ye'll die just like Matato.

Joseph depends on me. Dickson, even the Crown, depends on me.

And Dawson McTavish was too scared to act.

God, he felt miserable. His failure. All his.

"You're no murderer." Joseph had narrowed his eyes. "Didn't know how bad this would get."

"Here's the thing, even if I could see my way to shooting him now, we're all tangled up with these Arapaho. With McKeever alive, it's three against three. No telling what Wasichu'd do. We kill McKeever, we better kill them Arapaho at the same time."

"Dawson, we've never killed anyone before."

"No. But Joseph, if it comes down to it,

254

can you do that? Shoot one of the Arapaho? Maybe McKeever?"

"He scares me. Looks at me like I'm some kind of bug."

"He scares me, too. Scares Stone Otter and the rest. You can see it."

"And don't think the Arapaho haven't figured this out," Joseph said warily. "The fact they haven't tried anything? It's because we're three white men with rifles. That means if they start anything, one or more of them is likely to die. But you can bet they're planning for what's coming down the line. Somehow betting they're going to get all our trade, horses, and guns, as well as this Tylor's and some Snake plunder as well."

Dawson's stomach curdled. "Sort of puts us at the bottom of the heap, don't it?"

"Couldn't have called it better myself," Joseph agreed. "What about Wasichu? Which way will he break?"

"I think, like us, he's got more than he bargained for. When McKeever killed Matato, it sent a shiver down his soul. Back at the river, he thought: 'Don't cross the Scot. Do what he says, and wait for the moment to either get away, or for the Scot to reward you for good service.' And if the whites kill each other, and he's last man alive, he gets the trade.

"Then, like us, he's suddenly stuck with the Arapaho. Now, if we kill each other, there's nothing to keep the Arapaho from killing him. Arapaho and Tetons may be allies for the moment, but he's Santee. And with two packhorses of trade in the balance, what smart Arapaho is going to leave a Santee witness to tell the tale?"

"So, if it comes to it, Wasichu will side with us."

"For the time being." Dawson glanced sidelong at where the Arapaho rode some fifty yards to their right. That was the thing about the Arapaho. They never really let their guard down. Never rode with their backs turned, or where the whites could, on a moment's notice, shoot them down.

"I feel like a fool," Dawson said miserably. "We've been on the trail now for weeks, and you and me have just figured this out?"

Joseph glanced around, as if gazing at the lay of the land, then shot a nonchalant glance over his shoulder. "McKeever's known from the beginning. He's always where he can watch everyone. Whatever way this is going to end, we really need to figure out how we're going to get out of it alive. We've got to be smarter, Dawson. Otherwise it will be just pure dumb luck if we make it."

CHAPTER 31

In comparison to what Tylor had known in his marriage to Hallie, what he shared with Singing Lark might have been from a different lifetime, something magical, like a fairy tale.

In his old life, Tylor would have said his relationship with Hallie was more intimate than that lived by most married aristocracy. They had genuinely loved each other, had had a healthy sexual relationship, conversed about a variety of subjects in a manner most men would never have engaged in with a woman. They would never have considered each other as best friends, though they respected each other's intellect. Rare as that was between a man and a woman.

In the Carolinas a man's wife was legally the same as chattel. For most men in Tylor's circle, wives were essential breeding stock for the production and nurturing of offspring. A woman's job was to oversee the everyday operation of the household, ensure the servants were in line, that meals were prepared on time, that the floors were polished, and the windows closed in the event of a storm. She was to be a showpiece, immaculately dressed on social occasions and retiring in a way that reflected well of her lord and master's wealth and status.

As liberated as Tylor's relationship with Hallie might have seemed when set against the strictures of Carolina aristocracy, bounds remained that they would never have crossed. Their social roles had been as confining as if cast in iron.

What Tylor shared with Singing Lark would have been incomprehensible in North Carolina. From the beginning, their roles were reversed. This was her world, and she was the dominant partner, skilled in the intricacies of survival. Once she showed him how to do something, she expected him to do it.

Unlike in the east where lordly men and servile women's worlds were inviolately separate, Tylor and Singing Lark did *everything* together: cooking, hunting, gutting and butchering, defecating, packing firewood, teasing, arguing, caring for the horses.

Somewhere along the line he and she had

become two halves of a whole. The kind who enjoyed each other's company and had complete trust in the other. Somehow possessed of the knowledge that no matter what, each would be there.

That single realization stunned Tylor. He'd never known that kind of friendship with anyone — let alone a woman. Sure, as with Baptiste Latoulipe, he'd had friends, shared companionship — but a deep-seated reservation had always tempered the relationship. In the days following his capture in the wake of the Burr conspiracy, he'd been well aware of the limits and transitory nature of friendship.

That he and Singing Lark could share everything made him question all he'd known and been in the east. The world that had bred and raised him considered women frail and delicate, incapable of significant — let alone profound — thought, limited in ability beyond the simplest domestic responsibilities. After all, it was so plainly stated in the Bible: women were inferior in creation.

Given young Singing Lark's proficiencies, her ability to learn, and her remarkable acumen, he had to wonder if white women were naturally incompetent, if white men had bred the sense out of them through ages of selection, or if Shoshoni women just happened to be the pinnacle of brilliant accomplishment when it came to the female of the species.

Tylor's conjugal relations with Singing Lark were just as revelatory. He and Hallie had been active under the covers. Some in their world would have considered the extent of their enjoyment of the act sinful, but it had been structured, confined to both propriety and their bedroom. Almost ritualized. In contrast, Singing Lark had no inhibitions when it came to either his or her body, and considered copulation as natural and inevitable as she did any other aspect of daily life. She was happy to oblige at any time, and initiated the action whenever the mood struck, at times and places Tylor would never have imagined. Such as in the middle of fleshing a hide, right there on the sunlit grass.

So, who is right? My people, who are born in guilt and live in repression because Adam and Eve ate an apple and were kicked out of the Garden of Eden? Or is it Singing Lark's, whose people remind each other that in the Beginning Times the trickster, Coyote, carried a spare penis in a basket on his back in case his original equipment was inoperative?

"You are smiling," Singing Lark noted from her spot beside him at the fire. Outside, night had fallen, crisp, the night dark with clouds and a gentle snow.

"Wondering if I am James Sutherland."

"Who?"

"An older man who married a twelve-year-old girl. People made fun of him."

"Twelve? She had passed her first *hunni*?"

"I doubt it."

"That is wrong."

"Back where I come from, some would lift an eyebrow about you and me."

"Did you know that back among the people, they pitied you? Made fun of you behind your back?"

"Why?"

"They thought that I was playing with you. Making a fool out of you so that I could be selfish. That I married you so I could remain irresponsible. That I got everything, and you didn't even get the relief of *yokog* from the woman you married. Poor, pitiful Tylor."

He laughed. "I promised to be the responsible one, the adult taking care of you." He paused. "You are half my age. Do you really think you know what you want for the rest of your life?"

She shrugged. "My parents died from the rotting-face sickness. Gray Bear raised my sister and me. As a girl I dreamed of marrying a man who could hunt, who could fight, and who would keep me fed. We would have children, and they would grow strong and tall. That man didn't have hair on his face and coyote-like eyes." She gave him a teasing wink. "What I didn't dream was that such a man would let me be who I want to be. You are a puzzle to my people, Tylor, but I can't think of what life would be like without you."

As he considered that, she added, "As a rich and prominent man, the people are going to expect you to marry my sister when she has her first moon."

"Wait a minute! What?"

"A man does not marry sisters among your people?"

"No. One man marries only one woman at a time."

She turned, fixing him with her serious eyes. "We are not *Taipo*. We are the *Newe*. You had better start thinking about this. Or are you going to be as crazy marrying Yellow Breeze as you were about marrying me?"

"I don't know."

"If you do not like her, you can say no. But it must be done with respect, and you might suggest another man who would be better suited to marry her."

Tylor made a face, then rubbed his temples. On top of everything else, they expected him to be a bigamist? With Lark's sister?

She laughed, prodding the fire. "I see that confused look, husband."

"Thinking about the world I come from. Considering where we are. Right now. Beside our fire, with snow falling just beyond the shelter. Thinking about you and me. How different this world is from the one I left behind. I'm just coming to terms with the realization that I love you more than anything, in a way I never thought I'd love a woman, and you tell me I have to marry your little sister?"

"You must at least make the offer. She might want to marry someone else by the time she is a woman."

"How do you feel about it? Is that something you would want?" The implications were unsettling. Another . . . child?

"It would make our lives easier. She's a good worker, and I think she will turn out to be better at being a woman than I am. She's always been happier about gossiping, making clothing, tending to lodge fires, and doing woman's work. I would much rather that you brought her to our lodge than some other woman."

"Some other woman?" Tylor wondered. "Lark, what about us?"

"What about us?"

"You make it sound like a business arrangement. Marry my sister. She can go to work for us. But what about you and me? It will change things between us. I *love* you. I don't want someone else in our lives."

"Then don't marry her." Her brow lined. "You have told me about this thing you call love. We don't have a word like that, but talk about a longing in the *mugwa* for another, and warm caring, and dedicating one's life to another. But, this special feeling you have for me? Is your heart so small you can only share it with one person and not two?"

He blinked. "I . . . I don't know. Who do you think I am? Coyote? Like in your stories?"

She gave him her level and sober look. "Depends on how you think about Coyote. Lots of sides to him. But the world wouldn't have been the way the world is if Coyote hadn't been Coyote and Wolf hadn't been Wolf."

"Chaos forever in conflict with order," he murmured, stopping long enough to cut a short length of tobacco from the last of the twist he carried. "Too much of either is bad.

It's the *Newe* goal to strike a balance."

"What are the stories among your people?"

"God and his son, Jesus, are good. The Devil is evil. The choice is clear. Absolute. No balance to be struck between the two. Evil only exists because it's a force acting on its own behalf. The assumption is that the Devil will forever tempt people to do bad things, lead them away from God, and exploit them through their 'human' failings. That we're all flawed in our creation. What they call 'original sin' because we're born of copulation. We all start life on the wrong side. Have to fight to overcome the stain of being born bad."

"Born bad? Poor *Taipo*s. Among the *Newe,* some are born to be trouble. Others born to be helpful. I was six when Little Wolf was born. Something was wrong with him from the start. Perhaps he had some of Water Baby's Spirit in him. When he was three, his parents had a little girl. He hated that she got all the attention he used to get. When he was six, he took her out into the willows and used an obsidian flake to cut her into bloody strips."

"Definitely evil, I'd say."

"He didn't get all the blood washed off. When he went back, his parents were suspicious. They went out and found the body of his sister, of course."

"So, what happened?"

"His father stepped up behind him. Smacked him in the back of the neck with a club. Before his *mugwa* and *navushieip* could slip out of the body, they tied a sack over his head to trap the souls inside. Then they dug a hole, covered his body up, and rolled a big rock over it to keep his evil trapped forever."

"His parents killed him?"

"He was their child. Their responsibility. But, unlike in your world, most people are born good among the *Newe.*" She made a face. "I don't think I want to live in your world where all people are born bad."

"In my world, women are kept separate, a wife is little better than a slave. Men give the orders, women do as they are told. You and I couldn't live like we do." He snorted derisively. "Just the fact that we're married would be a scandal. I'm a white gentleman, you're a squaw."

"A what?"

"An Indian."

"I'm *Newe.*"

"Doesn't matter to them. Only the lowest classes of white men marry Indian women." Let alone *two* of them.

"Lowest classes? Explain."

"My people place different values on different kinds of people depending on who their parents are, what they own, where they live, what they do for a living, and what race they belong to. I came from the top, the chiefs. We are called the aristocracy, the landed planters."

She considered this. A crooked smile bent her lips. "You have gone from the top to the bottom?"

"I have."

"Miss being on top?"

He chuckled. "I think a person has to lose everything to really discover who they are."

She pressed her fingers together, that thoughtful look intensifying. "Among the Newe if a man orders a woman around like a slave, she'll just ignore him. Unless she's really a slave. Then she has to do what she's told or be beaten. But everyone has expectations about what a woman should be. A woman behaves in a certain way. Does certain things. She is expected to spend her time with other women, have children, talk about children. Tan hides. Cook. Gather food. Help other women."

"What happens when we finally find Gray Bear's camp again?"

The crooked smile was back. "I married a

267

Taipo. I've gone from the top to the bottom."

"I guess you have."

"In the beginning I married you to keep from being who they wanted me to be."

"How's that?"

"They could not have made me marry as long as Gray Bear and Aspen Branch took my side. I could have kept doing what I wanted, but it would have been hard. No one would have really trusted me. They'd have thought my *puha* was wrong. Maybe not tainted like Little Wolf's was, but having different *puha* than everyone else makes people nervous. Quick to lay blame if there's bad luck or illness."

"They won't say that if you're married to a *Taipo?*"

"Of course not. *Taipo* have different ways, that's all. And I was always different. It figures I'd do something crazy like marry a *Taipo.*"

He joined her laughter, then, in a serious voice, asked, "How is it working out for you?"

Her eyes were still sparkling. "As dumb as you are about so many things, I wasn't sure in the beginning. I still have to tell myself, he's a *Taipo,* and I would be as dumb in your world." She took his hand, lacing her fingers into his. "I think marrying you was the best thing I have ever done."

"What happens if we just stay here? Who would miss us?"

Her chiding look was back. "Not enough food. The sheep, deer, and elk have smelled too much of us and the horses and left. By the end of the next full moon, our bellies would be more empty than full. By now the raiding parties should be headed home. When the weather breaks, we'll slip south along the foothills, then over to Big River to look for Gray Bear's village."

"And then what?"

"We spend the winter in a nice lodge, tell stories, you trade. We hunt some. Enjoy each other under the robes."

"I need to trap beaver. I have to take trade back to Manuel Lisa. He's supposed to have a post at the mouth of what the Crow call the Big Horn River on the Yellowstone. You know where that is?"

She nodded. "I can find it. Follow our *Pia'ogwe* to where it joins the *Ge'te'ogwe*. The Fast River that some others call the Yellow Rock River."

"You will help me trap beaver?"

"It is hunting, yes. We'll have to be away from the winter village. Away from people telling me how to behave."

For a time they watched the fire burn.

"What comes after you take the beaver to the *Taipo* post?"

"What do you mean?"

"You have said you are not going back to the *Taipo* world, but what if they ask you to?"

"I can't go back. Ever. There are men back there who want to kill me. Men who hate me."

"Why?"

"I have an enemy back there. A man named Joshua Gregg. We were boyhood friends. We got into a fight as boys, and our fathers took it up. My father killed Joshua's father in a duel. Then we wanted to marry the same woman. She married me. I went west, to Santa Fe, in an effort to become . . . Well, a kind of great *Taipo Taikwahni*. The great chiefs among the Americans didn't like it, called me a bad man. Especially Joshua Gregg and a war chief called Jackson."

"Doesn't sound so bad."

"Hard to explain until you understand laws and governments. I escaped, but they want me dead. As long as Joshua Gregg knows I am alive, he will send men after me." He thought back to Fenway Mc-Keever, how close the big Scot had come to killing him.

Her gaze remained fixed on the flickering fire. "You think they will come looking for you?"

"I think Lisa will keep my secret." He gestured around. "This is about as far from the *Taipo* world as a man can get."

"I can take you even farther than this," she told him. "I can take you into the *Dukurika* Mountains, to the *Pa'do'ikint,* the place where the steaming water comes out. It is a place of the Spirits, filled with *puha.* The *Dukurika* live there. The Sheep Eaters. I have some cousins among them. It's a high land, cold in winter, with deep snows. No one but Sheep Eaters could find you there."

She giggled in that little girl way, eyes sparkling. "We could go to the *Pa'do'ikint* and never come back. Just live there. You and me, forever."

"There's worse things, I suspect."

Her gaze turned serious again. "What if the *Taipo* come hunting you?"

"Way out here?" He took a moment to consider the question. Jackson and Gregg would be able to trace him as far as St. Louis. McKeever would have reported to Joshua Gregg that he was onto his man clear back when Tylor had signed onto the Lisa expedition. William Clark knew that John

271

Tylor had traveled upriver. Clark had sent Cunningham as a courier, carrying Hallie's letter and a warning to Lisa. After Mc-Keever died that night in the Missouri, no word would be going back to Gregg.

Whether, in the midst of a war, Andrew Jackson would send anyone in pursuit was another matter. The rational assumption was that Jackson had a great many more pressing matters to attend to than an escaped traitor. But who would ever assume Jackson was rational?

"I think we have a couple of years," Tylor said at last. "No one will know what happened to me until Lisa returns to St. Louis next summer. Not that he'd surrender my secrets lightly, but anyone with enough pennies to get his returning *engages* drunk will hear plenty of stories about John Tylor. A persistent intelligencer will figure out that Will and I headed west into the plains. After that it's a gamble as to whether or not I'm still alive."

"How far is this St. Louis?"

"Very, very far."

"If anyone comes, we will hear." She seemed so resolutely sure of herself.

"Let's hope." But he kept thinking of that two-thousand-dollar reward Gregg had put on his head. And word was that Jackson had added another thousand. Money enough to goad any number of men off into the wilderness in Tylor's pursuit.

"Besides," Singing Lark told him. "If anyone comes, I have a rifle. I will shoot them."

"So, now you want to be a warrior as well as a scout and a hunter?"

"Why not?"

He had at least a year before anyone could travel from St. Louis to the Upper Missouri. Until that time, he could relax. Just be himself.

And know that in another couple of years, the people would expect him to marry Yellow Breeze when she became a woman.

Another couple of years?

Whatever made him think he'd live that long?

CHAPTER 32

The way led into the wind. The relentless
and everlasting wind. At night Toby and his
small command would make camp down in
the cottonwoods, along the banks of the
Platte. Just after the evening fire started to
burn down, the wind would usually die. In
the morning, after they'd cooked their
scanty breakfast and mounted up, the wind
would begin as a slight breeze, gathering
strength until midday, when it was a blow.

They had reached the long-sought fork of
the Platte, the channels running side-by-
side for miles, as the traders had said they
would.

"Where in hell are we going?" Silas Simms
asked as he huddled in his blanket and
stared up at the night.

They had camped in a hollow beneath a
steep embankment where a stream had cut
a loop into the side of a hill. Freshly shot
antelope sizzled where it was propped on

sticks over the coals. To the south, the broad plain of the Platte River was thick with cottonwoods. Above, the night was unusually clear, hoary with a million stars, and a faint sliver of moon in the east.

"Tired of adventure?" Toby asked, his own blanket around his shoulders. The night was cold enough their breath frosted.

"Funny thing." Danforth rubbed his bearded chin, staring thoughtfully into the flames. "Half the time I'm scared stiff. When we crossed them horse tracks today? There had to be what? Fifteen, twenty of them? That's a lot of Indians. And there's just the three of us? Way out here? If'n we's to be kilt, ain't nobody going to know what happened to us.

"And then I look around. See all this country. That's when the feeling sets in. I'm the first white man out here. Well, along with you fellers. I get this quiver down in my guts. Sort of says, by hell and tarnation, boy, yer the first! Ain't been nobody here ahead of you. And there ain't, right? Toby, you ever heard of any white man ever rode up the Platte to its start?"

Toby shook his head. Wished he had tobacco. "For all I know, we're the first. Might have been somebody ahead of us."

Silas smiled. "Kind of nice to believe we're

the first. Think, boys, we're seeing things even Lewis and Clark didn't. And, well, even if some fur hunters was to have gone this way, they might have been on the south bank, or down on the river. They ain't seen it the way we are."

"Sure was a lot of horse tracks we seen today," Danford reminded.

"Villages is down on the river," Toby said, thinking back to the last of the Pawnee towns they'd seen. From the high ridge they'd had a glimpse of the rounded earth lodges, tiny in the distance. The town had stood out only because a faint haze of smoke had hung over the lodges where the cold air lay. Toby had chosen a two-day detour to the north, staying to the low ground.

"Country's starting to change." Silas leaned forward to pull his skewered antelope from the fire. He blew on it, watching the steam rise. "Grass is getting shorter. Like that feller said back on the Missouri."

"We're making good time." Toby reached for his own meat. He figured that between them, if they recovered their bullets, they had powder enough for close to seventy shots. With the weather getting cold, meat wouldn't sour. They should be able to hunt for a couple of years at that rate.

Assuming they didn't get into an Indian fight. But then, if they shot up all their powder and lead, it wasn't a fight they were going to walk away from. He remembered Pap's stories about Fort Loudoun back in Tennessee. So much of winning and losing was about numbers, as the people fleeing the abandoned fort had discovered to their peril.

Toby considered his companions, and once again he admired Andrew Jackson's smarts when it came to assigning them to him. Tennessee hunters, all. Descended from families of long hunters who had braved the dangers west of the Appalachians and built homes beyond the white frontier. They had a spirit for adventure that had taken them to the army, and now lived unleashed in their breasts as they journeyed into the unknown.

Toby might not have known who John Tylor was, nor really cared, but it had surely sent him on the doings of a lifetime.

Simms's sky-blue eyes fixed on his cooling meat. "The bay packhorse is gonna throw that last shoe tomorrow. Might want to pull it in the morning."

"We'll save it along with the rest. No telling what we might need the iron for. Maybe trade, maybe repair something that's broke."

"I did a bit of blacksmithing," Danford said. "Hard part will be not having an anvil and the right hammer."

"Reckon we need to shoot a buffalo or two." Simms took a bite of his antelope. "My hide tanning on this prairie goat ain't fer shit. Never seen hair like this on a critter. Stiff, bristly, all hollow. The stuff just busts."

"Think we'll need buffalo robes?" Danford asked, his eyes on the starry night.

"It's nigh onto November." Toby bit off a morsel of his own antelope, having cooked it perfectly. The shooting of their first antelope had been one of those magical moments in a hunter's life. They'd heard about the prairie goats, stories having been carried all the way into the Tennessee forests. The first pronghorns they'd seen had dazzled them, left them in awe as the creatures raced away across the grass at a speed no horse could hope to match.

Danford had made the first successful stalk, shot one from ambush. Then the three of them had studied the beast from hooves to horns, and now found the meat the equal of elk and bison.

"These high plains is supposed to get damn cold," Toby said. "That's what that quartermaster back at the fort said. And I figger if they was a hard snow, blown by this miserable wind, it'd freeze a feller right down to his bones."

Danford frowned into the fire and retrieved his own skewered meat. "Way I figure it, we're making about twenty miles a day. That's about all the horses can take without wearing down. The important thing is their feet."

Somehow it had skipped Toby's mind to lay in a supply of horseshoe nails back at Fort Osage. At least Simms had been smart enough to pack a rasp so they could dress the hooves, though as the land had dried, they'd needed it less and less.

"Seems like the hooves have toughened on their own. Shouldn't be trouble unless we hit some rocky ground and the horses are loaded heavy."

"Couple of straps is wearing on the bay's packsaddle," Simms announced around a mouthful of antelope. "Buckle tongue is pulling through the leather."

"Can you fix it?" Toby asked.

"Reckon I can make a repair," Simms agreed. "Need to see to it in the next couple of days, though."

The eerie serenade of the coyotes carried in the night. The yipping, high-pitched squealings had sent the shivers down their backs the first time they'd heard them. Now, like the endless skies, that naked feeling of being small on the landscape, and the wheeling of the eagles and hawks overhead, the sound had become commonplace.

"Wish them French boys back on the Missouri had said how far we had to go west from the fork of the Platte," Simms muttered. "And how the hell do we know when we get there? Where the river runs north of the black mountain? How, out in the middle of all this, do we find Tylor?"

Danford asked dryly, "Ask the first buffalo we see?"

Toby scratched under his bearded chin. That was a hell of a good question. It was one thing to be standing in a room in Nashville when he made his promise to Jackson that he'd bring his man back. Another entirely when the traitor was thought to be in Lisa's company on the Upper Missouri. But now?

Toby Johnson was just beginning to get a glimmer of how fantastically large the land was, and the immensity of territory he was going to have to search to find a solitary man in this wilderness.

CHAPTER 33

From a high ridge, its top capped with a resistant dirty-yellow sandstone, the view was outstanding. The west wind gave off a harsh whisper as it bent and teased the ponderosa branches. The pines grew in sporadic patches just under the rimrock and along the broken slopes below. Sagebrush spikes shivered and tossed with each gust. In the wake of the snow, the sky was a remarkably clear blue, the sun glaringly bright in the southern sky. It cast a beautiful pattern of shadows in the northern slopes, in the drainages, and cuts.

Fenway McKeever pulled Matato's coat tightly around him in an effort to cut the wind's chilling bite. Didn't matter that the day was warm enough to melt the snow, the way the wind chill slipped through every gap sapped a man's heat.

"River you call Platte." Stone Otter sat on his horse and pointed off to the southeast toward a tall and forested mountain that ran east-west like a black wall. "River there. Under mountain. Black Lightning said he would winter there with his people."

McKeever squinted across the distance; lines of ridges and buttes — pale-looking basins and drainages interspersed among them — lay between their vantage and the mountain. His horse shifted under him, worked the bit, and tried to turn away from the wind.

"Close to the Snakes, aye? Ye said they'd be o'er yonder." McKeever pointed west toward the rugged bluffs and buttes that rose progressively into the southern flanks of the Big Horn Mountains.

"Black Lightning will have scouts. Watch for Snakes. Snakes have scouts, watch for *Hinono'ei.*" He used the people's word for Arapaho.

"Wee bit of a disputed border?" McKeever let his horse sidestep enough that the muzzle of his rifle could be shifted in a hurry. He never pointed it directly at Stone Otter. Just let it hint in the man's general direction.

Fox that he was, the Arapaho pretended not to notice. Stone Otter missed nothing in the dangerous game they played. He fully understood that he was the key to locating

Tylor in the vastness of the Powder River Basin, the Big Horns, and the Wind River Country beyond.

Over the month they'd been traveling together, McKeever had pieced the story together. How Stone Otter's party had tracked Tylor and another *Ni'otho* to their camp. Had approached in friendship and been shot down by the perfidious whites and their hidden Snake allies.

Not that McKeever believed it. Wasichu had overheard Red Bear Man and Wide Crane discussing how the Arapaho had killed Lisa's party under Champlain. For whatever reason, the *Hinono'ei* had come to the conclusion that whites were rather offensive. Some sort of ill-mannered and smelly rascals that deserved whatever exploitation the Arapaho deemed appropriate at the moment. That they came bearing an incredible wealth in exotic trade, that they could be played off each other — Spanish against British, British against American — was just the fat in the stew. Nor was there a thing the whites could do in retaliation. They were too few, too weak, and too disorganized.

One day that will change.

McKeever kept thinking back to that long-ago discussion he'd had with Tylor while they were on the river. About the Americans — a growing horde who raised corn, pigs, and kids in profusion. Tylor might be right, that they'd be coming in a flood that would wash across the plains in a few generations. Or McKeever might be right that it would take a couple of hundred years, but they would come.

"And what will ye do then?" McKeever pondered under his breath, a sidelong glance fixed on Stone Otter.

Not that it mattered. This was now. McKeever — through Wasichu — had learned that Tylor had shot Stone Otter's little brother. One of the Shoshoni had driven an arrow through a cousin. The other dead and wounded had been some sort of society brothers that Wasichu couldn't quite explain.

"We'd best be getting on aboot finding Tylor," McKeever told him. He pointed to the west, to where a valley marked a stream's course. "Ye said that way was the fastest to the Wind River, aye?"

"Snake that way," Stone Otter agreed, augmenting his words with signs.

"Let's be on then. Sooner Tylor's dead, the sooner what's a'tween us will come to a head. And then, laddie, she's Katy bar the door."

With that, he gave Stone Otter a disarming grin, gesturing that the Arapaho precede him back down the ridge to where the others were waiting.

Find me Tylor, ye heathen scum. After that, it'll be me pleasure to send ye to the Happy Hunting Ground so's ye and yer little brother can be together again.

CHAPTER 34

According to Singing Lark, the name of the stream was "Where-the-Buffalo-Drink." From their camp in the red sandstone wall, they had backtracked to the Middle Fork of the Powder River and traveled downstream. At the confluence with Where-the-Buffalo-Drink Creek, Singing Lark had turned them on to an established trail that followed the tributary. The valley led them south in a gentle curve around the flank of the mountains. By the end of the first day, the trail had curled around to the west, leading them into the setting sun.

Bounded by a steep ridge to the east and south, the valley was long, fed by drainages running down from the high slopes to the north that led up into the Powder River Mountains. The slopes and floodplain had grown thick with sagebrush, which, in the bottoms, rose as tall as a horse's head.

Along the stream itself, willows, chokecherry, sarvisberry, currants, and stands of both broad and narrow-leafed cottonwood grew, as did occasional box elders. Junipers dotted the higher slopes — sometimes thick enough to resemble forest. Occasional narrow-walled drainages cut through the mountain bedrock, and in their depths patches of aspen could be seen.

Tylor let Singing Lark lead the way. His wife rode as if one with her horse, her rifle squarely across her saddle. She followed a well-defined trail that paralleled the stream's left bank. Travel was easier there, given that so many of the drainages ran in from the west and north. At times, however, she would splash through a crossing to the opposite bank to avoid steep slopes, rock outcrops, or difficult passages where brush or terrain intervened.

Between them, the packhorses followed on their leads, lined out and delighted to be moving again, especially since their loads were lighter, consisting only of dried meat, hides, and camp gear.

Tylor had his newly tailored coat open, a testament to the day's warmth. Must have been in the mid-fifties if he was any judge. The low slant of the winter sun had them riding in shadow anytime they were close to the steep ridge where snow clung in and around the sage.

What a figure he cut, dressed in a fine antelope-hide shirt of soft leather that was topped by his sheep-hide coat. He'd been amazed at the fit Singing Lark had achieved — as fine as could be had by the tailors in Charleston or Philadelphia. His legs were clad in soft antelope; his sheep-hide leggings, tanned hair-on, were tied onto the cantle of his saddle. Shoshoni boots, also made from mountain sheep with hair-side in, now clad his feet. The only characteristic he hadn't grown used to was the seam that ran down the center of the sole. Though cushioned by hair and grass padding, the seam might become debilitating on a long walk.

While he rode with his head bare out of respect for the day, a fox-skin cap with a bill was rolled in his leggings. The jack handle rested sideways across his saddlebow.

He chuckled. *If I came to the west in an attempt to lay John Tylor to rest, my success is complete.*

Compared to the sartorial perfection of the man who had been received in London, Paris, and Amsterdam, he now might have been mistaken for a Mongol, Hun, or Vandal.

He reached up to finger Hallie's letter

where it rested in a pocket over his breast. At the sound of the paper crackling, he had to wonder what Hallie would say if she could see him now, dressed as he was. He suspected that she'd arch a skeptical eyebrow. Say something like, "Surely this is only for the moment. You will attire yourself as a gentleman as soon as you possibly can."

Her reaction to his marriage to Singing Lark, on the other hand, would be baffled incomprehension. He had been a Carolina gentleman. To marry an Indian was the act of a lunatic or someone mentally deficient. Proof of a previously unsuspected madness — the manifestation of which was only first glimpsed by his activities in the Burr conspiracy and the subsequent charges of treason.

Once upon a time, Tylor would have shared her reaction, considered the notion of taking an unlettered Native girl into his marriage bed an act of absolute scandal. A sort of perversity.

A sad smile bent his lips as he swayed in time with the black mare's steady walk, enjoyed the sunshine, and wondered just who in hell his people back in the Carolinas had ever thought they were. All that assumed superiority, the benefits of breeding, education, and station. And all the while, half the men were siring mixed-blood children off their negro slaves, while the women — overdressed and arrogant in their ignorance — couldn't have tanned a sheep hide if their lives depended upon it. What was the ability to keep a ledger of estate expenses compared to the talent and skill necessary to elude an Arapaho war party?

But then, were she to be dropped on the streets of Paris, Singing Lark would have been just as lost, terrified, and incapable of survival.

"It's a matter of where we are and what we know," Tylor mused a moment before his mare started; four mule deer burst from the willows and went bounding up the slope.

Reining her in, he turned his attention back to the trail and noticed that the chestnut packhorse in front of him wasn't walking as smoothly as it had been. Probably time to pull that last shoe. The miracle was that it had lasted this long.

He couldn't get over the feeling of revelation as he watched his Shoshoni wife riding ahead of him, her shoulder-length hair gleaming in the sunlight.

If he was to survive, let alone thrive in this new world, it would be because of her. That she had accepted him, shared herself with him, laughed with and cherished him, might have been the greatest wonder in his world.

"So, John, my boy, don't you ever take that young woman for granted. You'll never find her equal in this, or any other world."

Saying that, he threw his head back and laughed, satiated with the sheer joy of being alive.

CHAPTER 35

The camp that Gray Bear established sat in the cottonwood trees back from the *Pia'ogwe.* His small band had raised their lodges on the west bank, downstream from Dark Horse's village, which lay not more than a couple of fingers of time away by foot. A high bluff, capped with round cobbles, provided protection from the west wind, and the grassy bottoms had plenty of graze for the horses.

Their arrival had been accompanied by a flurry of activity and excitement in Dark Horse's camp. As Gray Bear's people set up their village, they'd been flocked by the entirety of Dark Horse's band, forty some people in all.

The first attraction, of course, was Cunningham. A *Taipo* who had come with trade. Everyone wanted to get a good look at him. Not that *Taipo* were as much a novelty these days. Dark Horse's band had met with the

Astorians under Wilson Price Hunt the year before as the *Taipo* expedition traveled through the Valley of the Warm Winds on their way to the Pacific.

The hawk had taken poorly to the arrival, upset at the number of unknown people who'd come to stare at him. The bird's fear ameliorated in proportion to the offerings of meat the new people brought.

Additional comment was stirred by the news that young Singing Lark had left as a wild girl, had become a woman in secret and without the usual rituals that marked passage to womanhood. Then, to top it all off, she'd married some other *Taipo,* and was last seen on the Pretty River. Speculation about her fate ran rampant.

And, of course, there were the guns. Most of the *Kuchendukani* Shoshoni were of mixed opinion about guns and their utility. Over the years occasional specimens had been traded up from the south. From the very beginning, the Spanish had forbidden the possession of guns by Indians — let alone any kind of trade in them. The few firearms that had been carried up the trails — most notably by Comanche cousins — and traded up to the *Kuchendukani* had been curiosities, most of them broken, rusted, and abused. Nor would anyone have traded it in the first place if it wasn't worn out and essentially useless.

Not to mention that to work, a gun needed both bullets and powder. While anything that fit down the barrel might have served for a bullet, gunpowder in any kind of sufficiency rarely made it as far as the *Kuchendukani*.

Then, a generation ago, had come the British up in the north. The problem was that they traded guns to the Blackfeet, Sioux, and Atsina — enemies all — and now the Arapaho were encroaching, and more and more often, they, too, had guns in number. Deadly ones that worked.

When the Shoshoni captured enemy guns, they came with only a limited amount of powder and a few balls. Whatever was carried by the enemy warrior at the time of his capture or death. The next problem was trying to learn how to shoot the piece. By the time any proficiency was reached, the powder and bullets were used up.

The arrival of Gray Bear's band, bearing brand-new rifles with powder, lead, and molds — not to mention a promised source for resupply at the mouth of the Big Horn — was a major cause for excitement.

And then there was Gray Bear himself: A man who had left as a hunter and returned from the distant Great River being respectfully called *taikwahni.* Everyone wanted to hear the story. That meant several feasts, a public recounting, and celebrity status for everyone in Gray Bear's little band after the story was told.

As an unseasonably warm day waned, Gray Bear sat before Dark Horse's lodge — a roomy four-pole tipi decorated with stylistic black horses on the run. Dark Horse's shield and bow rested on a tripod to one side, and an elk hide had been laid out for the guests.

At the hearth out front, Dark Horse's two wives cooked buffalo tongue and boiled a yampa-root stew crammed with rosehips. Their names were Sage Cup and Snow Flower, sisters, and they had born Dark Horse six children, of whom four had survived so far.

Dark Horse was in his mid-thirties, a broad-faced man with prominent cheekbones and a jutting chin. He wore his hair with the bangs curled back over the top of his head, the rest of his mane spilling down his back in waves. He leaned against a willow backrest, the sunlight emphasizing the golden hues of his elk hide jacket with its quillwork and faceted red beads in rose patterns.

Cunningham sat to the side, his long-stemmed pipe in his hand. He had traded for a newly tailored buckskin shirt and pants, but still kept his white man's boots. Now he watched Silver Curl, Dark Horse's auburn-haired, pale-skinned slave. The woman worked to one side, using a fleshing tool to hack the tissue from a buffalo hide. As she chopped the bits loose, she'd toss them to a big brown wolfish-looking dog. Gray Bear had seen her shoot Cunningham more than one curious long glance. The tall *Taipo* had reciprocated with a smile each time.

"What does this thing you have done mean?" Dark Horse asked as he packed kinnikinnick into the new ceramic pipe for which he'd traded a collection of otter skins. "You have nine guns and five men old enough to shoot them. Six if you count Eagle's Whistle, but he's still a boy. You say your people will trade the last three. For what? Who decides?"

"We all do," Gray Bear told him. "We all worked together. Everyone did his or her part. The guns belong to all of us."

"I would really like to have one."

"I will mention that. What would you trade?"

"How many horses do your people want?

I can offer three. Good animals. Solid. And I think one of the mares is pregnant."

"I will take your offer to my people."

Dark Horse shot him a measuring look. "Or maybe my people and I should travel to the mouth of the *Pia'ogwe* where it meets the *Ge'te'ogwe*. See how many horses the *Taipo* there want for *aitta*."

At that, Cunningham set his pipe aside so he could sign to fill in for Shoshoni words he didn't know. "You'll need packs of beaver. Furs. That or those white buffalo calf hides like Gray Bear traded. As to how many? That depends on the size and quality."

"It is not the first time the *Taipo* have tried to put a lodge at the mouth of the *Pia'ogwe* in the Crow lands."

Cunningham signed and said, "It's all going to depend on the river tribes and which side they choose in the war back east. If they side with Manuel Lisa and the Americans, that post at the mouth of the Big Horn will be open for trade. If Dickson and the British close the river to the Americans, all the guns will go to the Sioux, Arapaho, and Blackfeet."

"What can we do about this war?" Dark Horse asked.

"Nothing," Gray Bear told him. "It will

be fought in the east."

Cunningham was back to watching Silver Curl.

Black Horse noticed, took a draw from his tubular pipe, and exhaled. "I would sell her."

"Why?" Gray Bear asked. "She's known as a hard worker."

This time Dark Horse didn't sign for Cunningham's benefit, but spoke too quickly for the *Taipo* to understand. "I have these children to do a lot of the work. She's an extra mouth to feed. The men are constantly pestering her. She got a little too friendly with Belongs to Bow a couple of moons back. You'll notice his lodge is no longer here. His wife made sure they moved off for the Sage Grouse River after she caught Silver Curl and Belongs to Bow together. Beat Silver Curl half bloody and stripped her dress off in front of everyone."

Gray Bear grunted. That was the common behavior when a spouse discovered a cheating mate. Silver Curl was lucky to get off with just a beating and a little humiliation.

"That doesn't mean I'd let her go for cheap," Dark Horse continued. "I'd want a couple of horses for her."

"The *Taipo* only has that one horse. He won't part with it," Gray Bear said. "His other horses are either with John Tylor and Singing Lark, or enjoying life in some *Pa'kiani* or *Sa'idika*'s horse herd these days."

Cunningham asked in his broken Shoshoni, "What's this? I catch half the words. What about me and the girl?"

"Dark Horse wants to know if you'd like to buy her?" Gray Bear said.

"She a slave?" Cunningham asked. "Where from? Hair like that, those light brown eyes, light skin. Where'd she come from?"

"South," Gray Bear told him. "What you call Spanish. She was a little girl. The *Yamparika* took her. *Yamparika* used to be here, on what you call the Platte. Now they are in the land called Texas."

"Comanche?" Cunningham guessed.

"Sometimes they travel here, bring horses, metal, captives, things to trade for mountain furs and medicinal and Spirit plants, sometimes to visit kin," Gray Bear told him. "Silver Curl was maybe ten when Dark Horse traded for her. Sage Cup and Dark Horse's first child, Root, was little, and Sage Cup was full with the second, Lily. Snow Flower wasn't old enough to marry into the family. They needed the help."

"After ten years? Dark Horse really wants to sell her?"

"She's been a woman for five years now. She wants a woman's life," Dark Horse told him. "My family is getting too large; my lodge is too full. Silver Curl and Sage Cup would be just as happy to be away from each other."

In English, Gray Bear told Cunningham, "And you have a couple of packs of trade. Makes you as rich as anyone my friend here has seen in years."

"What if she doesn't like me after I buy her?" Cunningham asked in Shoshoni.

"Tie her to a post and beat her," Dark Horse told him. "She would be yours to do with as you want. Slave, yes? Not like a real wife."

Gray Bear tried to decipher the expression on Cunningham's face. Looked like he was trying to swallow his beard. Figured it was some kind of disgust.

"I would trade her for that *aitta* he carries," Dark Horse said casually, not signing. Perhaps in hopes of getting Gray Bear's reaction before making sure Cunningham understood. "The *Taipo* can always take her and go back to the Great River to get another."

Gray Bear kept his expression neutral. "I don't think Cunningham would trade his *aitta* for a woman."

The *Taipo,* who'd followed better than he let on, said, "*Kai.* No trade."

Dark Horse grinned. "Maybe you should take her for a couple of days. Put her in your lodge. Let her cook and keep your blankets warm. Then we can discuss this."

As Cunningham was considering this, Five Strikes appeared, his lathered horse splashing across the *Pia'ogwe.* The warrior, dressed in tailored deer hide, a buffalo cape over his shoulders, rode with his rifle held ready. The expression on his face looked even more grim than usual as he trotted up.

Gray Bear rose, remembering the protestations as he demanded that his men take turns scouting the backtrail. It was, some had declared, winter. Any raiding parties would have returned to their villages.

"What did you see?" Gray Bear demanded.

Five Strikes worked his mouth, his eyes hard as he reined his brown-and-white-spotted horse in. "*Taikwahni,* you remember those *Pa'kiani*? The ones who killed our people? The ones we left on Pretty River? They follow our trail." He jerked his head back the way he'd come. "Maybe fifteen of them. Same group. They still have some of the horses they took from us on the other side of the Red Fir Mountains. I figure they

301

will camp on the Bad Water tonight. They will see our village by midday tomorrow at the latest."

Gray Bear nodded, his heart dropping like a stone in his chest.

"Pa'kiani?" Dark Horse wondered. "At this time of year?"

"How do you want to do this?" Cunningham asked. "Way I see it, with Dark Horse's men, we've got close to twenty."

Gray Bear raised a hand to still any further comment. Chewing his lips, he thought about it. Considered the *Pa'kiani*'s guns. Thought about his own men, how they'd never fought with guns before.

Glancing from Dark Horse to Cunningham, he said, "I think this camp is looking a bit shabby. Too colorless. I want our peoples to winter in the *Ainga'honobita ogwebe.*"

"Do what?" Cunningham asked.

"These *Pa'kiani,*" Dark Horse said, "They'll just follow us over the pass, down into Red Canyon's Creek."

Gray Bear nodded, a grim smile on his lips. "My friend, for whatever reason, these *Pa'kiani* have dedicated themselves to destroying us. Maybe it's because Kestrel Wing drove an arrow into the war chief's shoulder, maybe because we were kind enough to leave them a full camp of meat on the Pretty River. Who knows? But if we fight them here, meet them man to man, we will kill a great many of them. They will kill a great many of ours. I'm tired of having to cut off my hair."

"You have guns!" Dark Horse cried.

Gray Bear smiled. "That's why we're running."

CHAPTER 36

McKeever was riding alongside Stone Otter as he and the Arapaho crested the gentle summit of a long ridge and faced squarely into the west wind. It batted at his elk hide jacket, pulled at his long red hair, and caused him to squint.

To the north rose the mass of the Big Horn Mountains, the slopes nothing like the near sheer wall he'd seen farther to the north, but gentler, rising hill after hill to a line of low peaks.

The western horizon vanished in a series of broken ridges, the country rumpled, irregular, and cut with drainages. To McKeever's mind, God might have taken a piece of paper and wadded it into a tight ball, then tried unsuccessfully to flatten it out again to achieve this kind of landscape.

To the southeast, the familiar long, east-west trending mountain lay dark on the horizon. Broken land, buttes, and sandstone hogbacks extended west into a low range of sage and juniper-studded hills to his immediate south.

From their windswept vantage point, the view was remarkable.

McTavish and Aird, along with Wasichu, rode up beside them, the packhorses blowing from the climb.

"Dear God," McTavish said through a weary exhale, the wind whipping the words away, "there's just more empty nothing."

"Doesn't it ever end?" Joseph Aird asked. "How in the name of the almighty are we ever supposed to find this traitor out here? Look at this! He could be anywhere."

"Ye've a lack of faith, laddie," McKeever told him. "According to Stone Otter, there be a . . ." He didn't finish, following Stone Otter's finger as the man pointed off to the south.

Red Bear Man and Wide Crane had split off that morning, Red Bear Man to the south, Wide Crane to the north. Each of the Arapaho was cutting for sign, any evidence of Tylor's party passing.

Stone Otter had assured McKeever that Tylor would not have crossed the Big Horns, not with the snows as deep as they would be atop the passes. Instead — so the Arapaho claimed — Tylor's party would skirt the southern flank of the mountains. Take the easier path on the way to whatever Shoshoni winter camp his band might be allied with.

Following Stone Otter's finger, he could see Red Bear Man atop his black-maned, dark-brown horse. And with him came yet another rider on a red horse. Even over the distance there was no mistaking: The second man was another Arapaho, his fringed winter coat blowing in the wind, his hair whipping.

"Who do ye reckon?" McKeever wondered as he tucked his coat more tightly against the wind.

"Hinon'ei," Stone Otter told him. Then, through signs, added, "Black Lightning's scout."

"Aye," McKeever said. "From the village ye said was wintering on the Platte."

They waited as Red Bear Man and the Arapaho scout climbed to their position.

Stone Otter rode forward, calling a greeting, laughing. The men clasped hands, chatting amiably in their heavily aspirated tongue.

"Ye catch any of that?" McKeever asked Wasichu as he leaned on his saddlebow and tilted his head away from the wind.

"Talk too fast," Wasichu said. "No signing."

"What now?" McTavish asked as he shared a meaningful glace with Aird.

That was one of the laddie's weaknesses. He'd do anything to protect the younger man. Sell his soul. The shite thought he was responsible for the boy.

Day by day, the two South West lads had grown ever more owly.

I'd hate to have to kill ye, laddies, so please, don't make me.

McKeever wasn't sure how it would play out in the end. Once Tylor's head was his, the fastest way back to St. Louis would be via the Upper Missouri. If Robert Dickson had dispatched as many agents to the tribes as McTavish insisted he had, the river might well be British by the time Fenway was back on its shores. In that case, he'd need McTavish's blessing. If, however, the river remained in American hands, he could offer up the British spies to Lisa, fair trade for passage back down the river.

Be a shame to have to kill McTavish and Aird and lose that leverage.

Now the Arapaho turned, the three riding back to where McKeever waited.

Stone Otter began signing and talking, Wasichu translating, "Black Lightning's village is on the Platte in a bend in the river below the Black Mountain. They are watch-

307

ing and waiting. A party of *Ni'otho,* white men, have come from the west. There are seven of them. On foot. They have built a lodge of logs at the Red Buttes."

"White men?" McKeever wondered.

"Probably Pacific Fur Company. Astorians," McTavish said. "Wilson Price Hunt, perhaps? He came upriver last year. Last we heard, he left the Missouri and followed the Grand River west. Disappeared into the mountains headed for the mouth of the Columbia. But that was with a lot more men."

"These are your friends?" Stone Otter asked in signs, his face like a stone mask.

"Enemies," McKeever signed back. "Americans."

"Hi'theti," Good. Stone Otter signed, "Black Lightning is waiting. The Americans will starve. Then the Arapaho will have their guns, the things they carry."

The scout said something.

Stone Otter, through signs, asked, "You would like to come with us? You have three good guns. You could lure the *Ni'otho* out. Then you could spend the winter with Black Lightning's band."

"Aye." *And no doubt come spring, we'd be scalped and the Arapaho would have yet another three guns, including that fine Philip*

308

Bond rifle McTavish carries.

Still, what if one of the men was Tylor? No telling but that the man could have run into a party of whites. While the man Mc-Keever had known on the Missouri had kept to himself, he was still a social sort. The kind who read books, liked to talk. Had been right close to Baptiste Latoulipe. Maybe the wilderness hadn't turned out to be as inviting as Tylor had hoped?

Would it hurt to see? To ride down and at least scout out the whites? If they'd put up a log cabin to overwinter, it might be worth knowing who they were and what they were about.

"How far to the *Ni'otho*?"

"Two days' ride." Stone Otter pointed almost straight south. "Red Buttes there. On Platte."

"A'ho!" The cry carried on the wind.

McKeever turned, staring north, searching the sage-blanketed ridge with its dips and rises until . . . Yes. There. Wide Crane's buff-colored horse could be seen picking its way through the sagebrush. The man was coming at a fast clip.

"Do these white men at Red Buttes have trade goods?" McKeever asked.

The question was proffered to the scout, who answered back, "No, they only have what they can carry on their backs and one old broken horse that is not worth the effort to steal."

By this time, Wide Crane was close enough to wave, calling, *"Beni'i'ho!"* over and over.

"What is that?" McTavish asked, his wary gaze flicking from one Arapaho to the next.

"Wide Crane is shouting, 'I have found him,' " Wasichu translated. "He thinks he has found Tylor."

McKeever grinned, a feeling of warmth spreading through the chill the wind had imparted to his chest. "Now, see, laddie? It's just like I told ye. A mon's gotta have a little faith."

And to think he'd been so close to turning his steps south. He'd have missed Tylor completely.

CHAPTER 37

It came down to one horseshoe. That was all the evidence. In Dawson McTavish's eyes, that made it about as flimsy as a pasteboard house. Hardly the thing to bet an entire venture on.

By the time Black Lightning's scout had departed, and Wide Crane had led them back to the narrow saddle at the base of the mountain, night had fallen, cold, windy, and bleak. They'd had to lay out camp in the sagebrush. Unsheltered from the wind.

Had Dawson and Joseph not rolled their blankets together, he was sure they'd have frozen. Nor was there so much as a chance for a fire. The wind blew it away even as they got it going.

Chalk it up to one of the most miserable nights he'd ever spent.

Shivering, blowing in his hands to warm them, morning was just as wretched. Breakfast consisted of raw and stringy sun-jerked

311

meat cut from a mule deer's carcass that Red Bear Man had killed a couple of days earlier. Thirst was slaked from crusted snowdrifts where the tall sage was shadowed from the weak winter sun.

Nevertheless, the line of tracks — made by four horses — led down into the headwaters of what Stone Otter called the Bad Water River.

From the Arapaho's careful inspection of the tracks, it was determined that two of the horses were ridden, and two, including the horse with the single right rear shoe, were pack animals.

Dawson wasn't sure how a person could tell, but having at least a modicum of ability as a tracker back in his home country, he assumed that the Arapaho were a lot better at the task than he was.

Clouds were building in the west and north just beyond the Big Horns. The wind — cold to begin with — just got colder as Red Bear Man led the way, following the tracks down into the drainage that emptied off to the west.

"Man and woman!" Wasichu translated Red Bear Man's call as the Arapaho pulled up and leaped off his horse to point at the ground.

There, in the sage, could be seen the

scuffed tracks where a woman in moccasins had stepped down from her horse, squatted, and urinated. And a little beyond, a man had dismounted and spattered his water a pace beyond his moccasins.

"Look!" Again Wasichu translated. "Snake. See the seam down the middle of the sole?"

"Where's the mon's boots?" McKeever muttered where he sat his horse, his rifle across the saddle before him.

"You knew him," Dawson said. "What kind of shape were his boots in to start with?"

"Aye, good thought, laddie. They was as worn oot as could be. Soles was splitting from the uppers. He must have traded fer moccasins."

"Or we're following two Snake Indians on a wild hare's chase," Joseph muttered.

"What aboot the horseshoe, laddie? Wasichu? Ye ever heard of a Snake Indian shoeing a horse?"

"Why only one?" Dawson asked skeptically.

"Only one to last this far from the river." McKeever was staring off down the valley. "Wasichu, ask Red Bear Man how long?"

The Arapaho pinched the urine-damp dirt, rubbing it between his fingers. "Dirt is frozen. Slightly dried."

"Last night," Stone Otter declared.

"We're close," McKeever said, his voice almost a hallowed whisper. "I've got ye, laddie."

McTavish resettled on his horse, easing his cold feet in the stirrups. He glanced up at the darkening sky, then stared down the long valley where it cut west at the base of the mountains. In the distance — like teeth across the storm-black western horizon — rose yet another mountain range, its high and snow-capped peaks eating at the storm clouds like some giant saw.

"Shoshoni owns those mountains," Wasichu told him, seeing where his gaze was focused. "According to the Arapaho, if we have to go that far, we probably won't come back alive."

"Then let's hope we don't have to," Dawson replied fervently. "Let's hope that these tracks really belong to this Tylor, and that he and this woman traveling with him have decided to hole up and wait out this storm."

"And hope that we can catch them before it hits," Joseph agreed, as he blew into his hands. "Otherwise, if we get caught in the open like we did last night? We're going to end up so frozen the wolves will have to chew on us for years to get a full meal."

Dawson wanted it over. Damn it, he could

feel the end coming. And somehow, he had to keep Joseph safe. Get the both of them out of this mess he'd caused.

CHAPTER 38

Gray Bear rode along the line as his people
climbed up out of the Wind River's basin,
their way following the ancient trail that led
up through a narrow valley in the *Mum-
bich'ogwe untoyabi,* or, in Shoshoni, the Owl
Creek's Mountains. The stone-littered
drainage they rode up offered one of the
few easily ascendible trails to a low pass that
pierced the Owl Creeks' southern flank.

That didn't lessen the seriousness of the
situation. Moving a winter camp at a moment's notice was a chancy thing. Especially
with the storm that was brewing in the
north. Each and every one of them knew
the risks. From the wind, the feel of the air,
this could either be a passing squall, or
could be the forefront of a massive snowfall,
howling blizzard, and subsequent drop in
temperature that the people called, "the
deep cold." The kind of cold where horses
froze on their feet, where a man could spit,

and have it crackle into a ball the instant it hit the ground.

Speed was everything. The people needed to make it over the summit and then down the other side to Red Canyon Creek in time to reach the springs where water, shelter, and fuel could be found. The lodges had to be set up, the supplies stored, and the horses attended to before the full wrath of the storm hit.

As Moon Walker carried Gray Bear down the line of worried people, the *taikwahni* called encouragement. "Hey, mother! You're doing fine." "Pine Nut, you look like First Woman with all those little children clinging to that horse of yours." "Hey, Red Bird, summit's not far." "Just a little bit of a climb, and then we'll be on the other side."

He kept his voice cheery as he sought to infect them with his optimism. But all it took was a glance overhead at the low black clouds scudding low across the slopes. Or the uncertainty of what was coming up the trail behind them.

What was it about this band of Blackfeet? Why were they so driven? They'd harried Three Feathers's original hunting expedition, essentially driven them out of the Powder River Basin, then doggedly pursued them down east of the Black Hills. After that victory a normal party of Blackfeet would have taken their captured horses, prisoners, and scalps back north. Would have celebrated their power, danced, and dispersed the captives and plunder among the people in their camp.

Instead, for whatever reason, most of the warriors had been prowling north of the Black Hills, as if hunting specifically for Gray Bear's band, anticipating their return from the east.

"That's it," Gray Bear called as Otter Tail chided Single Cup to keep moving. "Keep together. We'll make a warm and secure camp on the other side. Just a little longer."

He reined Moon Walker around, giving heel to the stubby horse, urging him up a deer trail that climbed through the sage to the rocky ridge top on the eastern side. From there he could look back in the fading light. The view was of the drainages, feather-patterned as they ran down from the foothills, across the basin, and became creeks that fed into the *Pia'ogwe*. The Big River's course could be seen where the dark line of cottonwood trees stood out against the pale sage and buff-colored buttes and ridges.

Back there, Five Strikes and the warrior known as Flat Finger were using their knowledge of the country to spy on the Blackfeet. Everything depended on what the enemy did next.

The sound of a horse puffing breath, hooves cracking on rock, and the creak of saddle leather announced Dark Horse's arrival as his black gelding scrambled up the rocky deer trail.

Gray Bear's counterpart pulled his blowing horse up, taking a position beside him on the narrow ridge top to follow Gray Bear's gaze back over the basin.

Dark Horse slumped over the saddlebow. "What do you see?"

"Nothing moving but a herd of buffalo over by the Sage Butte. The important thing is that there is no band of howling Blackfeet screaming up the trail right behind us."

"This storm is going to be bad." Dark Horse glanced up at the darkening sky. "I can smell it."

Gray Bear sniffed the cold wind blowing down the pass. "So can I. Feel it, that heaviness in the air?"

"I hope you are right about this, moving the entire village."

"How can anyone know?" Gray Bear shrugged. "We could have ridden out to intercept them. Might have been able to get close, maybe partially surround them before we broke cover and charged in to attack. It might have worked, and we'd have killed some, broken their line of travel. Taken some of the horses."

"But?"

"But they just as easily might have seen us. They have scouts, too. And if we hadn't had complete surprise, if something had gone wrong with our attack and not everyone was in the right place at the right time? They might have killed a lot of us, broken our attack, and we would have paid in blood. The village would still be fleeing, but in the middle of the storm. People would die."

"So, we're on the other side of Owl Creek's Mountains, what's different? They'll still track us, at least until the snow covers the trail. They'll know which way we fled."

"The difference is that I mean to finally bring this thing between that *Pa'kiani* war chief and me to an end."

"You're not a war chief, my friend."

"I don't want to be known as a war chief."

"What then? You taking this *taikwahni* talk seriously? You never wanted to be a chief."

"I could care less how people talk about me. I just want *my* people to be safe. I'll do whatever that takes."

"Then, what happens if this plan of yours

doesn't work?"

"Then we're right back where we started: We'll kill a lot of them, they'll kill a lot of our people."

As Gray Bear looked up, the first flakes of snow came spiraling down from the darkening sky. If it came down too fast, too hard, everything he'd planned was going to fail.

That was when Aspen Branch drove her horse up beside them. The old woman grinned, exposing the few brown teeth left in her jaws. "Hey, *Taikwahni.* I just had a talk with that hawk. Looked into his eyes. Got a message for you. He says to trust your *puha.*"

If only it were that easy.

CHAPTER 39

Once again, it had been Singing Lark who saved everything. From a high point on the trail, she'd seen the distant riders heading down toward the cottonwood-lined *Pia'ogwe* off to the west. She had extended a finger *Taipo* fashion, pointing them out for Tylor's less acute vision.

"They just never give up," Singing Lark growled under her breath.

"Who are they?" Tylor asked, the west wind beating at him. It always blew stronger as it crossed the high points. He shaded his eyes with a flat of the hand, staring across the sagebrush-topped ridges to where the line of mounted men crossed a distant basin; the horses made dots of color against the winter-gray branches of the greasewood and pale alkali-white soil. The riders, at this distance, were too small to identify.

"*Pa'kiani*. Don't you recognize the horses?"

"How can you recognize the horses? They're at least five miles away."

She glared at him with that "you're an idiot" look.

Then she led them back down into the Bad Water's valley, hurrying them down the narrow greasewood-and-sage-packed floodplain. Within a mile, she turned off from the Bad Water, heading them north into the mountains along the banks of what looked to be an intermittent stream. The creek bed was now dry, choked with sand and stone; scrubby-looking willows and currants were clinging desperately to its margins. The sagebrush they wound through on the narrow floodplain was as tall as Tylor's stirrup.

The way led upward, the foothills closing in, rising on either side. Occasional narrow-leafed cottonwoods began to dot the bottom. As the slopes on either side grew steeper, currents and mountain mahogany appeared in patches accented by scrubby juniper.

They passed a faint trickle of water that marked the end of the stream's reach before it faded into the sand.

Night was falling; dark clouds kept rolling across the sky from the north and west.

"Bad storm coming," Singing Lark called from where she rode in the lead. She pointed. "I don't think we're going to make it to the other side."

"What is this place?"

"Spirit Pass," she told him. "Old trail across the mountains. Maybe it goes back to the Beginning Times. Maybe it was first made by Coyote. We'll need to camp at the bottom. Need to collect rocks."

"Rocks?"

"For the Spirits."

They'd ridden until dusk threatened. Singing Lark stopped when they reached a meadow where the steep-walled valley opened slightly.

"Camp here," she told him, stepping down from her horse.

Tylor took stock. Where the creek ran along the steep eastern slope, a thick screen of narrow-leafed cottonwoods grew. The old ones had rotted in the centers, fallen, and provided a good supply of firewood. Thick stands of sarvisberry, squaw currant, rose-bushes, and chokecherry crowded up against the slopes. Juniper dotted the rocky sage-covered heights. Here and there, on the mountainsides above, bare granite, chunks of black schist, and splashes of quartz could be seen.

The temperature was dropping, Tylor's breath clearly visible before his face.

"What's the plan?" he asked, following as she led her horse over to the stand of cottonwoods. The packhorses trailed behind, nipping grass, looking around with curious eyes and pricked ears.

"Make shelter back in the trees next to the creek," she said. "We'll picket the horses at the top of the meadow. Get the packs off the horses first. Water them, then rub them down."

Tylor attended those chores, checking to discover that the shoe was now loose on the black's right rear hoof. In the morning it would have to come off. A last testament to the white world and Manuel Lisa's far-off post on the banks of the Missouri.

He used the lash ropes to tie a picket line at the top of the meadow, paying attention to the curious pile of stones at the side of the trail where it started up through the canyon.

"Spirit home," Singing Lark told him as she approached with two hefty cobbles in her hands. "*Temdzoavits,* the rock ogre, lives in this canyon and guards the pass. By tossing a rock onto the pile, we confuse him. He hears the rock clack onto the pile and thinks it's just another rock ogre passing."

"I see." Tylor took the rock, asking himself, *What if I don't believe in rock ogres?*

Nevertheless, he tossed the stone onto the pile, hearing it clatter as it added to the already chest-high cairn. If there was a rock for every party who'd ever passed here, that was a lot of people.

Singing Lark grinned at him, winked, and said, "I'm going to cut sticks to make a lodge frame. You need to go start the fire. We might be here for a couple of days. Depends on the storm." She glanced around. "Plenty of wood and grass. Protected from wind. There are worse places to be."

They pitched into the work, Tylor knowing the ritual now. He dug out the firepit in an opening between the trees, used the fire bow to get the flames started, and added fist-sized rocks to act as heating stones for the stew.

The first flakes of snow were falling as he and Singing Lark began construction of the lodge: a conical structure like a tipi, but laced together with branches into which sagebrush, juniper branches, and shocks of grass were woven.

Tylor retrieved the makings for stew as the snow began to fall in earnest. He made sure the manties covered the packs, and were tied in place.

One by one he added sticks to the fire.

326

"I'm going to get more wood," Singing Lark told him as she stepped up from the creek with a skin full of water. She laid it carefully into the hole she'd dug as a lining for an "earth pot" to boil the stew in.

Tylor watched her take her rifle and disappear into the swirling wall of white. He could barely see across the canyon now, the thick veils of snow swirling from dark clouds that rolled down the mountain.

Dusk was falling. The gloom intensified as Tylor went about rolling out their bedding inside the shelter. He placed their critical gear — things they didn't want to get wet — in the rear. His rifle, horn, and bullet pouch he set just inside the door.

The wind was howling up in the heights, whistling through the juniper up on the slopes. Tylor shivered, thinking what it must be like down in the flats with no place to shelter.

Nope, Singing Lark's camp was not a bad place to be at all. Protected as the canyon was, the snow just twirled down instead of being driven sideways by the wind.

Stepping back to the fire, he tossed another section of cottonwood branch on the fire, building up the flames.

When he glanced up, it was with a start to see a man standing, legs braced, in the firelight. A big man, snow caked to his coat, hat, and leggings. A trade rifle was pointed at Tylor's chest, cocked. The man's hand gripped the gun by the wrist, finger on the trigger.

At the sight, Tylor gaped, heart skipping.

"Who the hell . . . ?"

"Aye, laddie. And hell it is that I bring ye. It's been a long hard ride, and I've had the entire time t' think up how I'm gonna kill ye."

Even as McKeever spoke, men appeared, wraithlike, emerging from the swirling snow. Three, then four, six, a total of seven, all in a circle that cut off any chance to flee.

Tylor shot a sidelong glance to where the jack handle rested just inside the door to the shelter.

"Don't do it, laddie," McKeever warned. "I'll shoot ye dead if'n ye try. And, to tell the truth, I'd like to gloat a while before I cut yer head off."

CHAPTER 40

Dawson McTavish spared Joseph a sidelong glance when Fenway McKeever ordered, "Dawson, take yer wangs. Tie the good Mister Tylor up good and tight. Hobble his feet and truss him like a pig fer slaughter."

Dawson, his Bond rifle at the ready, stepped forward. This was the terrible John Tylor? The man was of medium height and build, dressed in a fine and warm-looking leather coat, a fox-hide hat atop his head. Frightened brown eyes, a thick beard the color of old tobacco, and a thin face turned Dawson's way.

"He won't give ye any trouble," McKeever said. "Just be sure ye don't get in the way lest I have to shoot him in the heart."

Dawson reached into his pack and retrieved the thick leather strings.

"You heard the man," Dawson told Tylor, and careful to keep from getting between McKeever's gun and Tylor, he pulled the man's arms around behind him, binding them tightly.

"Joseph," McKeever ordered, "See to the horses. Tie them off to the picket."

Dawson tugged the last of his knots tight as Joseph hurried off into the storm.

Stone Otter strode forward, his bow strung, an arrow in the nock. The man said something in Arapaho and drew his bow, the shaft aimed at Tylor. Red Bear Man and Wide Crane crowded in close, arrows nocked.

Wasichu, standing off to the side, translated. "Stone Otter says that now, with his relatives watching, he is going to show the . . ."

McKeever moved like a cat, using the muzzle of his trade gun to slap the head of the arrow up, causing Stone Otter to relax the bow's pull.

"Later," McKeever told him, standing almost chest to chest, as if ready for a shoving match.

"This man killed my younger brother," Wasichu translated, as Stone Otter shouted.

"Aye," McKeever thundered back. "And ye'll have his heart. All I want is his head. In one piece. It's worth a bloody damn fortune."

"His head is worth a fortune?" Dawson

asked. "Why?"

"He didn't tell you?" Tylor asked softly. "Fenway's a hired killer. A man back east wants me dead. Settlement for an old grudge."

"You're supposed to be some kind of agent. Working against the crown. Turning the western tribes against England."

"You're Dickson's men?"

"Aye, South West Fur Company. Sent to turn the Tetons against Lisa. A grudge, you say? McKeever says he works for John Jacob Astor."

"It's a lie. He's working for a banker, a man named Joshua Gregg. Astor knows nothing about it. McKeever's just using his name."

Dawson sat back on his heels, a sinking sensation inside. "It's all a lie?"

He turned his gaze to McKeever and Stone Otter where they stood chest to chest. The big Scot was grinning, his rifle cocked and at the ready. Stone Otter — his face like a molten mask in the flickering firelight — physically trembled. The Arapaho spoke, softly, passionately, as if fighting for control.

"He wants to kill Tylor now," Wasichu translated.

"Be ready, laddie," McKeever said from the side of his mouth. "This comes undone, ye're to shoot the mon on yer left."

That would be Red Bear Man.

Dawson eased to the side, recovered his rifle.

Both Red Bear Man and Wide Crane noticed immediately, each whispering a warning to Stone Otter.

"We find *Ni'otho*. Take trade now." Wasichu translated Stone Otter's next order.

"Aye," McKeever told him, "That was the deal. It's yers. I'll take Tylor's head, ye can have the rest of him and the trade. But meanwhile, no one's going anywhere in this storm. Not with a nice warm camp, a fire, and the makings of a stew." He paused, adding, "We're all friends here."

A pause. "Well, all but us and Tylor."

Stone Otter's lips twitched as if he were trying to form a smile but couldn't. He had to be achingly aware of the rifle pointed at his guts. Then he lifted the arrow from its nock, resettling it in his quiver. As he turned, he used the bow stave to slash sideways, caught Tylor across the face in a stinging blow.

"Coup," Wasichu explained as Stone Otter stalked off.

Before they followed, both Red Bear Man and Wide Crane used their bows to strike Tylor across his unprotected head.

McKeever's eyes narrowed, taking note, as Dawson did, that both Red Bear Man and Wide Crane hadn't slipped their arrows back into their quivers. Now the two Arapaho watched, uncertain gazes going from McKeever to Stone Otter. The latter had pulled up at the edge of camp, his head back, face lifted to the falling snow. He seemed to be struggling for control.

Joseph appeared from the darkness, head and shoulders caked with white. He had the action of his rifle tucked under his coat to protect the lock. "What did I miss?"

McKeever softly said, "Yer both Scots, aye? Ye've heard of Culloden? The great battle? Our esteemed friend, here, would be the Duke of Cumberland. See what happened to the Scots on the field of Culloden happen again. Right here. Are ye following me thread, laddies?"

"We are," Joseph said, voice unsteady.

Stone Otter, no matter how much English he might have had, couldn't have understood the illusion to Culloden. Wasichu certainly looked confused.

"It'll be coming any minute now, laddies. Keep yer powder dry." McKeever stepped back, crouched down, and extended his hands to the fire. His trade gun lay protected in his lap.

"Why don't they take the trade and go?" Joseph wondered.

In a low whisper, Dawson told him, "Somehow, I don't think McKeever ever meant to keep that agreement."

Joseph, looking scared, caught Dawson's eye and gave him a nod of understanding.

The Arapaho had collected on the opposite side of the fire, talking in low voices.

"Where is woman?" Wasichu asked as the tensions seemed to have abated.

"Woman?" McKeever asked, then nodded his understanding. "Aye." He turned. "Johnny, me lad. Whar be yer woman? Why don't ye call fer the charming lass to come in to the fire?"

"What woman?" Tylor asked innocently.

McKeever pointed. "The one that rides that Spanish saddle yonder. Oh, don't bother to deny it. We tracked ye long enough. We know she's oot there. Call her in."

"She doesn't speak English."

McKeever spun on his heels. "Ye'll call her, or I'm blowing a hole in yer knee. While I cuts off yer head, Stone Otter and his friends can start chopping yer guts out."

Tylor nodded, took a breath, and shouted something in a language Dawson had never heard before.

McKeever glanced curiously at Wasichu, but the Santee just shrugged, his eyes still on the Arapaho.

"Go find her," McKeever ordered the Santee. Then, standing, he tossed the young man his trade gun. "I told ye I'd get ye a gun before this was all over." He leveled a finger. "If'n she gives ye any fight or sass, laddie, shoot her dead. Some of these squaws can be real trouble. Ye up fer that?"

Wasichu grinned, examining the rifle. Dawson remembered how the youth had admired it when it had belonged to Matato. McKeever had just made a staunch ally.

As the young Santee vanished into the falling snow, McKeever pulled Tylor's ugly rifle from the protection of the shelter and checked the priming.

"Never liked this damn thing. Ugly as a witch's bloody broom."

"What next?" Dawson asked, nervous eyes on the Arapaho. They'd taken positions, bows still strung and at hand. Red Bear Man and Wide Crane kept their hard eyes on the whites. Ready to nock and draw at a moment's notice. Stone Otter, meanwhile, turned to Tylor's packs, grunting as he stripped off the manties and began pulling out dried meat. Then came hide bags of what looked like roots and dried berries.

"If they're going to make a move, it would be now, with Wasichu gone." Joseph reached up with a quick hand to wipe away a trickle where snow had melted on his cheek.

"Not yet," McKeever noted. "They'll wait. Figuring something will happen. Distract us. As soon as we're not fixed on them? That's when they'll try and take us."

"Listen to that wind," Joseph said, perhaps in an effort to cut the tension. "It's blowing like a bastard up high. Glad we're protected here and not out on the flats."

Dawson cocked his head. The sound of the wind blowing through the trees above was indeed vicious. It covered any sound outside of camp. Enough so that he wondered how Wasichu was supposed to find a woman out in that swirling storm.

"So, Fenway," Tylor asked, shifting as he tugged at his bonds. Snow was piling on his body and now caked as he struggled to sit up. "Whatever happened to your plan to become king of the Missouri? Thought you were going to wreck Lisa's expedition so you could go back and sell yourself to Gratiot, offer him control of the Upper Missouri? That all changed now that you've joined the other side?"

Dawson caught Joseph's puzzled glance, then whispered, "Later."

336

McKeever seemed undisturbed by the charge. "Johnny, me lad, nothing's changed. If anything, I'm more committed than ever. Dawson and Joseph, here, they're not the only agents Dickson sent to turn the river tribes against Lisa. I think Lisa's in fer a tough winter. And they's a bloody fortune in those packs the Arapaho want. Enough to set a man up right fine. So, for the time being, I'll play the British against Lisa. Be ready to step in when Astor finally moves on the river."

Through a sour smile, Tylor said, "And kill anyone who gets in the way. What were your words that night on the river? Ah, yes. People, you said, 'Who'll mysteriously die one by one.' Then I recall that you added, 'I've seen how taking out the right man at the right time can throw an operation into chaos.' Then you sounded so happy with yourself when you bragged, 'Made a study of it, I have.'"

Tylor frowned. "So, let's say the British do win. The war's over, and Dickson is the kingpin. Why do I suspect he's going to be found dead in his bed soon thereafter?"

"Life's a fleeting thing," McKeever granted noncommittally, his eyes missing nothing as the Arapaho emptied Tylor's packs.

Tylor flinched when they threw a book out into the snow.

Dawson clamped his jaws, eyes on McKeever as Tylor talked. The big Scot seemed completely at ease with the accusation. Dear God, that faint smile hinted that McKeever wouldn't just do it, he'd look forward to it.

"So," Tylor asked, "How do you get your two thousand dollars out of good old Joshua Gregg and another thousand out of Andrew Jackson when you're up here spreading chaos between Lisa, the South West Company, and Astor's Pacific Fur Company? Then, to sweeten the mix, God alone knows what Governor Salcedo is going to set loose down in Santa Fe? You'll be leaving it all to rot and ruin while you take my head back east."

"Figure I can find me a courier for that, laddie."

Tylor laughed hard, clearly amused. "Fenway, this is Joshua Gregg we're talking about. Think it through. Your courier arrives at Gregg Mansion in North Carolina, rides up the oak-lined lane to the big house. Knocks on the door.

"Gregg's manservant, Grady, answers, and when he hears your courier's tale, tells your man to wait. Ten minutes later, Joshua appears, demands to see my head.

"Your man opens the package, and there I am, all caked in salt. Joshua looks down, recognizes me, and the corners of his eyes tighten the way they do when he's in delight. His heart is pounding in his chest with triumph and exultation.

"But no expression crosses his lips, and without the slightest hint of emotion he tells your courier, 'That's not him. Don't come back until you have the right head.'

"And at that, Joshua will turn away, seem to pause, only to turn back as your man hits the bottom step. That's when Joshua will say, 'You might want to leave that here. If the authorities find you with it, they will charge you with murder. Especially when I tell them I know nothing about Fenway Mc-Keever, and to my knowledge, John Tylor is long dead somewhere beyond the frontier.' "

McKeever's expression had gone as cold as the falling snow.

"You didn't really trust him, did you?" Tylor asked. "I know the man. Grew up with him. He's not going to part with any two thousand dollars unless you have a gun to his head."

McKeever's expression had stiffened. The corners of his lips were quivering.

Dawson jumped as a rifle shot banged in the canyon above them, the sound echoing, only slightly muffled by the thick veils of falling snow.

"Too bad, Johnny," McKeever crooned. "I'd guess that Wasichu just found yer woman. Hope ye didn't pay too much for her."

CHAPTER 41

As the rifle report died away, McKeever studied Tylor in the yellow light cast by the fire. Damnation, the man had just raised a carbuncle deep in Fenway's soul. Of course that high prig, Gregg, would try and stiff him for the two thousand. Why hadn't he realized it from the start?

But something bothered him. Tylor's woman was dead. Soft as he was, the laddie didn't seem as horrified as he should be. Why? What did little Johnny have left to hope for?

"Thinking that perhaps Wasichu missed?" McKeever prompted. "Could be. In the storm and all. But the laddie had his bow wi' him. I've seen him with a bow and arrows. So, sorry, Johnny me lad, yer woman's dead. No hope in that direction."

McKeever shot a knowing look to where the Arapaho had straightened, fingers tight on the nocks of their arrows, as if some pending attack might come from the night.

They'd have to be taken out. But the moment had to be right. As it was, with McKeever's three against the Arapaho, all it would take was a single missed shot. Most likely from Joseph. He was the weakest link. If any of them missed, whichever Arapaho was left standing would skewer Dawson, McKeever, and Joseph before they could reload their rifles.

That was the conundrum. It had to be three shots for three Arapaho. And no mistakes.

McKeever shot a worried glance at Tylor. The man seemed to be studying on something. McKeever had learned to read Tylor's every expression back on the river. What was he counting on?

Was it that in the end there'd be no payment? In McKeever's mind, he could see Gregg, his mashed nose, the scar on his face, as he looked down into that keg of salt and said, "Never seen him before in my life."

Tylor was right, he'd have to take the head himself. And that knowledge sent a shiver of rage through him. He'd have to leave the river on hold. Hurry east with the head, and rush back to the Upper Missouri. Hope the war lasted long enough.

"Awfully quiet out there," Tylor noted, as

if offhandedly.

"Really?" Joseph muttered, nervous fingers twitching on his rifle as he watched the Arapaho watching him. "I keep hearing a lot of wind ripping around in the trees up above us."

"That could cover a lot of misfortune," Tylor said.

"What misfortune? That doesn't make much sense." Dawson kept his eyes on the Arapaho.

McKeever shifted his attention from the Arapaho back to Dawson and caught the subtle tones of anger in the young man's voice. Could see his conflicted expression. Too bad. That was the price of keeping Tylor alive this long. If Fenway had killed Tylor the moment he saw him, the Arapaho would have used the distraction to have murdered every white. For surely Dawson and Joseph would have been staring in horror at the blood gushing out of Tylor's severed throat. Wouldn't have realized the threat until arrows were sticking out of their backs.

The fact that they now knew they'd been played?

Alas, poor laddies, but no one lives forever.

Just as soon as the Arapaho were dead.

Ach, such a torturous balance, all having

343

to be orchestrated so carefully.

"Fenway," Tylor said reasonably, "You're going to lose."

"I'm not the one trussed up like a Christmas ham. With the snow building on me body."

Dawson, damn his soul, was looking ever more nervous, working his mouth, eyes darting from McKeever to the Arapaho, and back to McKeever, as if he couldn't figure out just where the darkest danger really lay.

Joseph, dumb as a post, was almost quivering with fear. It could be seen in the way the simpering fool kept swallowing, shifting, working his jaws.

They're going to fall apart on me.

"Laddies," he said softly, "this is going to have to be done quickly and just as I say. Now, don't say anything, don't even jerk yer heads. Do ye get the thread of what I'm saying here? Joseph, I need ye t' shift yer weight. Point yer shoulder in Red Bear Man's direction. But do it ever so slowly."

"I . . . what?"

"Yer the laddie most likely to miss. Now, Red Bear Man's the slowest. Takes the longest time to nock an arrow. So take a deep breath. Hold it. And shoot when you know you've got him."

"That's murder."

"That's living, laddie." He paused just long enough to let it soak in. "Dawson? Ye'll take Wide Crane. Center shot with yer fancy London gun. Like Joseph, I don't want you rushing anything. Make sure yer sight's centered in the middle of his chest afore ye trigger's the gun."

At that moment, Tylor raised his voice, calling out to the night. McKeever hesitated, gave him an irritated scowl, and bellowed, "Shut yer hole, ye shite, or I'll shut it for you."

The Arapaho figured it out an instant before McKeever did. They were nocking, drawing, as an arrow hissed through the night and drove itself into Stone Otter's chest. The man started, fumbled, his arrow releasing short to stick in the ground at McKeever's feet.

"Now!" McKeever cried, cocking Tylor's ugly rifle, taking aim at Stone Otter. He triggered it, seeing the flash an instant before the gun belched fire and thunder. Through the flame and smoke, Stone Otter collapsed as if poleaxed.

McKeever had a momentary glimpse of Red Bear Man's bow, extended, the string twanging as the man loosed an arrow.

Dawson McTavish's rifle boomed; Wide Crane staggered at the impact, his arrow flying off into the night. Then the warrior stumbled to the side. His left leg gave out, and he toppled.

An arrow hissed from the darkness, whizzed past Red Bear Man's face. The warrior spun on his feet. Staring out at the falling snow, he loosed an arrow into the darkness beyond. Then clawed for another arrow. Then he saw where his friends had fallen. McKeever caught that instant of understanding as the Arapaho spared him an evaluative look, then stared back at the darkness.

Red Bear Man turned, pounding off into the safety of the storm as a rifle boomed from the night. Muzzle flash shone out in the falling snow.

McKeever turned, searching the darkness. Arrows? A rifle? How many were out there?

He tossed Tylor's rifle to the side as useless, then glanced frantically around.

There.

Joseph sat frozen, terror wide in his eyes, an arrow sticking out of his belly.

McKeever ripped the unfired rifle away from the boy's right hand. As he lifted it, pointed it at the night, an arrow hissed. The impact on his cheek was like being slashed by a willow stick. A sort of sting. A pulling at his hair.

McKeever triggered the gun; the pan flashed before his eyes — followed an instant later by the boom and recoil. But all he saw was falling snow.

McKeever bellowed, "Who's out there?"

He was peering through the falling flakes when another flash, just a flicker, caught his attention off to the right. McKeever was running by the time the rifle's report sounded. Hang fire. Pan must have been wet.

Two rifles, an archer, there had to be at least three men out there in the dark. Meanwhile there he'd been, standing like a daft maniac in the firelight to be shot at. But for that hang fire, he'd be dead or dying in the snow.

In sudden panic, McKeever understood that his only chance was to run. Get as far from that fire as he could. With a bellowed curse, he charged off into the night.

"God's sucking damnation!" McKeever crashed into low-hanging branches. Dead stuff that broke, cracking and snapping; it dropped snow onto his head. He fled headlong. Hit a log while running full tilt. One moment he was upright, the next he hammered chest-first into the ground. Stunned, he gasped for breath, fingers clutching futilely at the snow.

Searching around, he got his hands on the rifle. Took two tries to get his feet under him.

Everywhere he looked was darkness, snow pattering on his head and face, melting to run down in cold trickles that slipped down past his collar. A burning traced along his right cheek and the side of his head. His ear stung as if a thousand wasps had been at it. He dabbed at it with fingertips, felt the gaping cut, found it warm, tacky. Had to be blood. To his dismay, the top of his ear hung by a flap of skin.

He could hear shouting, voices behind him.

With his left arm raised to fend off any obstacles, he shuffled his way forward. As his eyes were beginning to adjust after the firelight, the snow made the world into a dark gray haze.

Got to get away.

Outnumbered, armed only with an empty rifle, they'd kill him for sure.

That's when something moved ahead of him. Large. McKeever stopped short, raising his rifle like a club.

Horses! He saw horses! Two of them.

CHAPTER 42

Tylor's view of the camp was restricted where he lay bound in the snow. Beside him, Joseph Aird was gasping and shivering as he clutched the arrow. From the angle at which it was protruding, the point had driven deeply into his intestines.

Dawson was on his knees, making a mess of his attempt to reload his rifle. The man was shaking so hard he kept spilling powder, dropped two balls in succession as he tried to short-seat one in the muzzle.

"Wife!" Tylor called. "Hold your fire!"

"I can kill the last one."

"Wait," Tylor called. To Dawson, he said, "You want to live?"

"Who's out there?" Dawson was staring at the darkness, blinking at the falling sheets of snow that glowed in the firelight. He was trying to prime the pan.

"You better put that rifle down. Cut me loose. If you don't, she'll kill you."

"She?"

"Put the rifle down, Dawson. It's your last chance."

The young man, panting his fear, nodded too quickly, and laid the fancy rifle to the side. His shaking hands fumbled at Tylor's ties. Couldn't seem to manage the knots. He pulled his knife.

"Easy. Don't cut me," Tylor warned. "That's it. Take a breath. You're all right."

The bindings parted.

"Dear God," Dawson whispered. "What happened here?"

"Joshua Gregg and the spoils of hate," Tylor muttered, shivering himself as snow melted on his body and trickled down between gaps in his clothing to chill his skin.

Ripping the last of the leather wangs free, Tylor stood, walked over, and retrieved his rifle. "Check Joseph."

He took long enough to find his horn and bullet pouch, stuffed a load into the jack handle, and primed the pan. Tylor eased toward the closest of the downed Arapaho. The man was gasping, writhing in the snow. The blood draining out of his shattered hip looked like a black pool where it melted the snow. From the amount, a major artery was hit.

The second Arapaho stared sightlessly, the

fire's leaping flames reflected in miniature in those wide eyes. He lay on his side; Singing Lark's arrow stuck out from the man's ribs. The path of McKeever's bullet through the Arapaho's spine was marked by a bloody hole and bits of bone in the back of the man's coat.

Tylor retreated, hunching down beside Dawson where he worked on Joseph. The young Canadian was whimpering, making mewling noises as he tried not to move lest it jiggle the arrow in his guts.

"Why?" Dawson kept asking through tears. "Why did this happen?"

"You came here to kill me."

"He said you were working against us."

"The only thing I wanted was to be left alone." Tylor kept his eyes on the falling snow, nerves grating. He raised his voice, asking in Shoshoni, "What happened to the Sioux?"

"Dead," Singing Lark answered from the darkness. "The red hair said he should shoot me if I wouldn't come in. Besides, he had another rifle and I needed his bow and arrows."

"What did she say?" Dawson asked.

"The Sioux is dead. That was the first gunshot."

"She had a gun? A woman?"

351

"Mr. Dawson, the problem with making assumptions is that when they're wrong the consequences can be disastrous."

"How could this have . . ."

A rifle banged close by in the night, the report muffled by the sheets of falling snow. It was followed by an agonized scream. Then the sound of thrashing, a cough, and silence.

"Wife?" Tylor called, suddenly panicked. He stood, the jack handle shouldered, eyes searching desperately.

"It is all right, husband," she called. "The last of the *Sa'idika* came to the sound of my voice. His *puha* wasn't strong. Or maybe he just didn't think well."

Tylor ground his teeth. "McKeever's still out there."

A moment later, Singing Lark stepped into the firelight, a rifle dangling from each hand, a bow and quiver over her snowy shoulders. "He is gone. Two of the horses got loose. He caught them before I could kill him. From the sound, he's moving fast."

"Which way?"

"Back down to the Bad Water. He is a man alone in country he does not know. The *Sa'idika* and *Pa'kiani* are out there. If he finds the *Kuchendukani,* we will hear about it. I don't think he will last long."

"Don't count him out. I thought I left him drowned back in the Missouri River."

Joseph shivered, gave off a croaking sound, and turned his tear-streaked face to the night. Beside him Dawson dropped his head into his hands and wept, whispering, "My fault. All my fault."

CHAPTER 43

The feeling was like a band was being tightened around Dawson McTavish's chest. As if he couldn't draw a full breath. His heart kept hammering at his breastbone, and his stomach felt sick. Like he wanted to throw up. And all the while a voice was screaming inside his skull: angry, scared, and afraid.

A voice that he didn't dare allow to break through his tight throat.

"Dawson?" Joseph whimpered. "You'll not leave me?"

"Not going anywhere." Dawson stared past Joseph's head to the falling snow where it was illuminated by the leaping flames of the fire. He sat in the shelter, Joseph cradled in his arms. The position was awkward given the arrow still protruding from Joseph's gut. He'd been hunched forward, so the arrow entered just under the ribs, had cut down through the intestines, and from the angle

354

and length of the shaft protruding, the iron tip had probably lodged in Joseph's pelvis somewhere near the spine.

Any attempt to lay Joseph straight pulled at his guts and caused a terrible pain. The only thing Dawson could do was sit awkwardly cross-legged and support his friend so the arrow was mostly held straight.

"Hurts. Every time I breathe. Like a burning. Acid, you know? My belly's on fire, Dawson."

"Shush now. We'll fix it. You heard Tylor. We'll have to wait until morning. He says he's got to have light to see to try and take it out."

Joseph swallowed hard. "He's lying, you know."

"He's done this sort of thing before."

"I never heard him say that."

"You were —"

"Dear God, I have to shit. No, please. Don't let me. Please, no."

"We can get your trousers off. I'll just have to —"

"Please, no, Dawson. It'll hurt too much. I'll hold it. 'Fraid . . . 'fraid if I let go, it'll all be blood. My guts will shoot out with it. Couldn't . . . couldn't stand that."

Joseph swallowed hard again, shivering, whimpering with the pain.

Dawson kept his hold on his friend. Wondering how long it would take, knowing it could be days.

Tylor had been blowing wind, saying they'd need daylight to dig the arrow out. Of course that was a lie.

Sometimes it took as long as a week for a man to die from an arrow to the guts. A week. Seven long days of holding Joseph. Feeling his agony.

" 'Member when we was back at Michilimackinac? When we was kids?" Joseph asked through a whisper. "Remember when we mixed gunpowder into old Jacques Beauchamp's pipe tobacco?

"Never forget the look on his face when he touched that burning stick to the bowl. Singed his eyebrows and blackened his forehead. Remember how he jumped, dropped the pipe. His eyes was so wide I thought they'd pop from his head."

"Would o' been better if we hadn't started laughing," Dawson agreed. "He chased us over half the post. If he'd a caught us, he'd a beat us half dead."

"Good times back at Michilimackinac. I'm glad your cousin, Robert, took it back from the Americans. Wonder how he's doing attacking Detroit?"

"Don't worry about Robert Dickson. He's

like an army all in one man," Dawson forced reassurance into his voice as Joseph tensed, yipped in pain. The sound of his bowels emptying in his trousers could be heard.

"God, no. Please, God, no," Joseph kept whispering.

"It's all right," Dawson soothed. "There's a creek just yonder. I'll wash them out in the morning."

"It's like a fire in my guts," Joseph said weakly. "I just want to die, Dawson. I can't stand this. I don't want to die like this."

"We'll get you fixed up."

"God, it hurts."

Out in the snow, Tylor and the woman — not much more than a girl actually — appeared in the firelight. They were snow-packed, heads and shoulders along with the folds in their parkas clotted with snow.

Tylor stepped over as the Indian woman bent to Stone Otter's body. Without hesitation she placed a foot on the dead Arapaho's chest, grasped the arrow by both hands, and grunted as she pulled.

From where he sat, Dawson could hear the sucking sound it made as she pulled the iron point through the man's lungs and out of the ribs. The wound gave off a hissing exhale as the dead man's chest relaxed.

Joseph must have heard, for he began to sob.

Tylor bent down in the doorway, asking, "How's he doing?"

"Joseph's as strong as they come," Dawson told him bravely.

"God it hurts," Joseph barely managed to whisper. "Don't let me die this way."

"We'll be trapping and trading yet," Dawson told him. "You'll see. Just like we've been. Friends forever, aye?"

"Scared. There's a fire in my . . ." Joseph tensed, trying to keep from crying out, but like the corpse, a flatulent sound could be heard around the arrow's shaft as gases vented from the wound.

Dawson did his best to keep his expression calm; when the smell of it came to his nose, it was all he could do to keep from throwing up.

Tylor's expression, though shadowed, was worried. "Singing Lark and I are going to haul this last one out into the brush with the others. We'll be back as soon as we can."

"We'll be here," Dawson told him with false bravado.

Together he and Joseph watched as Tylor and the woman grabbed Stone Otter by the arms, pulled his corpse around in the snow, and dragged it out into the storm.

"It will be all right," Dawson crooned. His own back was in agony. His muscles beginning to tremble at the strain of holding Joseph up so that the arrow didn't pull.

"Please . . ." Joseph whispered. "I don't want to die like this."

A week. It could take a whole week.

Again the voice shrieked in Dawson's head. He and Joseph, they'd been inseparable since Joseph had been six. Been through so much. How had they come to this place, only to have Joseph take an arrow through his guts?

A week. It could take that long . . .

I can't stand this! God, make this stop!

CHAPTER 44

Gray Bear considered himself to be a mere speck — like a buffalo gnat, tiny and insignificant in a world of white. White sky, white land, even white air, for this high on the pass they were in the clouds. Adding to the effect, lightly falling snow drifted down to mix with Gray Bear's frosted breath every time he exhaled.

He lay with his belly down in the snow, a snow-caked buffalo robe over his back. His position was on the crest of a rocky ridge. Before him was the narrow defile through which the trail passed. Most of the storm's fury had spent itself in the night. Now the air had gone still, and if they had any chance of disaster, it would be because of the wind. That it might carry their odor down to the *Pa'kiani*.

He heard snow crunching, but didn't break his cover as Dark Horse wormed his way up beside Gray Bear's position. The man's wolf-hide parka was dusted with snow. The lines of his diamond-shaped face were curiously softened by the weak light, his weather-browned skin black against the backdrop of white.

"Think they are coming?" Dark Horse asked. "Can't see more than a half an arrow shot across the trail."

"Five Strikes and Flat Finger said the *Pa'kiani* had followed them as far as the mouth of the canyon. The enemy knows the route we took. If they are not here by midday, we'll send scouts to see. Hard to think they would have come this far, stayed this long away from their people, only to give up now."

"Five Strikes said they barely stopped at our village site."

"Why would they? They knew they were only a couple of hands of time behind us. That they came so quickly?" Gray Bear allowed himself a slight shrug. "I'd say they bit down on the bait."

"Why? This doesn't make any sense."

"Maybe it doesn't make any sense to us, but it must to the *Pa'kiani.* That war chief leading them isn't to be underestimated. He's kept his warriors on the trail when we both know they'd rather be back in their villages up north. That takes someone with *puha,* or a special kind of personal charm. Some kind of fire in the soul. Whatever it is, he knows how to lead."

"Does he, my friend? If he comes up the pass, he's going to lead his party right into our ambush."

"Tell me what my orders were."

Dark Horse made a face. "You said he would send two scouts. To let them ride past if they didn't discover us. Just let them go. Then, when the rest of the party rode through the gap, everyone was to count. You gave every warrior a number, put number one at the top, number ten at the bottom of the ridge. The warriors count back from the leader to the rider that has their number. Our warrior number six, counts to their warrior number six, and so on. Then, when you shoot, they shoot the warrior with their number."

"As long as your people follow my orders, we will win this thing."

"My people? You question them?"

Gray Bear gave a dismissive tilt of the head. "They just heard the words. They don't really understand what I'm trying to do." He paused. "Not any more than that *Pa'kiani* war chief will understand until it is too late."

"This only works if they ride into the

ambush."

"Or, Black Horse, as you told me. It's a terrible place to fight a battle."

"Hope you are right."

"That's two of us."

After a time, Dark Horse asked, "You think that *Taipo* will trade for Silver Curl?"

"Maybe. If the price is right. And if we ever get the time for him to figure out if he wants her."

The sound of a hoof striking rock down in the canyon could be heard.

"Shhh." Gray Bear nodded. "Now, slither back down out of sight. You and the rest of the archers will get your chance."

Gray Bear's heart began to pound. The notion ran through his head that this was as crazy as Coyote. So much could go wrong. The scouts could spot the ambush. Or, as the tension built, one of his warriors could squeeze too hard on a trigger. A premature shot would ruin it all. In their excitement, everyone could miss.

"You have to trust me," he'd told his anxious warriors. "Like the buffalo hunts of old, this has to be done just so."

Why would they listen to me when a line of enemies is riding past? It will be so tempting.

Snow crunched, someone climbing up beside him. Dark Horse with some last question? The man was going to ruin the whole thing.

"I said you'll get your chance," Gray Bear hissed. "Now get back to your —"

"Come to sing the *Puha*," Aspen Branch's hoarse voice was barely a whisper. "Going to concentrate the Power, call the Spirits to blind the *Pa'kiani*. That chief, he's had the *puha* his way for too long."

"Grandmother, I don't want you here. All it would take is a single arrow, a bullet, and you're right up here where —"

"I've made my *puha, Taikwahni*. No bullet will touch me."

Gray Bear made a face. "Thank you, Grandmother."

It couldn't hurt. Besides, she'd been right since way back in Three Feathers's camp in the Powder River Basin. He turned his attention back to the trail.

He could almost physically sense the moment the first of the scouts appeared out of the fog. A tension, electric as rubbed fox fur, ran up the line of hidden warriors.

A horse blew. He heard the distinctive sound of a hoof dislodging a rock.

Then he saw it: movement. A single rider, young, maybe in his middle teens. He rode with his blanket pulled tightly around his shoulders, wary eyes glancing this way and

364

that as he followed the trail. From the direction of the breath puffing from his horse's nostrils, the slight breeze was blowing up from below. That was a blessing, for it carried the scent of the Shoshoni away from the approaching Blackfeet and their horses.

The youth carried only a bow and arrows. His mouse-brown horse had a sure-footed gait. Seemed to have good wind given the climb it had just made.

His heart beating in his throat, Gray Bear almost trembled with anxiety. His blood was pulsing, muscles quivering with the tension.

Please. Please. Tam Apo, don't let anything go wrong.

He could barely hear Aspen Branch's soft voice, like the whispering of the wind. Her rising and falling tones sent a tingle of *puha,* of rightness along his skin.

By the time the youth had ridden past, beyond the ambush, into the fog and widening saddle where the canyon opened into the pass, Gray Bear's jaws ached from the stress. As tightly as he'd had his jaws clamped, he considered it a miracle that he hadn't cracked a molar.

The sound of horses — almost ignored in his half panic — grew louder from down below.

Aspen Branch's whispering intensified.

Somehow, as the first of the riders appeared in his field of view, a sense of inevitability settled on Gray Bear's shoulders. He took a deep breath, stilling his hammering heart.

He began counting as one by one, the *Pa'kiani* rode into view.

Chapter 45

The horses kicked a trail through fetlock-deep snow as Singing Lark, Dawson, and Tylor crested the summit of Spirit Pass. They had quite an outfit now: their own belongings, ten horses, one of the South West Fur Company trade packs, and assorted bows and quivers.

Looking back to the south, the view across the basin was stunning. Tylor was delighted when Singing Lark called a halt to rest the horses. He was able to turn in the saddle and stare back at the snow-white basin they'd left behind. It glittered a soft shade of blue in the low light of the winter sun. In the distance he could see the far-off low green mountains that Singing Lark called "Pine Stand." Back to the east was the Black Mountain, and beyond it, the endless plains of the Platte.

Somewhere out there, Tylor hoped, Fenway McKeever was stiff and dead, ice glittering in his red hair and on his lashes, those terrible green eyes grayed and frozen through. He could imagine the man's freckles, stark against the frost-pale skin of his face, the lips pulled back, ice crystals dancing on his teeth.

McKeever would have his arms pulled tightly about him, his body in a fetal position where the snow had drifted around it.

"Too good to be true," Tylor muttered.

Then, looking to the north, it was to see another basin opening before him. The line of up-thrust foothills on the west gave way to the steep slopes of the Powder River's Mountains. The tops were white, irregular, humped, and faulted above thickly forested shoulders, peaks, and valleys.

The basin before him stretched in a great open bowl, cut by ridges and drainages, bounded in the distant north by the low slope of a far-off mountain. A plume of what looked like steam could be seen down in the basin immediately to their left.

"What's that?" Tylor asked.

"We call it *Pagushowener,* the Hot Water Stand. Steaming hot water boils from the ground beside the *Pia'ogwe.*"

It was to the west that — spectacular as the rest might be — the view actually took Tylor's breath away. There lay a range of shining fantasy mountains that humbled the Alps: a broken confusion of high, sheer thrusts of stone. Snow-packed, majestic, like a hundred sawing peaks all risen into the sky, they stretched for as far as the eye could see.

The sort of mountains that would have awed Viking gods, and cowed Zeus himself.

"My God, that's stunning," Tylor uttered in disbelief.

"Those are the *Dukurika*'s mountains," Singing Lark told him.

"People live in those heights?"

She nodded, resettling her rifle over the bow of her saddle as she stared thoughtfully at the distant mountains. "It's a good life. I have relatives there. Far into those peaks, up at the head of the rivers, is a big lake and country where the hot water shoots from the earth. The *Dukurika,* the Sheep Eaters, have lived there since the Beginning Times. You want to get lost? That is where you go."

"Maybe we will," Tylor told her.

Dawson had ridden off to the side, staring back at the line of tracks they'd made leading out of Spirit Pass. His face was a conflicted study. Tylor could see the grief, the anguish, all frothing in confusion and mixed with a terrible guilt.

Tylor had been standing back from the fire, hidden by the falling flakes. He'd watched as Dawson McTavish had reached out, clasping a hand over his friend's face and mouth.

Tylor had knotted his fists, had made himself stand there in the pattering snow, as Joseph Aird struggled, kicking, thrashing, and bucking. Had watched the young man's arms flail ever more weakly as they reached back and clawed at Dawson's head.

Had ordered himself to witness the final quivers as Joseph Aird finally relaxed, body limp, legs quivering.

Through it all, Dawson had kept his hand clamped over his friend's nose and mouth. Even long after Joseph ceased to suck for breath. And not once did McTavish stop sobbing.

Sometimes the price of love was more than the soul could bear.

"Nothing you could have done," Tylor had told the man later. "It was a blessing that Joseph was dead by morning. It's a hard and terrible way to die, rotting away on the inside from punctured guts."

But something had gone dead inside Dawson McTavish's eyes. The man's movements had been wooden, mechanical, as if some part of his brain had shut off.

Now Tylor walked his horse over, meeting the man's eyes. "You changing your mind about coming with us?"

Dawson's jaws clenched, his gaze thinning as he looked back to the south. "He got away with two horses and one of the packs. That's South West Fur Company property. Took Joseph's rifle. I was responsible. My cousin trusted me to bring the Tetons over to our side. I failed him. Failed us all."

Tylor said, "Don't know if this will help, but once upon a time, I served a cause that I thought was bigger than myself. It destroyed me. You're a free man, Dawson. Go hunt McKeever if you want, but if he's alive out there, and you can find him, he'll kill you. If he's dead, and you manage to stumble across that packhorse with its trade intact, you're a man alone in the heart of Arapaho, Crow, and Shoshoni country. Not to mention that we saw a party of Blackfeet just before the storm. If you somehow, incredibly, make it back to the river, turn Black Buffalo and the Tetons to the British, the Americans are going to win in the end."

"You don't know that. The might of the British empire —"

"Is meaningless out here, Dawson." Tylor gave the man a knowing squint. "Britain has enough on its plate dealing with Napoleon. I don't give a fig who wins the war. I could care less. The Americans are coming. Not the army, not the fur companies, but the people. Like a great wave, they're going to wash over everything."

"That's absurd. It's nothing but wind, buffalo, and grass. Who'd want the plains?"

"All those farmers back east who are raising corn, pigs, and too many kids. And these are unruly Americans, not 'subjects.' Any time you get three or more of them together, they just can't turn down the itch to form a government. No matter whose territory they're in for the moment. That's the thing neither the British, nor French, nor Spanish understand. I suspect that Jefferson, Jackson, and some of the others do, but in the end, it will be the tide of people that determines who holds the land."

"So, what should I do about it?"

"Nothing." Tylor turned his eyes back to the distant Dukurika Mountains. "But it's your life. Like we discussed before, you're free to live it like you want."

Dawson chewed at his lips, still staring south with those haunted and guilty eyes.

"My advice? Come with us. Winter with the Shoshoni. Then, come spring. You can figure out what you're going to do."

With that, Tylor reined his black mare

around. "Come on, wife. Let's go see the Hot Water Stand. Maybe splash around in the hot springs."

She shot him a knowing smile, flipped her black hair back over her shoulder, and started down the long slope that led to the red sandstone hogbacks below.

When Tylor glanced back, Dawson was following in their tracks. But the expression in the young man's face was listless, somehow mindful of a man who had lost his soul.

Under his breath, Tylor whispered, "Discovering that you are entirely free is a terrible thing, Mr. McTavish. The rare few can fully embrace it. But for most people, it's too terrifying to endure."

CHAPTER 46

Gray Bear should have been elated. Like the rest, he should have been screaming his triumph to the crystalline-blue skies, shaking his fists, waving the long-haired black scalp from his slain enemy. He should have been singing, his breast fit to burst with the hot thrill of victory. That exaltation should have been bred into his blood — legacy of a thousand generations of *Newe*.

Instead, as he led the way down the gentle slope on the north side of the Owl Creek Mountains, a feeling of wary disquiet filled him.

He couldn't get the images out of his head. What he'd done, seen. The terrible thing he'd wrought back on the pass. Oh, he'd had the moment of exultation as he triggered his gun, saw the *Pa'kiani* jerk at the bullet's impact. He'd been the sixth man in line. Shot through the center of his body, the *Pa'kiani* had slumped off his horse's side

374

as the animal reacted to the thunder of gunfire. The *Pa'kiani* had hit the ground like a bag of rocks.

The banging of the guns was somehow faint in Gray Bear's memory. The welling wall of blue-gray smoke. The Blackfeet warriors tumbling from spooked horses. The few who remained in their saddles had been stunned, dazed, unable to comprehend. Before they could react, Dark Horse's bowmen had rushed over the ridge top, stopping only to shoot, rip another arrow from their quivers, and shoot again.

After it was over, as the *Pa'kiani* horses were gathered, as the last of the wounded Blackfeet were dispatched with war clubs and arrows, Gray Bear had walked the length of the ambush. One by one, he'd stared down into the faces of the dead. They lay trampled in the bloody snow. Some barely more than boys, others older, expressions gone slack, eyes sightless, mouths agape as blood drained from their punctured bodies to melt the calf-deep snow.

He had kept telling himself, over and over, *These are the men who killed Soft Dawn, Willow Stem, Yampa Root, and poor young Tidy Frog. One of these men urinated in the sockets of Three Feathers's gouged-out eyes and stuffed those severed genitals into his mouth.*

Filled with hate, they had been coming to kill Gray Bear's people. And, filled with hate, Gray Bear and his warriors had destroyed them. Right there in the narrow confines of the pass.

But after having walked among the bodies of the dead, having looked into their sightless eyes, and watched his warriors cut the dead apart and scatter their limbs to bleed out in the snow, he just felt numb.

Not even a night's sleep could still the anxiety in his breast.

"Worried?" Aspen Branch asked where she rode by his side. "I can see the torture in your eyes."

"Where does it end, Grandmother? I know it goes back to the Beginning Times. We kill them, they kill us, we kill them. Is it endless? Or does it ever stop? And, if it does, who stops it? Them? I don't think so. They hate us from all the times the *Newe* murdered them from on horseback while they were on foot. We took their women and girls, made slaves of them. Made them bear our children. Then they got horses and *aitta.* They murdered us in our camps, took our women and girls, made them slaves, and made them bear their children.

376

"That chief, the only reason he chased us the way he did was because he hated us. Wanted us all dead. Somehow his hate was powerful enough to convince his warriors to follow him this far into the winter and this far from their homes."

"And his warriors died."

"He didn't. He got away. Filled with even more hate because we lived and his warriors died."

She frowned, the lines in her wrinkled face rearranging. "I felt his hate. That's what I used against him. Power can be turned upon itself. He wasn't strong enough to turn it back at me."

"Then I guess I had better be very thankful that you were there with us."

She gave him a squint-eyed, knowing look. "Yes, *Taikwahni,* you should. But part of the *puha* was yours. It gave you the wisdom to use the *aitta* in a way no one else would have thought of."

She chuckled. "The finest of leaders are those who don't want it."

Gray Bear looked back at the line of warriors, twenty-one of them and the captive horses they'd taken, including Three Feathers's beloved gray war horse. His men rode with their rifles across their saddles, singing the old victory song that had been on the lips of his ancestors all the way back to the Beginning Times.

Sticks with scalps waved back and forth in time to the gait of the horses. All in all they made quite a caravan as the horses cut a deep trail through the powdery fetlock-deep snow.

And the chewing sense of wary unease lay like a stone under Gray Bear's heart.

When the trail opened into a wide swale, Will Cunningham kicked Cobble forward, snow puffing from under the big horse's hooves. He pulled up alongside, Cobble matching Moon Walker's dogged plodding. Cunningham shot a long look at Gray Bear. Gave a nod to Aspen Branch.

"You look pretty darn grim," Cunningham said, half in English, half Shoshoni. "I'd a thought ye'd a lost that fight instead of shot the ever-loving stuffings outa them Blackfoot bastards."

Gray Bear winced, sucked at his teeth, then said, "I know that Tylor would understand. But you might have a sense for it."

"For what?"

"Back on the pass. What happened there. Our world changed, Will Cunningham. Since being at Lisa's post, I've had the feeling." He touched his chest. "Here. Inside. The knowledge lives that nothing will be the same. It was the way we destroyed the *Pa'kiani.*"

"Three of them got away."

"Twelve of them did not." Gray Bear snapped his fingers. "Like that, ten *Pa'kiani* were dead. In another five heartbeats, Dark Horse's warriors rose, and their arrows took down the rest. By the time we could reload the rifles, the *Pa'kiani* were dead or fled. All but that poor scout. And you shot him off his horse as he came riding back to see what happened."

Cunningham narrowed an eye, squinting against the glare off the snow. "Felt bad, shooting that kid."

Gray Bear tried again. "Is this what war is coming to? It was not even like clubbing rabbits in a net. There is effort to that, you have to exert yourself. Look the rabbits in the eyes as you kill them." He lifted his right hand, twitched his finger. "That's all it took. No work. No effort. And they were dead. Never had a chance."

"Better them than us."

Gray Bear gestured his futility. "I do not think human beings should have this kind of power. These *aitta,* they are the sort of thing Coyote would have invented."

Aspen Branch chuckled in bitter agreement.

379

Cunningham nodded, beard working as he chewed at his lips. "I don't know the right or wrong of it. I'd say it just is, coon. Sort of like my wife dying. It just happens. One minute ye lives one way. The next something's changed, and ye'll have to figger out how to live different. I think I foller the line of yer thinking here. Suddenly your world just got a might more spooky."

Gray Bear grunted his understated assent. "But, coon, back in the white world I come from, entire armies fight that way. Think a couple thousand men, lined up, marching up to each other. And a couple thousand rifles fire at once. The sound louder than thunder in a summer sky. It's an old reality for white folks."

"My people are not white folks."

Cunningham — a deep sympathy behind his brown eyes — said, "I'm sorry. Deep in my heart. But a storm is headed yer way, and whether it's brought by the Blackfeet, the Arapaho, or Crow, it's going to break right over the people's heads."

"How do we avoid this?"

"Can't. All you can do is know it's coming and figure some way to be on the winning side when it breaks."

"How do we know this winning side?"

"It's whichever one the *Taipo*s is on."

380

"That might be difficult. You people upset things."

"Then I'd say the *Newe* need a smart leader like you, *Taikwahni,* to help them make the right choices."

"I'm just a hunter."

"Uh-huh." Cunningham pulled a carrot of his wonderful tobacco from his pouch, cut a bit from the twist, and plopped it in his mouth. After getting it juicing, he spit, then said, "Masterful job setting up that ambush. Me? I think the people have a damn fine leader."

"Did you want something? Or did you just ride up here to depress me?"

"See, yer learning. Fact is, I been thinking about that Silver Curl. Sits wrong with me to think of buying a woman. This child don't hold with slavery. But she's been shooting me these looks. You know, like that a woman gives a man when she's interested."

Aspen Branch chuckled under her breath, a knowing smile on her old brown lips.

Gray Bear told him, "You killed two *Pa'kiani.* Two of those horses back there are yours." And one of them was the gray that had belonged to Three Feathers. Cunningham had shot the warrior who was riding him. "But one horse would do. I'd offer

381

Dark Horse the mouse-colored one that scout boy was riding. I would like to trade you for the gray. It once belonged to a friend of mine."

Cunningham nodded, as if thinking it through. "The gray is yours."

"In exchange for . . . ?"

"A gift, coon." A twinkle grew behind Cunningham's eyes. "That's what friends do for each other. Me? I ain't going back to the white world. Maybe I'll stay, assuming that's all right with the people."

What friends do for each other?

Gray Bear, his heart somewhat mollified after the carnage back on the pass, smiled. "I thank you for the gift. I am sorry it sits wrong with you to buy a woman, but Cunningham, as ugly as you are with that hair all over your face? That sickly color of skin and weird pale eyes? Stupid as you are about the way a well-mannered *Newe* man should act? The *only* way you are going to get a woman is to buy one."

"I can make you a love charm," Aspen Branch told him. "Say, in exchange for a string of those blue beads in your trade. Make you irresistible to Silver Curl."

Cunningham ignored her, eyes on Gray Bear. "You saying no woman would take me?"

382

Gray Bear shifted his attention to Aspen Branch. "If you take his beads in return for a love charm, that's theft. Nothing. Absolutely nothing, could make Cunningham attractive to a self-respecting woman."

" 'Tarnal hell." Cunningham almost spat the words.

In return, Gray Bear just gave the man his most placid smile.

CHAPTER 47

To lie back and float in the hot water as steam rose around his body was a sensation Dawson McTavish couldn't have imagined. Adding to the miracle, he watched snowflakes fall from the frigid gray sky to vanish in the heat. Not even in his wildest dreams. Well, maybe if he'd been in the throes of a terrible fever and half out of his mind, but never when he was in possession of his wits.

Yet, here he was. Floating on his back, naked as a newborn, body as warm as it would be on the hottest day. Didn't matter that his beard and hair were frozen in the cold air. The idea that hot water would just bubble up from the ground was like magic come true.

The problem was that he was here, living the magic. Joseph's lonely body lay out in the snow, under a pile of rocks. Cold, frozen. Dead.

As he stared up at the stormy sky, little

fits of wind stirred the thick cloud of steam rising around him. As it did it wove shapes and images, phantasms that alternately haunted or teased him.

Raised Catholic like he was, he couldn't help but wonder if they were demons in the mist. Come to judge him for his failures. The only thing he was sure of was that he'd been played for a fool. The central character in his own tragedy. That he'd been a coward all along. Right up to the moment he'd smothered Joseph.

All the determination, the dedication and will to succeed that had driven him when he departed for the Missouri, had been a lie. Mere self-deception. He had failed from the moment McKeever had stepped into camp.

How worthless can a human being be?

The moment of his fall had been when McKeever slammed Matato to the ground. At that instant, Dawson should have stood, raised his Bond, and shot the cowan bastard dead.

He clamped his eyes shut, thinking, *But I was afraid.*

"Thought it was better to have believed McKeever's lies, and lived." That was the falsehood he'd told himself . . . and Joseph.

Poor Joseph.

That was the failure that damned him beyond redemption. Reaching out, suffocating his best friend. Dawson could lie to himself, tell himself he'd acted out of sympathy for his beloved friend. But he hadn't. He'd done it for himself, because he couldn't bear to sit for days and watch sweet Joseph die. It had all been about him, what he could or could not stand.

Blinking at the sweat that ran down his forehead, he lifted his right hand — the hand that had murdered his best and most trusted friend. He studied his fingers, pruned by the water. Flexed them. Let his eyes follow the patterns in his palm.

How did a man redeem himself after falling so far?

Joseph's face formed in the steam, smiled in the most ghastly manner, and twisted away with a breath of breeze. The pain of that moment when Joseph stiffened and finally went limp lay upon Dawson like a granite weight. And the worst of it was that Joseph, kind Joseph, had he still been alive, would have forgiven him. Dawson could almost hear his voice: "We played it as best we could. Who'd a thought the man was a devilish liar like that?"

Wasichu, too, had died as a result of Dawson's negligence. As much as he wanted to blame Singing Lark for shooting the Santee, she'd been out there. Had heard McKeever's order. His command that if she gave him trouble, Wasichu was to kill her. Couldn't fault the woman for protecting herself or her husband.

"My fault. If I'd shot McKeever in the back that morning when he killed Matato, we'd be on the Missouri, in some Teton lodge, doing our jobs."

And there was Wide Crane. In the Indian trade, killing was always a risk. Something he'd considered himself prepared to do. Then, when it finally came, he'd been so shaken that the shot he'd aimed at Wide Crane's heart had blown out the man's hip. And that from less than six paces.

Bad enough that he had fallen apart so entirely; he couldn't help but relive the moment he'd stood over Wide Crane's body. Seen the blood, the look of agony that had fixed on the man's face as he died.

I knew him. Ate at his side, laughed at his jokes.

Dawson flexed his trigger finger, remembering the feel as the Bond rifle bucked in his hands.

Matato, Joseph, Wasichu, Wide Crane, Stone Otter, and Red Bear Man. Dead.

Men who would be alive but for Dawson

McTavish's cowardice and culpability.

Joseph's whimpering moans as he fought to rip Dawson's hand from his mouth and nose echoed in Dawson's ears. Until he died he would relive those moments as his best friend struggled, the arrow tearing sideways in his guts. His lungs sucking at Dawson's palm and fingers.

Dawson exhaled, as if he could drive the shame from deep inside.

Good men are dead, and Fenway McKeever rode away free and clear with a pack of expensive South West Company trade.

"I should have gone after him."

"A man alone? You'll be dead within a fortnight at most, by tomorrow at the earliest." Tylor's words from the Spirit Canyon camp haunted his ears.

True, Dawson hadn't been dressed for the cold. Wouldn't have known where to look. McKeever's trail would have been long vanished in the blowing snow out in the flats.

So, where would the bastard have gone?

Would he have headed east, back toward the river, figuring he could continue with his insane plan to corner the river fur trade? Tylor made no bones about the fact that McKeever had deluded himself into believing he could become the king of the Upper

Missouri. Or would McKeever remain here, in the west, knowing that Tylor was still on the loose. That to ever obtain his two thousand from Joshua Gregg, he was going to have to take Tylor's head back to North Carolina himself.

How to atone? Easy. Kill McKeever. Send his black soul to hell.

But how did Dawson find him? Where did he even begin to look?

"Give me a sign, Lord. Please. Just a simple direction."

He stared up into the swirling steam, trying to scry a pattern from the bending and twisting streamers.

But nothing formed, no holy cross in the sky, no voice whispering down from above.

The only sound was the distant mocking call of a raven flapping over the river.

Eventually, God would have to answer.

"McKeever will kill you," Tylor had said, and with the conviction of a man who knew of what he spoke.

Didn't matter. So far as Dawson McTavish was concerned, he was already dead.

In the swirling mist, Joseph's face formed, his eyes blazing with betrayal. As it slowly faded, a scream sounded in Dawson's head and slowly echoed into a consuming darkness.

Dawson clamped his eyes shut, pressed his hands over his ears, as if that would block that horrible scream.

Just as he had done from the moment McKeever had walked into camp, he was deluding himself. Deep down he understood that if he ever found McKeever, the man *would* kill him. McKeever would fix him with those cold green eyes, and Dawson's heart would stop. His muscles would freeze, and the fear would rise to seize his heart.

An ordinary man can't kill the Devil.

Joseph's face reformed in the patterns of mist, haunting, terrified. Dawson reached up into the rising steam, tried to grasp the image. His fingers closed on nothingness.

Sometimes atonement lay forever beyond a man's grasp.

And when it was?

I have lost it all.

Rising from the water, the cold air sent a prickling tingle along his skin.

Sloshing out of the hot spring, Dawson walked over to his clothes and kit. His fingers tried to stick to the cold metal of the lock work as he lifted his Bond rifle.

Staring up into the steam Joseph's face wavered in the mist.

"My fault," he whispered. "All my fault."

The cock clicked under his thumb.

CHAPTER 48

Moon Walker splashed across the rocky ford where the *Pia'ogwe* ran across bedrock. The river — dotted with clear sheets of floating ice — was shallow here, running fast across the rock. This was one of the few easy fords this side of where the channel emerged from the Owl Creek Mountains. There not even a trail followed the river's sheer banks as it churned, thrashed, and cut its way through the narrow and precipitous gorge.

Reaching the far shore, Gray Bear looked back, seeing the gentle slope of the mountains as they rose to the southern horizon. Around him, a series of red sandstone hogbacks lifted at an angle, the country faulted, broken, and topped by gray travertine that merged with the snow. He led the way, urging Moon Walker up the bank, through the willows, and around the boles of cottonwoods before breaking out on the sage flats. A couple of bowshots to the east, a sandstone ridge covered with juniper hunched like one of the Beginning Time giants.

Behind him Cunningham and Silver Curl rode their wet horses up onto the floodplain, and last of all came the hawk, riding imperiously atop its packsaddle.

The bird stared around with a piercing gaze, as though disdainful of this new country to begin with and irritated that it was packed up on a horse and forced into such an inconvenient journey.

Turning Moon Walker, Gray Bear followed the bank, letting the horse pick its way through the stirrup-high sagebrush. Immediately ahead, thick palls of white steam rose at the base of a round-topped knoll, then flattened as they hit the cold air cap where it hung low in the bottoms. Streams of steaming water feathered out from the springs to flow over stone and trickle down steep travertine bluffs and into the ice-dotted river.

The first signs of horse tracks were paired with places the grass had been grazed off.

Gray Bear reined Moon Walker to the right, seeing where a shelter had been built on the terrace; the location was tucked back against the red sandstone and protected from the north and west wind. The camp had a southern exposure; the snow melted away despite the temperature.

Their arrival wasn't a total surprise. John Tylor stood on one of the sandstone boulders that had tumbled down the slope. His ugly rifle was cradled in the crook of his left arm, his right raised in a wave.

Not that Gray Bear could have recognized the man from his clothing. The beard, brown and full, gave him away. As had the horses.

Gray Bear pulled up at the foot of the slope and stepped off Moon Walker. He took only long enough to hobble Moon Walker's front feet, then stepped back and lifted the hawk from the packsaddle, careful to ensure the bird's talons didn't shred his hand.

Cunningham had already climbed up to the camp and was slapping Tylor on the back, howling a greeting, as the two of them cavorted and danced around. Silver Curl stood to one side, watching curiously.

Gray Bear picked his way carefully up the trail. Be a disaster if he slipped on the ice and fell. The hawk would use the opportunity to rip his face, arms, and hands to ribbons. He'd learned quickly that the bird didn't take to upsets and had no sense of humor.

Tylor disengaged from Cunningham, a smile beaming from behind his bearded lips. "Gray Bear, hello, my old friend."

"Tylor, we've been worried about you. I brought you your hawk. We're all tired of working for it. The bird thinks humans were born just to feed it. Screams like a water baby in a fire if it's not fed on time."

Gray Bear carefully shifted the bird to Tylor's saddle where it rested to one side under a screen of interwoven sagebrush. The bird immediately fluffed its feathers, raised its tail, and squirted a white smear down the side of the saddlebow.

Tylor made a face, then sighed. "How'd you find us? Where are the rest of the people?"

"Five Strikes. He was scouting on the other side of the river. Heard a gunshot late yesterday. When he rode over to check, he saw your horses. Came to tell us. We're camped at the *Ainga'honobita ogwebe* springs. Just over that way." He indicated with a lifting of his chin to the southwest.

Tylor took a deep breath. "That gunshot." He shook his head. "Sad story there. Young Canadian man. Shot himself. Lark and I buried him up on a ridge overlooking the river. Worked for Robert Dickson. Seems he got tangled up with Fenway McKeever."

"McKeever?" Cunningham said with a snort. "Thought that coon had done gone under."

"Oh, he survived drowning in the Missouri. Found a party of Dickson's agents, two young men and a couple of Santee Sioux sent to beguile the Tetons into turning against Lisa. McKeever bullied them into chasing me. Along the way they picked up some of the *Sa'idika* we tangled with back above the Grand River. Caught up with Singing Lark and me in Spirit Pass." He paused. "It's a long story. McKeever got away."

"He around here?" Cunningham asked.

"Last we knew, he was headed south into the Powder River Basin with two horses and a rich pack of trade goods. That was into the teeth of the blizzard. He might be frozen for all we know."

"Let's hope," Cunningham muttered, eyes narrowing.

Tylor said, "You should also know this. There's a party of Blackfeet south of the Owl Creeks. Or were, last time we saw them."

"Not anymore," Gray Bear told him. "They followed us from the Pretty River. It's a long story. Three of them got away."

Cunningham said, "Prettiest thing you

ever seen. Gray Bear laid an ambush. They rode right into the fusillade."

Tylor glanced at Silver Curl, asking in English, "And who might you be?"

"Silver Curl," Cunningham told him. "I just bought her. We're figuring out if we like each other." Cunningham fingered something — a little leather pouch hung from a cord around his neck.

"Auburn hair, white skin, light brown eyes? I thought for a moment she was white." Tylor glanced at Cunningham. "Bought?"

"Spanish. Stolen from down New Mexico way."

"*Buenas dias, señorita. Me llamo* John Tylor."

Silver Curl gave Tylor a stunned look. "*Mucho gusto, señor. Muchos años han pasado casi hablar en Español.*"

Gray Bear and Cunningham listened incredulously as the two prattled on in Spanish.

After a pause, Tylor cocked a brow and glanced at Cunningham. "She says you've got a chance, that you're the handsomest man she's seen since she was stolen away by the Comanche."

Cunningham grinned, then fingered the pouch again.

And it hit Gray Bear as to what it was: love charm. Aspen Branch was richer by a string of beads. He'd only been kidding when he told Cunningham no woman would have him.

But then, looking at Silver Curl, maybe the charm was working.

Singing Lark, rifle in hand, appeared from around the edge of the bluff, stopped short, and charged forward.

The laughter, the wide grin, reminded Gray Bear that she wasn't much more than a girl. Especially as she laid her rifle down and leaped into his arms, hugging him fiercely. "My heart bursts with joy! *Taik-wahni!* I have missed you so!"

"We have worried about you. Hoped that you had not been caught by the *Pa'kiani.* Seeing you brings tears of joy to my eyes." He pushed her back. "And look at you! I would swear you are a hand taller. Perhaps the most beautiful woman I have seen."

She beamed at him in response. "I am free."

"Thought you were married to the *Taipo?* What? Has he thrown you away?"

"Still married," she told him happily. "It is a trial. Tylor takes constant care. He doesn't know the simplest things. Constantly getting into trouble. Just the other

397

night I had to rescue him from a bunch of *Sa'idika,* a Sioux, and a couple of *Taipo.*"

"You did?"

Tylor said, "She may be the most remarkable woman alive."

"And how did you do this?" Gray Bear asked.

"By walking very softly and shooting very straight. It was luck that I was out of camp when they came on us. I should have seen them. Would have but for the storm."

"I am so relieved that you are well," Gray Bear gave her another hug. "But please, do not hold this over the women's heads. Don't brag and make them crazy."

She looked up into his eyes, her own sparkling. "There is only one man who could ask such a thing from me."

"Tylor? Will you ask your wife not to cause trouble?"

Tylor said, "Lark, the chief would like it if —"

"Him?" Lark cried. "He's just my husband. You're my *taikwahni.* So, yes, because you ask, in this one instance, I shall control myself and not go about bragging in front of the women."

Tylor lifted his hands in mock defeat.

"Looks like we all dodged the bullet," Cunningham noted. "Reckon we got a whole winter t' get our trade together, Tylor. Come spring, we need to haul a couple of packs of fur to the mouth of the Big Horn and meet up with Reubin Lewis at Lisa's post. He's supposed to have rebuilt Fort Raymond."

"You've still got those traps Lisa advanced us?"

"Yep. And the weather's cold enough the fur should be prime."

"Maybe McKeever's finally had enough. Hell, alone, in the middle of the winter, and riding around with a pack of trade, he'll be lucky to keep his hair even if the cold doesn't kill him. If we stick to the mountains, keep our heads down, the world will finally forget that I exist."

The hawk screamed, fixing its glaring eyes on Tylor.

Would the bird ever fly again? Gray Bear wondered. Lifting his eyes, he looked up at where the thick column of steam rose against the cold winter sky. The *puhagan*s said they saw images from the underworld when they studied the patterns in the rising steam, that sometimes they could see the future.

But as Gray Bear studied the patterns, he could see nothing. The future would have to wait for another day.

CHAPTER 49

The fact that they'd found shelter was a miracle. That, or Toby was getting good enough at knowing the plains that he'd begun to develop a sense for the weather. That nice warm day had left him slightly nervous, caused him to stop early where a mustard-yellow sandstone outcropped above the cottonwood-thick floodplain above the Platte.

To the south, grass-covered terraces were set back from the river before giving way to long slopes that led up to the mass of the great black mountain. It lay east-west, rising to block the southern horizon. The channel of the Platte had bent to the south, cutting close to the western base of the mountain. There, irregular red sandstone bluffs rose from the river's northern shore, impeding further travel.

He had delegated Silas to wood detail while he and Eli Danford cared for the horses, built a shelter, and stowed the packs.

That night the storm had roared down from the north, and Toby and his little command had been as snug as could be with a crackling fire and dry bedding.

"Never known nothing like this," Simms had blurted, his blanket pulled tightly around his shoulders as he hunched under the canvas shelter they'd made of the pack manties.

Overhead the wind had howled, blowing snow in blinding veils that had obscured the cottonwoods no more than fifty yards away. On their pickets, the horses had stood head down, tails flagged as snow packed their rumps. A fine filtering of powder white was constantly sifting down through any gap.

"We'd a froze out in an open camp," Danford agreed. He had shot Toby a look. "What kind of country you brought us to?"

"Well, we found the black mountain," Toby told him with a grin. "If Tylor's out here, this has got to be the country he come to."

But the problem had gnawed at him. As they'd traveled up the North Platte, the country had grown wilder, rougher, sometimes causing them to circle wide around canyons and broken hills where the river ran fast and white.

Then had come the great black mountain, and now here, where the Platte again entered a narrow chasm. What should he do? Keep following the river? Head out across the plains? And if he did, in which direction? Assuming Tylor was still alive, where, in all this open country, did he find the man? How did they do it and avoid detection? What happened if they were discovered by Indians?

Three days ago, they'd seen a large party of mounted Indians. Some thirty riders carrying shields, bows and arrows, and some lances. Again, Toby's instinct was to hide first, take chances later. Just as well, they'd barely avoided a large village of tipis set back from the south bank of the Platte. Maybe a half-mile-long stretch of lodges, smoke rising from the tops. To be safe, Toby had detoured them north a half-day's ride.

How did a corporal with two privates tell who was who out here? Arapahos? Sioux? Cheyenne? Snakes?

"Think we can get 'em to carry flags? Maybe wear uniforms like the lobsterback British?" Danford had wondered wistfully.

"Poor planning on someone's part," Simms had muttered in reply. Then he'd grinned. "Bet ya'll there's money to be made when we get back. Bet they's a news-paper, or one of them writers who'd pay us for the story. We can be famous. Think of the tale we can tell. Into the wilderness and back, and us bringing in a bloodthirsty and terrible traitor just afore he brung the savage heathen hordes down on America."

"I ain't seen no savage heathen hordes," Danford had muttered. "Lessen that village we passed is one."

Toby, as befitted an officer, had let them talk.

That was the thing about being an officer. He was the one who had to come up with the answers, and as the storm raged, he wasn't coming up with many. Danford and Simms just figured all they had to do was follow orders. That either it worked out that they found Tylor, or it didn't. Either way, it wasn't their concern. They were both in it for the adventure. Having the time of their lives, going where — as they figured — no white man had ever gone before. If that meant the occasional cold camp, gaunt belly, or discomfort, why, that was just part of the challenge.

They hadn't made the promise to General Jackson. That had been Toby's doing.

Sometimes, being an officer was an all-fired complication.

The third day the storm finally broke. The sky dawning clear, the air felt glass-sharp cold and froze the nostrils. The kind that bit at any exposed flesh. Condensation puffed in white clouds with each breath the horses exhaled while they pawed at the snow for grass.

Most of the firewood was burned, Danford having made a few forays to augment the supply as the wind had exhausted its strength the night before.

A thin column of smoke rose from the fire, threading up past the sandstone overhang to vanish into the remarkable blue.

"How cold you all reckon this to be?" Simms asked.

Toby — a section of blanket wrapped around his mouth, a strip of rag tying his hat brim down over his ears — muttered, "Well, there's cold. Bitter cold. Damn cold. Bitter damn cold. And finally there's really bitter damn cold. I think we're closing in on that last one."

"What do you want to do today?" Simms asked, his eyebrows frosted. He was a curious bundle of blanket-wrapped oddity, looking more like a cocoon than a soldier.

"Not sure," Toby told him. "I'm betting we can swing north of these buttes, circle around, and hit the river again like we done downstream. But it worries me about what happens if we're out in the open and the wind whips up. Might freeze us and the horses."

"Heard tell of that back in Tennessee," Danford said, his head hidden by a peculiar deer-hide hat he'd fashioned for himself. He wore the God-awful creation hair-side in. The rawhide had hardened, sort of like a helmet. Both Silas and Toby had made fun of the thing, but about now it was looking remarkably warm. "Pap knew a man what froze his feet off in the mountains up Pigeon Creek way."

"Might be best to stick to camp here." Simms clasped his arms tighter around his blanket-wrapped chest and fought a shiver. "We got wood, Toby. The horses ain't shy on graze. This cold's gotta break sometime soon."

"Got half a deer left," Danford agreed. "Cold like this? The meat sure ain't souring none."

"Hell, it's done froze solid," Simms chortled. "Have to whack pieces off with the ax to get cooking size."

"I think maybe we ought to —"

"Halloo the camp!" a voice called from the bluff above.

Toby blinked, half unsure if he'd heard

what he thought he'd heard. Had to be. Danford and Simms were looking wide-eyed, startled.

"Who in hell?" Toby muttered, oddly unfazed that he didn't immediately cringe and expect his father to appear out of the air to damn him for his profanity.

The three of them bundled their way out of the snow-capped shelter, peering owlishly up at the figure on the ridge above the caprock.

Had Toby not grown so used to looking at his companions and their manner of tacked-together dress, he'd have thought it an apparition, some mockery of a human, bundled, snow-packed, and windblown as it looked. A rifle was held crossways, and the man was riding bareback.

"Hello yerself," Toby called. "My God, what are you doing out here? Who are you?"

The man reined his horse around, the animal blowing white clouds as it half stumbled, looking exhausted as it followed the trail around and down to the floodplain. Behind followed a weary packhorse, ice clinging to its hair on the windward side.

The rider pulled up, took two tries, and finally slid off his horse. He barely caught himself, looking as if his legs were about to fold.

"Eli, help me give him a hand. Silas, see to those poor horses."

Toby hurried forward and got an arm around the man's shoulders. Snow cracked loose and Toby could feel the man shivering in his layers of blankets. A bundle of what looked like cloth had been wrapped around the man's head, the right side dark and . . . bloody?

Together Danford and Toby got the man into their shelter, easing him down in front of the fire. Long red hair — filled with ice and frozen blood — hung over his collar; the freckles on the man's pale face stood out. But the green eyes turned keen as the big man reached out to the fire.

"Aye, and I half figgered meself wolf meat," he whispered. "Yer the Astorians, then?"

"Who?" Toby asked.

"Heard tell from the 'Rapaho. Black Lightning's village is here about somewhere. Seven of Astor's Pacific Fur Company men were wintering at the Red Buttes. I found the cabin ye built. Can't figure for the life of me why ye'd leave it fer this?"

"Pacific Fur Company? Astor?" Eli had a puzzled look on his face. "Who's that?"

"Must be that rich feller up in New York," Toby said. Then to the man, "Sorry, mister.

Haven't seen no other white men. We're soldiers. First Tennessee Volunteers. I'm Corporal Toby Johnson. This is Private Eli Danford, and that fella seeing to your horses, he's Silas Simms. We're under orders from General Andrew Jackson. Hunting a dangerous traitor."

The man's green eyes had narrowed. "Hunting a traitor? Aye, and in all the world, I wonder if it wouldn't be John Tylor?"

"You know him?" Toby almost gaped in wonder.

"Aye, laddie. Who'd ye think give me this?" He indicated the clotted blood on his cheek and the head wrapping.

"Can you take us to him?"

The man gave Toby a crafty sidelong look. "He's with the Snakes."

"Do you know how to find them?"

"Aye, laddie." A smile bent the man's lips, the fire's heat beginning to melt the ice frozen in the red beard. The first drips spattered on the big man's chest. "I'm Fenway McKeever. Glad t' make yer acquaintance."

ABOUT THE AUTHOR

W. Michael Gear is a *New York Times, USA Today,* and international best-selling author with over 17 million copies in print worldwide. His books have been translated into 29 languages. A Spur Award–winning author, his western fiction has been taught in university courses in both Western literature and anthropology. Gear lives on a remote Wyoming ranch where he raises trophy-winning bison with his wife — author Kathleen O'Neal Gear — two shelties, and a flock of wild turkeys.

The employees of Thorndike Press hope you have enjoyed this Large Print book. All our Thorndike, Wheeler, and Kennebec Large Print titles are designed for easy reading, and all our books are made to last. Other Thorndike Press Large Print books are available at your library, through selected bookstores, or directly from us.

For information about titles, please call:
  (800) 223-1244

or visit our Web site at:
  http://gale.com/thorndike

To share your comments, please write:
Publisher
Thorndike Press
10 Water St., Suite 310
Waterville, ME 04901

FOL

SEP 0 6 2024